BOOKED TO KILL

Danielle M. Haas

HARLEQUIN®
ROMANTIC SUSPENSE™

Recycling programs
for this product may
not exist in your area.

ISBN-13: 978-1-335-73821-9

Booked to Kill

Copyright © 2022 by Danielle M. Haas

Harlequin Enterprises ULC
22 Adelaide St. West, 41st Floor
Toronto, Ontario M5H 4E3, Canada
www.Harlequin.com

Printed in U.S.A.

He walked behind her up the three floors.

When they reached the landing to her hallway, she came to a quick stop and Jack bumped into her. Instinct had him latching his hand to her hips to steady her. His chest heaved with the feel of her pressed against him, but warning bells went off in his head. "What's wrong?"

She shifted her head to the side and kept her voice low. "There's a man standing in front of my door."

Urgency propelled him into action and he swept her behind him. He rested his palm on the butt of his sidearm secured at his hip, hidden behind his jacket. He stared at the broad back of the man who stood in front of Olivia's door with something in his hands. A box?

Without moving, he yelled, "Whoever the hell you are, take a step away from the door and put your hands in the air."

Dear Reader,

I'm so excited you've decided to take another ride with me. Since I've been home in Northeast Ohio more than usual the past couple of years, I wanted to take another trip to one of my favorite places: New York City. Even if that trip involves murder and took place in my mind before I put it down on paper.

When figuring out who I wanted to take this trip with, I homed in first on my heroine. In *Booked to Kill*, Olivia Hickman is a young widow who is trying to get her life back on track. I feel like she's someone we can all relate to. I know I've had times in my life when things haven't gone as planned or I find myself back at the beginning of a journey I thought would be in my rearview mirror. Olivia embodies some of the qualities I admire most—loyalty, bravery and kindness.

Detective Jack Stone enters her life when she's at the lowest of lows, barely able to put one foot in front of the other. He doesn't swoop in and clean everything up for her. He stands beside her and gives her someone to lean on as she learns to take those steps on her own. Jack shows Olivia that her past is special, something that brought her to the present. Honestly, out of all the heroes I've written, he reminds me most of my own hero, my husband, Scott.

Thank you for making the choice to read *Booked to Kill*. I appreciate you more than you'll ever know.

With all my love,

Danielle M. Haas

Danielle M. Haas resides in Ohio with her husband and two children. She earned a BA in political science many moons ago from Bowling Green State University but thought staying home with her two children and writing romance novels would be more fun than pursuing a career in politics. She spends her days chasing her kids around, loving up her dog and trying to find a spare minute to write about her favorite thing: love.

Books by Danielle M. Haas

Harlequin Romantic Suspense

Matched with Murder
Booked to Kill

Visit the Author Profile page at
Harlequin.com for more titles.

To my mom, Brenda Hill. You've stood by my side through my lowest lows and highest highs. You've listened to every chapter I've ever written. My success wouldn't be nearly as sweet without you.

Chapter 1

Olivia Hickman stopped in front of the white-stone apartment building she'd once called home. The morning sun warmed her skin, and she sucked in a deep breath of the springtime air. The winter had been long and hard, and she wanted nothing more than to enjoy the vibrant green leaves on the tree-lined street and the subtle scent of flowers that mixed with the baking bread. Instead, she tipped her chin to take in the six stories that housed the loft where she'd once spent most of her time.

Happy times with a husband she loved in a life that seemed as if it existed only in her dreams.

Her nerves danced in the pit of her stomach as she steeled her resolve and barreled through the front door to the lobby. Walking into a place that held so many cherished memories and love never got easier—scrubbing away the presence of strangers who should have never been there in the first place was never fun.

She couldn't dwell on that now. She should count her luck there was never a shortage of tourists in need of a reasonable place to stay in Manhattan. Especially when her loft offered plenty of space and high-end upgrades in the two-story apartment. Much more than anyone could find in a small hotel room surrounded by the constant noise of the city. And although it hurt to give strangers free rein of the loft, she needed the income from the rented space if she wanted to keep her focus on her art and not some soul-sucking job she took just to keep her head above water.

Pushing down the strobing ball of apprehension, she took a left to the stairwell, then bounded up the two flights to her old apartment. With her keys nestled in the palm of her hand, she let herself in and tears dotted her eyes.

A stab of grief pierced her heart. She and Dave had envisioned a long life with children running through their home. She never imagined she'd be forced to rent out the loft on one of those vacation rental sites. Selling wasn't an option, at least not yet. Not when the closest she felt to Dave was in the brief moments she went back to the loft, even just to get it ready for the next renter.

Dark wooden floors ran the length of the open space, making the whitewashed brick of the walls pop. The same deep brown, suede couch she and Dave had purchased with money from their wedding occupied the corner, a shaggy cream-colored rug beneath it, a square coffee table anchored in the middle of the plush piece of carpet. An overnight bag sat open beside the couch, and Olivia frowned.

Crossing the large room, she peered into the bag. Women's clothing spilled out the side. She puffed out a frustrated breath. The woman who had rented the loft was supposed to be gone an hour ago. If she was still here, it would push back Olivia's entire day. "Hello?"

No response.

A slight shiver of trepidation zipped through her veins, and she licked her chapped lips. The lockbox attached to the door allowed her to rent out the space without ever coming face-to-face with the people sleeping in her home. Not meeting her lodgers made it easier to forget people invaded this sacred space with their own happy memories and loved ones.

She tiptoed to the kitchen, taking stock of every inch her gaze landed on and checking to make sure nothing screamed to her something was wrong. The poker rested in its place against the fireplace, and nothing had been disturbed from the bookshelves. The dishes she'd set out on the long table separating the kitchen from the living room were still perfectly set, the white orchid still in its pot on the marble countertop.

She lifted her chin to the second-story loft that took up half the area upstairs, leaving the second portion above the kitchen with high ceilings, allowing the exposed black beams to become the focal point. Clear glass encased the bedroom, giving an illusion of privacy while still keeping the open concept intact, and large windows lined the top of the walls, letting warm light flood the inside.

"Hello? Is anyone here?" She called out.

Nothing.

The stillness in the tidy apartment sent chills up her spine. Her heart picked up its pace and sweat collected in her palms.

Stop overreacting. Nothing happened. She's probably still asleep.

She rounded the table toward the stairs. The woman *had* to still be in bed. She must have started packing her things the night before, then slept through her alarm. There had to be a reason she wasn't answering. Why she hadn't taken her stuff and left.

A crumpled body lay at the base of the stairs, a pool of blood seeping into the floor. Dark hair swirled around a woman's face, her eyes wide and lifeless. Her lips parted as if her life had been cut short in the middle of speaking—or screaming.

Olivia's hand flew to her mouth, capturing the shriek that poured from her throat. Her heart raced and fear clouded her vision.

This couldn't be happening. Not again. Not another death.

Irritation made Homicide Detective Jack Stone's skin itch as he stood in a rented-out loft in the Meatpacking District. One young woman lay dead on the floor. Another woman, a knockout redhead with fear in her eyes, huddled on a sectional in the living room.

"You want to talk to her, or do you want me to?" Jack's partner, Max, asked, dipping his chin toward Mrs. Hickman.

"I'll talk to Mrs. Hickman. You take a look at the body." He'd looked up information on the loft owner while Max had driven to the scene. Made more sense for him to speak with her, even if her beauty had been a punch in the gut at first sight.

Max nodded, then strolled over to where a young officer stood by the staircase, an unneeded bodyguard for a woman who'd already met her fate.

Jack kept his focus on Mrs. Hickman. As he crossed the room, he couldn't help but be impressed with the clean, modern lines and the sheer size of the loft. The questions brewing in his mind couldn't keep him from noticing the gleaming countertops in the droolworthy kitchen or the built-in bookcases lining an entire wall.

Mrs. Hickman sat hunched over her knees on the sofa, her blank stare lifting to meet his gaze. An oversize gray T-shirt hung loose on her slim frame, and her socked feet were planted on the rug.

"Mind if I sit?" He grabbed a notepad from his back pocket and waited for her response. No color settled in her ivory cheeks and a glassiness settled over her hazel eyes.

Sniffing back tears, she cleared her throat and gave a half-hearted attempt at a small smile. "Please do."

He opted to sit on the cushion that gave him a better visual of her, his portion of the sectional adjacent to hers. He wanted a good read of her facial expressions as he took her statement. He smoothed the lines of his face, making sure no hints of sympathy—or even suspicion—came across. "My name is Detective Jack Stone. I'm sorry to cross paths with you this way. I know this conversation won't be easy."

She pinned him with her wide stare, lips pressed in a straight line. "I can't believe this is happening."

The quiet astonishment in her voice squeezed his heart. "Did you know the victim?"

She shook her head. "She was a renter. I list the loft on one of those vacation rental sites. She was staying for a couple nights." Tears clung to her lashes, and she dashed them away with long, slender fingers.

He wrote down the information, not wanting to forget any details. "When did she check in?"

She ran a palm over her smooth forehead. "She was here for two nights. Scheduled to leave this morning."

He made a quick note before meeting Mrs. Hickman's wide-eyed stare. "Was she alone?"

Mrs. Hickman shrugged. "No other name was listed, but I never know when someone brings in a guest."

He lifted his gaze to the ceiling. "Any chance you have security cameras inside?" He'd spotted cameras outside the building, but any cameras inside the loft could clear up a lot of questions.

She wrapped her arms around her middle and sank into the back of the sofa. "No. I don't have the money to invest in something like that right now."

He raised his brows at her excuse, forcing himself not to ask the question sitting on the tip of his tongue. The loft was high-end in every way. How could the owner not afford to put up a few cameras for safety? He'd talk with the building manager about getting the footage for the outside cameras and hope he got lucky. "Can you tell me exactly what happened when you got here this morning?"

She sucked in a deep breath. "I came in and found a bag. I assumed the woman was upstairs." She flicked her wrist to the opposite end of the couch. "I was frustrated at first and called out for her, but no one answered." Her voice trailed off, and she dropped her gaze to her clasped hands on her lap.

He spotted the bag on the floor. Something to go through and see if they lucked out with a clue. Probably just clothes and toiletries, but he could always get lucky. He shifted back to her. "Was the door locked when you opened it?"

She scrunched her nose. "I think so. I mean, I used my key but didn't pay attention to if the lock actually turned or not."

Interesting. Forced entry didn't appear to be at play. "Then what?"

"I went into the kitchen, then headed toward the stairs. That's when I saw the body and called the police." Her voice caught on the last word. "Was this just a horrible accident? Could she have tripped down the stairs and hit her head?"

Weirder things had happened, but he wouldn't bet his paycheck on it. Neither would he throw out half-baked theories to a woman he didn't know. "I can't tell you that. All I know is we will need access to your apartment until we clear the scene."

She squeezed her eyes shut, the fear and concern clear as day on the soft curves and slopes of her face. Opening her eyes, she refocused on him, but a sadness lingered in her expression. "Of course. Whatever you need. Can I go now?"

Standing, he tucked his lips at the corners then fished into the back pocket of his trousers. "Sure. Take my card."

"Thank you," she said, rising on unsteady legs.

He frowned. "Can you make it home all right? Is there anyone you can call to be with you?"

She managed a small smile. "I'll be fine."

A weird pull in his chest made him want to walk her home and make sure she was safe and sound. "I'll be in touch." The woman had been through hell, and even if he couldn't ignore her connection to a suspicious death, a part of him wanted to protect her from going through any more tough times.

Instead, he offered a stiff nod and watched her walk out the door before joining Max beside the young woman whose life had been cut tragically short.

Max rubbed a palm over the back of his neck. "She have anything useful to say?"

"Woman was renting for a couple nights, and Mrs. Hickman walked in this morning to find the body. She was pretty shaken up. I'll give her some time to absorb everything, then pay her a visit a little later. Right now, we need to focus on the victim." His gut lurched as he took in the pool of blood spread around the dark hair like a disgusting halo of death. Even though he'd made the decision months ago to move from behind a desk where he worked for the Cybercrimes unit to time in the field solving homicides, the sight of death still turned his stomach.

That and the smell. The stench of fresh blood and the beginning stages of decay that mixed with the normal scents of lavender and vanilla from some plug in the wall was nauseating.

"Do you think she knows more than she's saying?" Max asked, his blue eyes trained on the woman at the base of the stairs.

Jack cut his gaze to the door Olivia Hickman had walked through moments before. He'd need to dive in deeper and see if she was connected to the woman found in her loft. Even though a killer could be on the loose, a nagging feeling told him the hardest part of this investigation would be keeping a tight leash on his unwanted attraction to the beautiful woman at the center of it all. "I can't say for sure, but you can bet your paycheck I'll find out."

Chapter 2

The sidewalks bustled with activity, New Yorkers hustling to the next important place while tourists meandered through the crowds and vendors searched for easy targets to purchase their knockoff goods. The morning was young, but exhaustion weighed down every step Olivia took as if she'd been awake for days. Sleep sounded amazing, but going home alone wasn't an option, at least not yet. Not back to a quiet apartment with nothing but her scattered thoughts and images of death to keep her company.

Not knowing where to go, she allowed her legs to move of their own volition, her mind unable to stop replaying the moment she'd turned the corner and found a dead body at the base of the stairs. She couldn't handle the stress—couldn't carry around the worry and despair on her slim shoulders anymore. Not like she was given a choice. Life just kept throwing more and more crap on her plate until cracks and splinters threatened to break the damn plate in two.

The scent of coffee wafting from an open door penetrated the fog in her brain. She blinked, taking in her surroundings. A humorless snort puffed through her mouth, and she pushed her way past the cluster of people near the doorway of the bakery she'd been a patron of since it opened.

Since the day her best friend had poured her heart and soul into her entrepreneurial baby, The Mad Batter.

Black-and-white tile covered the floor while gray matte paint with a sprinkling of purple glitter coated the walls. A smattering of round tables with curved metal legs littered the room and a long glass-covered counter display case housed a variety of pastries. Teacups and gold stopwatches hung from the ceiling in front of the window, giving off the same whimsical vibe as *Alice in Wonderland*.

The sweet scents of vanilla and cinnamon mingled, mixing with the lingering smell of blood and death attached to Olivia's nose, and turned her stomach. Images splashed back in her mind, making her knees shake. The chatter around her mixed with the whizz of an espresso machine and rang in her ears.

"Olivia?" Christine's brisk voice broke through the noise. Concern lined her forehead. "Is everything okay?"

Olivia latched her gaze on her best friend and almost whimpered in relief. Words wedged in her throat, so she shook her head.

Sensing her turmoil, Christine led her through the room and past the trays and platters filled with sugar-dusted pastries.

Olivia clung to her friend, needing an anchor to keep her steady. She was barely hanging on by a thread, and that thread was unraveling faster than the kid in the corner was shoving a doughnut in his mouth.

Reaching the office, Christine opened the door wide, letting Olivia pass before securing the door. Flour smudged her cheek, standing out like a beaming light against her dark skin. Her blond hair was cut in a short bob, the left part exaggerated to show off the shaven side of her head. Worried eyes watched Olivia behind thick red frames. "What's going on?"

Tears spilled over Olivia's dark lashes, and she struggled to put words to the nightmare that was her life. Bracing herself against the wall, she rubbed her foot against the warped wood floors that Christine hadn't gotten around to replacing, focusing on the motion as she struggled to string together a coherent thought.

"Come sit." Christine pulled out the lone chair shoved behind the desk.

Olivia fell onto the seat, thankful she'd managed to keep herself upright until then. "The renter who stayed in my loft last night is dead." The words croaked out of her dry throat, and she rubbed a palm over her collarbone. Her heart beat an erratic rhythm beneath her hand.

"What do you mean?" Christine asked, settling onto the edge of the desk. She crouched down to eye level and rested her hands on Olivia's knees. "What's going on?"

"I found a dead woman in the loft." She drew in a

shuddering breath. "I went in to clean and found the renter. How is this my life? I've barely been able to put one foot in front of the other since Dave died, but I've tried. I've moved on as much as I can. And now I've found a dead body. In my home. In *our* home—the one place that was always mine and Dave's. It's too much. I can't handle any more shit in my life."

Christine dropped into a crouch, securing Olivia's hands in hers. "Oh my God. That's horrible. I'm so sorry. For all of it. I know this year has been difficult, but you're tough. So much stronger than you know. You'll get through this, too. Now tell me what happened."

Olivia sniffed back her tears, preparing herself to relive the horrible moment. "I entered the loft to clean up after another renter. The woman was at the bottom of the stairs. Blood everywhere." She squeezed her eyes shut, but the image of the dark hair matted with thick, crimson ooze made bile creep up her throat and she opened her eyes wide. "Am I cursed? Did I do something horrible, and karma is kicking my butt?"

Realization that she was making a tragic death all about her had her pinching the bridge of her nose. "I'm terrible. I'm a terrible person. A poor girl is dead. She's the victim here. Not me."

"Stop it. You've been dealt another devastating shock. You're allowed to be upset. Anyone would be. Especially after Dave's accident." Christine winced, her small mouth pushing outward. "It sounds like this woman might have tripped on the stairs. That it was just another terrible accident."

Olivia shrugged. "Is it weird to say I hope so? The detective I spoke with wouldn't say much."

An image of the blue-eyed detective flashed in her mind. Well, his blue eyes were more gray than blue, made more alluring by the dark scruff that hugged his jawline. His hair was a little shaggy, like he was overdue for a cut and the strands didn't know which way to bend—and the attraction Olivia had felt when first laying eyes on him had been swift and cutting. Something she wouldn't admit, even to her best friend.

"Did he ask you any more questions?" Christine asked.

Thinking back on her morning, she let out a long breath. "Just a few, but he said he'd ask more later. I'll pull up whatever information I have from the woman— Courtney—and hand it over. Besides that, I don't know anything."

Christine's skin paled, looking ghostly against the red of her glasses. "Did you say Courtney? Are you sure?" Her words came out in a strange octave, shaking slightly.

Olivia struggled to pull forward more details of the woman who'd stayed in her loft but came up short. "I think so. I can't recall the last name though."

"Bailey? In her twenties? Dark hair? Tall and curvy?" Christine's eye shifted back and forth in a frantic motion, as if searching for the answers on Olivia's face.

Olivia swallowed past the image of the blood-covered dark hair and awkward angle of the body she'd found. "That sounds familiar. Why? Who is Courtney Bailey?"

"Eli Seal's little sister." A misty sheen shimmered in Christine's amber eyes.

A wave of grief crashed against Olivia, and she covered her mouth with her hand. "Eli Seal? As in your high school boyfriend?" Christine and Eli had dated all through high school, parting ways amicably when they left for college. His sister had been much younger, and Olivia had never known the girl, but knew who she was.

Christine nodded and stumbled backward, sitting on the wide-planked wood floor. "She married not long ago but was going through a divorce. She wanted a weekend away from the messiness of it, and their family had moved from the city. I recommended your loft, then never heard anything. I can't believe this." Tears dripped down her face, smearing the patch of flour.

A crushing blow pounded down on Olivia, crumbling her insides. She'd told Detective Stone she didn't know Courtney, and now she discovered that wasn't true. She had a connection to the woman who wound up dead in her home. A nagging sensation clawed at her brain. *What in the world could that mean?*

Jack studied the list of tenants beside the door until he found the one he needed. Chills rippled down his arm. The shadowed spot in front of Olivia Hickman's apartment building was out of reach of the warm rays of the afternoon sun, and in his haste to leave that morning, he hadn't bothered with a jacket.

Or the effect may have had more to do with the information he'd uncovered regarding Courtney Bailey than the cool temperatures.

Instead of making assumptions regarding Mrs. Hickman's knowledge of the woman she'd rented her loft to, he pushed his finger against the stained buzzer on the side of the stone building. He didn't want to believe

Mrs. Hickman had knowingly withheld information earlier, but the only way to know for sure was to ask.

"Hello?" A wispy voice crackled through the speaker beside the list of tenants in the building.

"Good afternoon," he said into the little box. "This is Detective Stone. I'm here to speak with Olivia Hickman."

"Umm, okay. Come on in." Another buzz sounded, indicating the door was unlocked. "I'm on the third floor. To the right. Elevator's broke."

Grabbing the door before the lock clicked back into place, he entered the building with a small snort. Riding the elevator to the third floor wasn't a habit of his, or most New Yorkers he knew. He scanned the shabby entryway for the staircase, surprised by the lack of amenities and state of the lobby.

Okay, lobby might be an overstatement. Grubby subway tile lined the floor. Rusted metal mailboxes hung from one wall. A closed door marked Maintenance was located opposite the elevator, the dark stairwell beside it. Not what he'd expected from the owner of the upscale loft.

Shoving that interesting tidbit in the back of his brain, he jogged up the three flights of stairs, only a little winded when he reached the right floor and found the apartment number. He knocked on the door, taking note of the faded carpet on the narrow hall as he waited.

The door swung open, and Mrs. Hickman stood beside it, her hand clasped on the knob as she stared at him with those wide, haunting eyes. "Detective."

Pressing his lips in a thin line, he nodded his hello. He needed to keep a tight lid on the twinge of excitement that tightened his stomach muscles at the sight of her. The messy red hair swirling around her shoulders and pretty pink polish on her bare toes had him clenching his hands into fists to keep from doing something stupid. "I have a few questions. Do you mind if I step inside?"

She waved him in, then took a step back, closing the door behind him.

He scanned the studio apartment, again shocked by the space. A queen-size bed was shoved in the far corner—neatly made with a colorful comforter. A small desk was tucked at the foot of the bed, separating it from the kitchen. A couch was adjacent to the bed with a small stand between the two pieces of furniture. A glass coffee table sat in front of the sofa and a television was mounted on the wall. A hallway led to what he assumed was a bathroom.

"What can I do for you?" she asked, worry spilling from her every pore.

She drew his attention back to her. He planted his feet wide on the dark wood floors and shifted gears to the questions he had prepared. "Are you aware that the woman you found in your loft this morning went to your high school?" He didn't want to believe she'd kept that information from him. Hell, Courtney Bailey had been six years younger than Mrs. Hickman, so the two women might not have ever met. But the connection had to be explored.

Mrs. Hickman crossed her arms over her middle and rested one hand at the base of her neck. "Yes."

His head reared back at her admission. Irritation crawled up his throat, and he tried to maintain his cool.

"When we spoke earlier, you claimed not to know the victim. Had you forgotten that she was an acquaintance of some kind?"

"I've never met her, and honestly, her name didn't ring familiar until I spoke with a friend this morning." She sighed, then backed up until her knees hit the couch and sat. "My friend told me she'd recommended my loft as a rental, but then hadn't heard anything more on the subject so never brought it up to me."

He untucked the slim notepad he kept in the back pocket of his slacks. "So Courtney Bailey was a friend of a friend?"

"She was the little sister of my friend's high school sweetheart," she said, her eyes glued to his. "She'd been married, so the last name didn't ring a bell, and apparently she wanted to get away for the weekend. Christine thought my loft would be a good place for her to stay a few nights." The last words came out tight, as if barely able to squeak through Mrs. Hickman's throat.

"Christine is your friend? Her last name is?"

Mrs. Hickman nodded. "Roberts." She dropped her gaze to her hands resting in her lap. She rubbed one finger over the other, as if one part of her body had to remain in motion.

He scribbled down the name. One more person to track down.

"Have you uncovered if the death was an accident?" Hope lifted her voice.

After everything that had happened to Mrs. Hickman, he wasn't sure if the truth would be that much easier. But she deserved to know what really happened, even if he couldn't give her all the details. If nothing else, it might convince her to invest in a decent security system. If she chose to keep the loft at all.

Besides, he couldn't cross her off the list of suspects. Not yet. Not after this.

Schooling his expression to remain passive, he said, "I'm sorry, but Courtney Bailey's death has been ruled a homicide."

Chapter 3

The ominous statement pounded against Olivia like a hammer, breaking her down until all she wanted was to curl into a ball and cry. But she couldn't fall apart. At least not yet, with Detective Stone standing over her with suspicion burning in his blue eyes.

Not like she blamed him. Hell, if a woman had been murdered in someone else's property, she'd be wary of them, too.

Unshed tears burned the backs of her eyes, and she struggled to keep her composure. "That's awful."

"Do you mind if I sit?" Detective Stone asked, dipping his chin toward the opposite end of the sofa.

Sniffing, she scooted to the far end of the couch, giving him plenty of space. "Sure."

Settling onto the rose-colored cushion, Detective

Stone leaned forward and rested his forearms on his knees. He shifted to the side, angling his large body toward her. "Where were you last night between the hours of 8:00 p.m. and 3:00 a.m.?"

His legs were so long, his knees invaded her personal space, but it was the question he asked that raised her temperature, not the closeness of his body. She swallowed past the fear building inside her. All she had to do was tell the truth, then the detective would leave her be and spend his energy searching for the real killer. "I had dinner last night with my brother. Then came home—alone—and spent some time working. I was in bed by ten."

He hooked up an eyebrow. "Working? Where?"

She nodded toward the hallway. "Here. I'm an artist."

He flitted his gaze toward the hall, then settled his stony stare back on her. "Can I get contact information for your brother to verify your statement?"

"Yes." Her voice cracked, even though she had nothing to hide. She held out her palm. "Hand me your notepad, and I'll write it down for you."

"Can you write down your friend's information as well? I'd like to speak with her." He offered the notepad and pencil, and his fingers brushed against hers.

Her body temperature went from warm to scalding hot. She yanked away the pad, and the pencil fell to the floor. She bent to retrieve it and knocked her head against Detective Stone's on the way down. Bolting upright, she pressed her fingers to the throbbing spot on her forehead. "I'm so sorry."

He chuckled and ran his hand over the top of his head, making the wayward strands of hair stick straight out. "My fault. Here, let me get it." He scooped up the writing utensil and offered it to her.

She made sure to grab the tip, not wanting any more contact with his skin. Embarrassment over her reaction to this stranger combined with anxiety crept up the back of her neck, making her aware of every inch of her own body. In an effort to calm herself, she smoothed a hand over her hair and mentally cringed. For the first time since Dave died, she wished she'd actually applied some makeup and run a brush through her tangle of hair.

Guilt swept in, destroying any other emotions brewing inside her, and she quickly scribbled the information Detective Stone had requested for her brother and Christine. She needed the sexy detective out of her apartment and out of her life as soon as possible. "My brother might be difficult to get a hold of. He usually can't answer his phone while working and is on call pretty much all the time." Instead of handing back his things, she set them on the coffee table.

Detective Stone grunted his acknowledgment and retrieved his notepad. "What can you tell me about Christine's relationship with the victim's brother?"

Olivia scrunched up her nose, recalling long-ago days when Christine had been madly in love with Eli. "There's not much to say. They were high school sweethearts who parted ways when they went to college."

"Any animosity between them? Any reason for your friend to hold a grudge against her ex or his family?" He shot the questions out in rapid succession, as if not understanding his implication.

She bristled. Being asked about her whereabouts made sense. Questions regarding Christine's intentions for making an innocent and helpful suggestion to an old friend did not. "No animosity. No grudges." Answering questions about her friend left a sour taste in her mouth. A friend who'd pulled her out of the pit of despair, then stayed glued to her side until she realized life was still worth living.

Silence beat an uncomfortable cadence between them. Detective Stone stared at her as if in some kind of challenge to spill secrets that could reveal a deep-seated desire her friend had to exact revenge on a love from her past. The idea was downright ridiculous. "Do you have any other questions for me?"

"Does anyone other than you have access to your loft?" he asked, eyes narrowed. "A friend or relative?"

She fought the urge to roll her eyes. "Just me. I don't use a cleaning company to maintain the apartment. I do it all. A key is in the lockbox hooked to the door. I have a key on my key ring and a spare key in my junk drawer."

He furrowed his brow, head tilted slightly forward. "Junk drawer?"

Sighing, she rose and skirted around the coffee table to a drawer wedged between the wall and the small refrigerator she hated with a passion. She might only be one person, but the stupid thing barely fit her milk and daily yogurt cups. Out of all the things she missed from her loft, the gourmet kitchen with high-end appliances was at the top of her list. She reached the drawer and yanked it open, waving her hand over the top of the litter of mismatched items inside. "You don't have a junk drawer? A place where all your random crap ends up because none of it has a designated place?"

He stood and crossed to her side in four long strides. Leaning over her shoulder, he glanced into the drawer and frowned. "How can you find anything in there?"

"Just have to rummage around a little." She lifted old takeout menus, rubber bands, and random notes she'd made herself from the drawer. Loose coins and paper clips cluttered the bottom.

"I don't see a key." He leaned over farther, pushing into her personal space.

The heat of his body so close to hers curled her toes. The scent of his cologne—a mixture of orange peel and a smoky, almost whiskey aroma—hit her senses, making her core throb. A reaction that was as unexpected as it was unwanted. "It's in here." She moved around the random items, but no key.

Her heartbeat picked up. She tossed the menus and notes on the floor, throwing out other scraps of paper. "I don't understand," she said. "The key is always in here. I haven't touched it in months."

Detective Stone edged her gently to the side and ran his palm along the lining of the drawer. He picked out bobby pins and batteries until nothing was left inside.

She shook her head, not understanding what was in front of her. "It *has* to be there. The key not being in there makes zero sense."

Detective Stone fixed a hard stare on her. "I now have a crime scene that someone had a key to get into. Because if you don't have this key, someone else does. And that someone might be a killer."

Jack swished his closed mouth side to side as the implications of what the missing key meant smashed against him like a tornado, twisting everything he thought he knew about the case upside down. If some-one had a key, it would explain why there was no forced entry into the loft. It also meant his assumption the vic-tim let in her killer—that the killer was someone she knew—might be bullshit. Not to mention a possible waste of his time and energy.

"I need a list of everyone who has been inside your apartment over the last month," he said, annoyance making his skin tight and itchy. He shoved a hand through his hair. "Make it two months."

Mrs. Hickman's mouth fell open. "Seriously?"

"Yes, seriously. I need to know who had access to your kitchen. Anyone who could have known where you kept a spare key. Friends, relatives, hell—even a deliv-eryman who might have brought up a package that was too big for you to carry and placed it near the kitchen while you dug for cash in your purse."

She shook her head over and over again, as if refus-ing to see the truth even as it glowed brighter than the lights in Time Square. "No one would have stolen my key. Why would they? If they wanted inside the loft for whatever reason, all they had to do was ask."

"Mrs. Hickman. If someone had ill intent, do you think they'd make those intentions clear to you? Or do you think they'd wait until your back was turned and grab what they needed?"

A splash of red invaded her cheeks and showed off a smattering of freckles under her eyes. "Call me Ol-ivia, and please don't question me like I'm an idiot. If I thought someone close to me could kill an innocent woman, don't you think I'd have told you that already?"

"Olivia," he said, the name sounding oddly intimate on his tongue. "I'm sure you would have, but in these cases, people are usually surprised to learn secrets that have been tucked away, sometimes festering for years."

She dropped her chin, as if she couldn't carry the weight of her head on her shoulders for one more second. "Fair point."

A strange sensation tightened his chest and an unfamiliar urge to comfort her took hold of him. He'd read about her husband's tragic accident the year before. Understood how a loss that deep could cut away pieces of your soul until you were no more than a shell of the person you once were. But that didn't mean he could give her any special treatment.

The opposite was true. The empathy swelling inside him combined with his growing attraction for the woman meant he needed to keep things as professional as possible. "So will you write that list for me?"

"Sure," she said, the word coming out in a long sigh. "Do you need it right now?"

"The sooner the better, but I understand going through two months of memories might take a while. Tomorrow would be great, though."

Olivia slumped against the stained wood counter and rubbed circles in the middle of her forehead. "There has to be another explanation."

Fine. If she wanted to go down this road, he'd play along. Although she'd like what he was about to say a lot less than his first idea. "Okay. Say you're right and no one you know or who has been let inside stole your key. What option does that leave? One, you misplaced the key." He ticked this option off the pad of his index finger.

She grimaced. "I mean, I guess it's possible, but I highly doubt it. I don't even remember the last time I needed the spare."

"Then two." He lifted his middle finger, now displaying a peace sign for a situation that was anything but peaceful. "Someone broke in and stole it."

She gasped. "You don't really think that, do you?"

He shrugged. "Someone has that key. How are your locks?" He glanced toward the door and cringed. He could tell that it wouldn't take much to bust through the flimsy lock attached to the handle.

"The locks are fine. I've never had any trouble. It's a safe neighborhood." Her defensive tone told him she was trying to convince herself as much as him.

"Are you sure about that?" he asked. It wouldn't be the first time someone had broken into an apartment in the city where the tenant wasn't aware. "Have you noticed anything missing? Items misplaced or in weird locations?"

The color drained from her face. "My perfume."

"What about it?" He took a step toward her, his spiked pulse telling him what she was about to say was important.

She licked her lips, then flicked her wrist toward the skinny stand sandwiched between her bed and couch. "I always wear the same perfume. Have since I was a teenager. A while back, I misplaced my perfume bottle. I figured I must have accidently thrown it away or something."

He rubbed the back of his neck, kicking himself for

not asking about a possible break-in at her apartment earlier. "Is that something you'd do? Accidently throw something away?"

She shook her head. "I'd just purchased a new bottle the week before, and the stuff isn't cheap."

"I need you to go through your apartment and see if anything else is missing. Anything you might have overlooked. And what was the name of the perfume?" He grabbed his notepad to write it down.

"La Femme Fleur. I have a bottle on the stand if you want to look at it." She studied the apartment, her mouth moving in noiseless whispers, as if she was giving herself a pep talk.

He wrote down the name of the perfume, then took a picture of the bottle with his phone. If the killer stole her perfume, finding the missing bottle could help build a case. Tucking his phone and notebook away, he watched Olivia meticulously search the rest of the space, then hurry to the hallway. He didn't want to creep her out by following her to the bathroom but needed to keep an eye on her.

He walked down the hall, surprised by its length, then took a few steps to the doorway Olivia had disappeared through. He turned into the unexpected room. Beams of sunlight shone through the floor-to-ceiling windows, showcasing the explosion of colors on mounted canvases. Splashes of paint covered a protective tarp thrown over the floor. A narrow wooden table took up one wall and was topped with brushes of all shapes and sizes. Rags huddled on the corner, and hand-drawn sketches were tacked up on a thin strip of corkboard. "What in the world?"

Olivia dug through a thick stack of paintings nestled against the wall. "This is my studio," she said without sparing him a glance. "The apartment is small, and this should be my bedroom, but the light in here is amazing. It's the perfect place to paint. My brother is subletting me the place, and he said as long as I didn't damage anything permanently, I could do what I wanted with the space."

Jaw dropping, he took a step inside. He didn't know a damn thing about art, but the deep sea of blues and bold reds splattered on the canvas set on the easel by the window drew him in—reminded him of the grief and pain and loss he'd battled for so long. Sadness overwhelmed him, and he braced himself against the table, unable to speak, his focus glued on the painting.

"It's not here." She stood in the middle of the room, turning in a slow circle as if trying to find something she'd missed.

Olivia's panicked screech pulled him out of his head. He cleared his throat, zeroing in on the ashen tone of her skin and wide, terrified eyes. "What's not here?"

"One of my paintings." She dashed to the opposite side of the room and searched through another mound of canvases. "A picture I painted of a church. The church Dave and I were married in. It's gone." She faced him, fear and confusion knitting her brow. "Oh my God, someone was inside my apartment."

Chapter 4

The smell of lemon disinfectant hung heavy in the air. The pungent solution stung Olivia's hands, making them cracked and dry. She should have searched for rubber gloves before scouring the lingering presence of a stranger from her apartment, but she'd left all her industrial-strength products at the loft—including her gloves. She couldn't go back to a crime scene where her sense of security and safety had been violated before ridding the exact same energy from her home.

Throwing the wet sponge in the lukewarm bucket of water, she sank onto the floor and leaned against the cabinet. She used the back of her wrist to brush aside hair that had slipped loose from her high ponytail. Tears dotted her eyes.

Getting the phone call that her husband had been

killed in an accident had been the lowest point of her life, but today was a very close second. The image of that poor woman lying at the bottom of the stairs would never leave her. Nor would the guilt that burrowed in her chest, as if she was somehow responsible for the young woman's grisly fate.

A sharp knock on the door set her nerves on edge, and she shrank against the hard cabinet. Fear froze her movements.

"Olivia? Are you home?" Her brother's voice penetrated the thin wood.

She shot to her feet and hurried to let him in, throwing her arms around his neck in the doorway. "What are you doing here? I'm so happy to see you."

Jason gave her a tight squeeze, then pulled away, keeping a soft grip on her shoulders. His short brown hair was perfectly groomed, but worry shone bright from the hazel eyes so much like hers. "I got a call from a homicide detective. Are you all right?" He studied her face, as if he'd be able to detect any form of harm.

But the harm today's events had caused couldn't be found on the surface.

Not needing to pretend to be okay, she let the tears hovering in her eyes fall and shook her head. "It was so awful. I still can't believe this is happening."

Dropping his arms, Jason closed the door, then steered her toward the sofa. He waited for her to sit before crossing to the stove. "I'm sorry. This sucks. But you're okay. That's the important thing." He snaked the silver teakettle off the gas stove and filled it with water from the tap before setting it back on the burner, igniting the flames underneath it.

Sniffing back her raw emotions, she rubbed the chills from her arms. "What did Detective Stone say when he called?"

Jason leaned against the laminate counter and hooked his ankles. "He asked me where I was last night. I told him I was with you, which sealed your alibi," he said, shaking his head. "So freaking weird. Why do *you* need an alibi?"

The indignation in his voice warmed her. "Because an innocent woman was killed in my loft."

Jason hooked a dark brow, making his oval face even longer. "How do you know she's innocent?"

She bristled at his words. "No matter what happened, I'm fairly certain she didn't ask to be murdered. She's an unfortunate victim."

He retrieved two cups from the cabinet and set them on the counter by a pad of paper. "What's this?"

She rose, glancing over his shoulder at what he'd found while searching for tea bags. The enormity of what Detective Stone had asked of her sat like a stone on her chest. "The spare key to the loft is missing. So is a bottle of my perfume and one of my paintings. Detective Stone thinks either someone broke into my apartment, or someone I know grabbed the key while they were here. He wants me to write down anyone I can think of who's been here."

Jason picked up the pad of paper and irritation puckered his brow. "Seriously? These are all friends. Family. Clara? Really?"

She shrugged as heat slammed against her cheeks. Writing down each name on her list had felt like aiming an arrow into their backs. But she had to name everyone she could think of, even her brother's soon to be ex-wife.

"Why would anyone you know and trust steal from you? This is a waste of time." He threw the notepad back on the counter.

A shrill whistle sounded, and Olivia removed the kettle from the burner. She scooted one cup her way and filled it with water before dunking the bag of chamomile tea into the steaming mug. "I agree, but it's better than sitting around doing nothing. Or scrubbing this place until my hands bleed."

He let out a sigh. "You're right. I'm sorry. This is all just so surreal. And after everything with Dave…"

Her husband's name made her heart lurch. Jason had taken Dave's death almost as hard as she had, as the two had been friends since middle school. More death and stress were the last thing either of them needed.

He blew a long breath from his mouth and cast one more look at the list of names on the yellow legal pad. "You need new locks on your door. Here and at the loft."

A dull ache thudded against her forehead. "I can't afford new locks."

"Then maybe it's time to consider selling the loft." He spoke as if trying to keep his patience while explaining math to a child.

Clenching her jaw, she carried her cup back to the sofa and sat. "We've been over this. I'm not sure if I'm ready. I've had to say goodbye to so much. I don't know if I can put everything Dave and I loved behind me."

"Come on. It's time. You're living in this shit hole when you could take the money from the sale and move into a decent place. Keeping that loft won't bring Dave back. You have to move on. Move forward."

"I don't have to do a damn thing," she snapped, her hands trembling from her brother's harsh sentiment. "Dave didn't leave me like Clara left you. I'm not angry and bitter and eager to get on with my life. I want to keep Dave and my memories alive, and there isn't another place in this damn city where he feels closer to me than in our home. I'm not ready to let that go."

"I'm not eager to move on from Clara. I just don't have a choice in the matter." Jason winced, a mixture of guilt and irritation flickering on his face. "At least let me lend you the money for some locks. You can't live in an apartment someone's already busted into, and you can't leave a lock on the loft that someone might have a key to."

As much as she hated accepting her brother's charity, her shoulders sagged in relief. She'd sleep a lot better knowing she was just a little bit safer. "Thank you." She stayed quiet about his relationship. He was a grown man and knew how she felt about the breakup of his marriage. There was no reason to rehash her irritation at his and Clara's inability to get past whatever had shoved a wedge in their marriage. Especially when she feared she might be that wedge.

Nodding, he fiddled with the knot on his baby blue tie. "I don't mean to be harsh. It just seems that maybe this is a sign. A sign to say goodbye. Dave wouldn't have wanted you to be so reliant on renting that place out week after week."

She took a sip of the tea, and it burned the top of her tongue. "This isn't a sign. It's a tragedy. And just like the last tragedy, I'll do whatever it takes to put it behind me. And that starts with doing what Detective Stone asks of me so the police can clear the loft and I can put the listing back up until I can figure out my next step." She just hoped that once that happened, life would calm down and she could get back to nursing her broken heart.

The setting sun shimmered through the towering buildings, the muted light sparkling against endless glass. Little grains of fatigue scratched against Jack's eyes. The day had been long and frustrating. All he wanted was to prop up his feet with a glass of scotch in one hand and the remote control in the other. With his roommate and fellow detective working tonight, he had the apartment to himself.

But before he could trudge through the rush hour traffic to get home, he had to stop by Olivia's apartment to grab the list she'd come up with. He'd almost asked her to just shoot him an email with the names she'd remembered, but the thought of laying eyes on her was too tempting.

He pressed the button he'd used earlier that day, prompting Olivia's sweet voice to crackle through the speaker.

"Hello?"

He leaned forward and projected his voice. "It's Detective Stone."

"Come on up."

The buzz sounded and he hurried inside, bounding up the stairs to Olivia's place.

She sat in the threshold of her apartment, the door wide-open, with her strawberry blonde hair piled on the top of her head in some kind of messy bun, a bandanna tied in a knot to keep loose strands from falling into her eyes. A smattering of tools lay on the dingy carpet beside her.

He slowed his steps as he studied her furrowed brow. Dammit, if she didn't look cute in her frustrated heap. "Everything okay?"

Sighing, she slumped against the doorjamb, tilting her chin up so she stared at the ceiling. "Not even a little bit."

Crouching beside her, he picked up a discarded doorknob. "What exactly are you doing?"

Angling her face toward him, she met his stare. "Failing."

Her matter-of-fact tone curved his lips. "Care to elaborate?"

She puffed out a breath that made the loose stands of hair falling in her face dance in the air. "My brother bought me new locks. Said I needed them if someone had broken into my apartment."

He nodded along with the words. "Smart man."

She frowned, then gestured toward the mess at her feet. "Well, Mr. Smarty Pants was called back to work before he could finish installing the doorknob and new dead bolt. Hopefully he'll be back, but I can't just sit around and wait all night. What if there's another emergency surgery at the hospital he's called in to take care of? What if it's the middle of the night before he can make it back here? I can't just hope no one comes around or tries to break into my apartment again." Her voice hitched higher with every word, while her eyes grew wider as if each new thought caused a new thing to worry over.

"Since none of those are good ideas, how about I

help?" He unbuttoned his tailored shirt at the wrist and shoved up his shirtsleeve, then did the same with the other arm. Having a maintenance worker who was scarcely around the building had made him more self-sufficient in the last few months.

Her lips formed a small O, as if she wasn't sure how to answer the question.

"I promise I won't break anything. I'll just pull up a video on my phone. I'm sure it won't take long." He fished his phone from his back pocket and searched for a how-to video. "See. Tons of help just a click away."

Her mouth morphed into a thin line, and she narrowed her gaze, leaning forward for a better glimpse at his screen. "I'll be darned. I'd never thought to search online. Thank you."

Picking up the screwdriver, he watched a few seconds of the clip, then made quick work of securing the new knob into the door.

"I don't know if I should be impressed or angry that you made that look so easy," she said.

A quick glance over his shoulder told him exactly which way she was leaning. With her arms folded over her chest and a scowl pinching her face, she definitely didn't look pleased. "I'm sure if you'd have watched the clip, you could have done it just as quickly. Do you want to try the dead bolt?"

She swished her lips to the side. "Sure."

He brought up a video to help and held it at eye level. "You might need this." He extended the tool he'd used for the knob.

With her eyes fixed on the phone, she reached for the screwdriver. Her fingers brushed against the back of his hand, and she jumped back. A pretty pink flared to life on her face and she dropped her gaze to her feet. "Never mind. If you work on this, I'll grab the list. That way you won't have to wait any longer than necessary to get on with your evening. I'm sure you're busy."

The lump lodged in his throat refused to let him speak, so he nodded and went to work while she disappeared inside. Heat crept up the back of his neck. He tried to keep his focus on the stupid video, but his mind kept wandering back to Olivia and the way his body reacted to a simple, innocent touch.

No! This was the last thing he should be doing. Had he not learned his lesson? The last time he'd let a woman get into his head like this, he'd almost botched a high-profile child trafficking case and a woman he'd come to care about was killed.

He needed to get it through his thick head that Olivia Hickman was off-limits, not storm into her life with some stupid hero complex and fix her locks. She might insist she didn't have the money for proper security cameras at her rental property, but eyes didn't lie. Her loft told him she had plenty of money at her disposal, despite the head-scratching lack of amenities in her current residence, and she could no doubt afford to hire a handyman to install her damn locks.

Olivia came back into view and hovered nearby. She held a folded piece of lined paper in her hands. "I divided people up based on how I know them. Family. Friends. Acquaintances who stopped by with the latter. I also wrote down the restaurants I order takeout from."

"Now, that's impressive," he said, fastening the lock in its place. "Done." He stood and handed her back the screwdriver before wiping his hands on his pants. Not like it'd been a dirty job but sweat moistened his palms just being near her and he didn't want to smear the ink on the paper.

She accepted the tool, then handed him the slip of paper. "I listed telephone numbers for the people I know. If you have any questions, I'll answer whatever I can. The sooner we find out who did this the better."

He tucked the paper in his pocket. "Agreed."

"Do you know when I'll have access to my loft?" she asked, twisting her mouth.

Her question wasn't out-of-bounds, but the meaning behind it tightened his jaw. "Not yet. I'll let you know as soon as I find out."

"It's just that I need to rent that loft as soon as possible." Her gaze dropped back to her bare toe that she swiped back and forth across the floor. "The longer it sits vacant, the more money I lose."

"Understood. I'll be in touch." Not wanting to say something he'd regret, he dipped his head, then turned and walked away, leaving her staring after him. He resisted the urge to tell her to be safe, to get inside quickly, and lock up tight. She wasn't his responsibility, and she'd made it clear that her priority wasn't keeping anyone safe.

It was money. And as much as that disappointed him, it forced him to shove any unwanted attraction for Olivia Hickman out of the way so he could focus on the case. Find a killer. And put the pretty widow as far behind him as possible.

Chapter 5

Heat penetrated the thin cardboard barrier around Jack's paper to-go cup. Just enough to have him transfer the cup from one hand to the other after each long sip of the strong, black coffee.

"You getting something to eat?" Max asked, taking the spot beside him after placing his order and stepping down the line to wait.

Jack shifted forward, allowing space for an elderly woman to squeeze through. "Nah. My stomach's a wreck."

Max's single pat on the shoulder and tucked-in lips told him his new partner understood where his issues stemmed from. After years of working at a desk, solving cybercrimes from behind a computer, speaking with the loved ones of the recently murdered woman didn't sit well with Jack. After years as a homicide detective, Max had learned how to tolerate them a little better.

The barista approached the counter with a large cup and brown bag and handed them both to Max, who dipped his chin in gratitude.

"Let's take a seat and regroup," Jack suggested. The late-morning hour had cleared out most of the patrons who'd lingered before work. He spotted a two-person table shoved in the corner of the cluttered space and led the way, weaving between people loitering with friends or staring down at a phone screen.

Max sat across from him and lifted a muffin from the bag, taking a bite before sipping his coffee, then leaning back in his chair. He might seem relaxed as they discussed their morning, but intensity never left his light blue eyes. "Mr. and Mrs. Shipley weren't a wealth of information. I'd hoped they'd have more to share this morning, after the shock of their daughter's death had worn off a little."

He and Max had taken the bridge over to Jersey first thing, wanting to speak with Courtney's parents in person. They'd made the notification of her death via the phone and hadn't wanted to press for details at that time. The trip had gotten him out of bed painfully early and hadn't helped one bit. He'd left with the memory of two heartbroken parents with nothing but sadness haunting their eyes and countless questions.

Max circled his palms around his cup and blew out a long breath. "Just a couple names. The ex-husband's story clears him for his whereabouts at the time of death if it checks out, and the parents didn't jump to any suspicions that he was involved. But we still need to speak with him. He'll have a different take on the victim than her parents."

Nodding, Max nibbled his breakfast. "From their account, she was a perfect daughter. Sweet girl who everyone loved. But that's what most parents say. Her friends and ex might paint a different picture."

"She got the idea to stay at Olivia's loft from Christine Roberts, Olivia's friend," Jack said, taking a sip of the strong, black coffee and praying the caffeine kicked in soon. "Could be a coincidence Ms. Roberts knew both the victim and the owner of the loft, but I doubt it, since Olivia has items supposedly stolen from her apartment, including the key to the loft. Then someone is murdered in her rental."

Max arched his dark brows. "Olivia?"

Jack hid a scowl behind his cup as he took another long sip. "She asked me to call her Olivia. I complied. Don't make a big deal about it."

Smirking, Max lifted his palms. "No deal at all. But back to your point. The killer could be connected to Olivia," he said, her name coming out on a huff of humor. "Instead of Courtney. And Christine Roberts is connected to both, which needs to be explored. We'll set up an interview."

"Already did. She owns a bakery a couple blocks from where the murder took place. I thought it'd be interesting to take a little walk and see what kind of path one would take to get from one location to the next." He retrieved the paper Olivia had given him the night before and laid it on the table. He twisted it to face Max. "Do you see any other listed names that ring a bell? Any that you've come across while doing research on the victim?"

Max ran an index finger down the paper as he read

through the list. "Nope, but we only need one. When are we speaking with her?"

"After you finish shoving that muffin in your face." He slid the paper back toward him and put it in his pocket. "I just want to run through what we know. No forced entry in the loft tells us that the victim either knew her attacker, or someone let themselves in when she was unaware."

Max tossed the last bite of food in his mouth and crumpled the brown bag in his hand. "Blunt force trauma to the back of the head has me leaning away from crime of passion. But we can't cross it off the list. The crime scene, as well as no defensive wounds on the victim, reads as though someone struck her from behind, then she either fell or was pushed down the stairs."

Jack drew in a long, steadying breath. "There are some sick sons of bitches out there."

Max ran a hand over his mop of dark hair. "The level of depravity of mankind never ceases to amaze me."

Not wanting to dive deeper into the grisly side of human nature, Jack changed the subject. "Speaking of the crime scene, when will the loft be cleared for Olivia to gain access?"

"We've secured all the evidence we need, and the crime-scene unit has already been through the property with a fine-tooth comb. All we need to do is take the police lock off the door, and she can have her loft back."

"She'll be happy." The bite in his voice was as potent as the strong coffee in his mostly empty cup.

"What's that all about?" Max asked, lifting himself to a half-standing position. He leaned to the side and threw his trash in a nearby receptacle before sitting back down.

"I don't know what you're talking about." Ignoring his friend's questioning look, he wiped crumbs off the table into his hand before throwing them in the trash.

"The tone. Like it's weird Mrs. Hickman would be happy to have access to her loft." Max narrowed his gaze, as if his hard stare was searching for some unseen answers on Jack's face.

"Nothing," he said, kicking his legs out in front of him. "She just seems awfully eager to get her loft back on the rental site. Like it doesn't bother her someone was murdered there. As long as she gets paid, it's fine."

Max shrugged. "So what? That's her business. We don't know her reasons, and as of now, we don't need to know her reasons."

He wouldn't admit this to his partner, but that first bit of logic was the only reason he hadn't used his computer skills to uncover everything he could about Olivia Hickman. That, and the intense invasion of privacy he just couldn't bring himself to commit. But he'd tossed and turned all night with thoughts of the doe-eyed widow.

"Good point," he said, standing. "Let's head out. Our interview with Christine is in fifteen minutes."

Then he could call Olivia and let her know her loft was no longer a crime scene. It was hers to do what she wanted with, and Max was right, it wasn't his concern. Besides, the less time spent thinking about the widow and her ways the better.

A restless night's sleep had done absolutely nothing to quell the quivering nerves jangling through Olivia's body. The walls of her apartment were suffocating, not even the natural lights filtering into her workspace sparked creativity. Needing some fresh air and hopefully a different perspective, she paired a denim jean jacket over a fitted gray T-shirt and red joggers.

Just like the morning before, she walked down the sidewalk with a mind full of problems and memories filled with hideous images. She thought she'd feel better after handing her list of names to Detective Stone, but now she worried what her friends and family would think when they found they'd been singled out. Her brother hadn't been thrilled. A heads-up might not be a bad idea. Especially for Christine, who already felt guilty that she was the one who'd recommended the loft.

She could stop by The Mad Batter, then loop around and see if she could get back into her place. Everything had happened so quickly the day before, shock and fear leaving her shaken and details murky. She wanted to take stock of the loft and see if anything needed to be addressed before relisting the space to be rented.

Horns blared as annoyed drivers crawled through traffic, trying their hardest to drown out the sound of birds chirping overhead. A gaggle of tourists with wide, plastic visors clogged the sidewalk, and Olivia pushed past them, increasing her pace until she approached her best friend's bakery.

As she reached for the handle, a man from inside used his back to push open the door.

She took a step back, allowing him space to leave. When he turned to face her, the sight of his deep blue eyes sucked the air from her lungs.

Detective Stone's eyes widened, and he stopped in the doorway.

"Dude, what's the holdup? Keep moving." Detective Green shoved at his shoulder, spurring him forward.

Olivia moved her mouth into an O of surprise. "Hello." She hoped the men before her couldn't hear the hitch of nerves in the single word.

Detective Stone cleared his throat, then fiddled with the knot of his tie. "Hi."

Confusion beat through the thrum of unwanted excitement at seeing the handsome detective. "What are you doing here?"

Detective Green offered her a tight smile. "Nice to see you, Mrs. Hickman."

Understanding dawned, and a punch of guilt tightened her core. "Are you here to speak with Christine?"

The two men exchanged a glance, then turned somber stares her way.

"We're just following leads," Detective Green said. "Now we need to part ways. I just got a call from the station. Jack, you're good to take things from here, right?"

Detective Stone nodded.

She offered a small wave and watched him go before turning back toward the man who caused way too many feelings to stir inside her. "Did you talk to her?"

"We did." He dipped his chin, making eye contact.

She waited for him to elaborate and sighed when nothing else followed. "Is she okay?"

"Shaken, but that's understandable." He shifted, putting himself in the center of the bakery window.

She peered past his shoulder and spotted Christine working the cash register. The stone-faced expression told her that her friend was doing whatever she could to hold herself together. Maybe right now wasn't the best time to talk.

"Listen, I have to get going," Detective Stone said. "Was nice seeing you. I'll be in touch soon about when you can get inside your loft. I just need to check some things first." He nodded a goodbye, then made a move to walk past her.

She bit the inside of her cheek as indecision warred inside her as she watched him walk away. "Wait, Detective."

He swiveled around, a smirk on his full lips. "You can call me Jack."

The sexy smile made her stomach flutter. "Okay," she said, with one slow nod of her head. "Jack. Are you going to my place now?"

He tilted his head to the side, his eyes narrowed. "Yes."

"Can I come with you?" She nibbled her bottom lip, unsure of how much she wanted to divulge. "I don't want to go inside by myself. At least not the first time seeing the place after walking in on a crime scene. I'd feel better if someone—you—were with me." She dropped her gaze to the cracked sidewalk. She'd much rather watch the crumbled trash blowing along with a swarm of stomping feet than see any hints of hesitancy or unease on his face.

"Umm, I guess that'd be all right."

She lifted her gaze in relief, stepping in sync beside him. Not knowing what to do with her hands, she plunged them into the shallow pockets of her jacket. "Any chance you've caught the person responsible?"

He snorted out a humorless laugh. "Not yet. Trust me, we'll let you know when that happens."

"*When*, not *if*?"

Halting his steps, he turned toward her with nothing but sincerity in his somber expression. "When."

She forced a smile and kept walking, needing the movement to expel her nervous energy. Nervous about being so close to him, but also nervous with the throngs of people milling around her.

Growing up in the city, she'd always taken comfort in the fact she was never alone. Never exposed or vulnerable to the types of chaos she watched in horror films when she was younger. The bad guy hiding in a cornfield or stalking his prey through a forest. No way some guy with a machete could sneak up behind her with hundreds of people always on the street.

But now an unfamiliar sensation prickled at the back of her neck, as if someone was hiding—waiting and watching until the moment was right to strike again. And with Dave gone, she was alone. Vulnerable in a way she'd never been before.

So she kept moving, in this moment at least protected by the man beside her with a badge clipped to his belt and no doubt a weapon hidden somewhere on his body.

With the approaching white-stone building, the subtle scent of the flowers in their window boxes brought her back to the day before. The scene eerily similar. Beams of sun broke through thick white clouds overhead and a slight breeze rustled the leaves of the trees dotted along the congested street. But unlike yesterday, fear rooted her to the sidewalk.

The doorman opened the door with a nod of his head.

Olivia followed Jack, focusing on the way his crisp white dress shirt molded across his back as he swung his arms with each long stride. Unease tapped against her spine, and she all but held her breath until they made it to her door. Jack fiddled with the police lock before letting her pass through.

Flashes of the morning before appeared in her mind as her sneakers squeaked on the hardwood floor. The bag beside the door. The neatly set table in the dining room. The orchid on the kitchen counter.

The dead body on the floor.

She pressed a hand to her mouth to stifle a sob. This loft once held only cherished memories, an aura of love and hope permeating the walls. The space was tainted now. Maybe Jason was right, maybe selling was the right move.

"I just want to make a quick sweep through each room. Are you okay?" Jack asked.

She nodded and stepped farther inside. Jack crossed over to the sofa, his attention fixed squarely on whatever his mission was today. Turning her back to him, she treaded lightly to the one spot she didn't want to see. The stairs. She passed the beautiful table, dishes still laid out, and took a deep breath. She had to get this over with—had to push past the jitters.

Steeling her resolve she pivoted to the place where the beautiful young woman had lain only twenty-four hours before. A hiss of terror pushed through her. No body laid sprawled on the floor, but white petals were scattered along the ground, the color glaring and pure against hard red bloodstains.

Chapter 6

"Jack!"

The screech of his name had Jack racing around the corner, terror at what he was about to find zipping through his veins.

Olivia stood beside the marble island with one hand over her mouth and the other extended in front of her—index finger pointed toward the floor. "Blood. Dried blood still on the floor. And the petals. Someone scattered ripped petals on the stain."

He followed the long line of her finger to the base of the stairs. The stain was from the day before, the team in charge of examining the scene was not responsible for cleaning the mess. But the petals. Those were definitely new. "What the hell? Where did those come from?"

Olivia whipped around to face the kitchen, her frantic gaze taking in every inch of the space. "The orchid. Where's the orchid? Did the police take it?"

"Wait. What?" He lifted his palms, mind racing to make sense of the sudden change of subject.

Swirling back to face him, she swept her arm toward the bewildering sight on the floor. "The petals. They look like torn-up orchid petals. I had a white orchid on the counter, and I don't see it."

If he remembered correctly, the potted flower from the kitchen wasn't taken in for evidence. And he was 100 percent certain no police officer or crime-scene investigator had busted into the crime scene, torn apart a plant, and thrown the petals on the same spot where the body had lain—the wood stained red from the now-removed blood.

Pushing all questions to the back of his mind, he sprang into action, removing a pair of rubber gloves from his pocket and shoving them on his hands. "Stay close, okay? Someone was in here, and I need to make sure they've left. Try not to touch anything," he said, removing his sidearm. If someone was still inside the loft, he wouldn't be caught unprepared.

She bobbed her head up and down and fell into step behind him. Hunching low, as if trying to make herself small, she stayed close to his heels.

The heat of her body skimmed his back as he made quick work of clearing the first floor—checking every nook and corner in each room. Nothing was out of place, the only items unaccounted for were things already taken in as evidence. Skirting the bloodstain as best he could, he climbed the stairs to the bedroom. Plush cream-colored carpet covered the floor. Modern art with clean black lines and splashes of bold red hung on the walls. The crisp white bedspread lay in a heap in the middle of the bed.

An open door led to a small bathroom. He padded across the carpet. One more space to check to make sure he and Olivia were alone. No one hovered in the bathroom or hid in the shower. Whoever had been inside was long gone.

A narrow window that sat high on the wall caught his attention. He stood on the edge of the bathtub and ran his fingers along the unseen seam where the window should have met the white, wooden ledge. Instead, a sliver of air rushed against the pad of his finger. "The window's open. Is there a way for someone to climb up to it and squeeze through?"

She closed her eyes, her nose scrunched in concentration. "The fire escape is on that side of the building. The landing is outside the kitchen window, but the ladder going to the next apartment would be close."

He shoved his gun back in the holster at his side, then locked the window. "Let's head back downstairs. I need to call this in."

He trailed behind her as she made her way back to the dining room, the sound of their footsteps echoing off the high ceiling. He pulled out the chair that would position her back to the petals on the floor. "Can I get you some water or something?"

She nodded, rubbing her palm over the exposed skin above the collar of her shirt. "That'd be nice. I keep bottles of water in the refrigerator." She was silent for a beat, her unblinking gaze staring straight ahead. "This can't be happening. I don't understand."

Yanking off his gloves, he skirted around the island to the stainless steel appliance. He opened the door and grabbed two bottles before joining her at the table. After sliding one in front of her, he unscrewed the cap off the other bottle and took a long sip before placing a call to Max.

"What's up?" Max asked after the first ring. "I only have a second. I'm about to talk to the lieutenant." A hint of annoyance lifted Max's gruff voice.

"Someone broke into Olivia Hickman's loft again. Left ripped flower petals, possibly from an orchid Olivia had on the counter, over the spot where the victim was found."

"Shit. We need to look at the building's security feed. Did you secure the place?"

"The place is cleared. Looks like someone got in through a window in the upstairs bathroom. I need someone to get here to check for prints." He glanced at Olivia from the corner of his eye, relieved to see a little color back in her cheeks.

"I'll send someone right away."

Jack uttered a goodbye, then set his phone on the table, screen facing up so he wouldn't miss any incoming calls or messages. "I need to stay here a little while longer. I can take your statement, then you're free to leave."

"Will you need to take over my loft again? I have a renter tomorrow night. I really don't want to cancel the booking."

He hid his annoyance over another swallow of water. "What has to happen next shouldn't take too long, but I'll let you know once I have the details. But you really should have some extra security measures put in place. New locks. Cameras. Alarm system if possible." All standard in a place like this, but for some reason not for Olivia. Was the bottom line that important to her?

"I'm getting new locks in as soon as I have clearance and have someone on standby to come and clean before the new renters arrive." With one hand cradled around the base of her untouched water, she used her free hand to pinch the bridge of her nose. "Why would someone take my plant? Use it to do something so despicable?"

He shrugged, confused by her distress over something so unimportant. "People do things for all sorts of reasons. I'm sure you can find another orchid somewhere in the city."

She narrowed her gaze, her stare now hard with a hint of fatigue. "Someone sent that plant to my husband's funeral. Seeing it every day was too much—brought to mind too many horrible memories. But I couldn't let it die." Her voice cracked, and she hung her head. "Having it here was like knowing a little piece of Dave was always home where he belonged."

Her confession tightened his chest. He'd been too judgmental, assuming the worst when he had no right to jump to any conclusions about this woman he barely knew. What seemed like a molehill to one person was someone else's steepest mountain. And what was a simple potted plant to him represented so much more to Olivia.

"The orchid may be gone, the petals ruined, but your husband's memory will always live on. I can't put that flower back together for you, but I can find out who destroyed it. And when I do, I'll make sure they pay."

* * *

Streaks of late afternoon sun streamed in through the floor-to-ceiling window, drowning Olivia's workspace in light. The day's events played on repeat in her mind, dragging her down. Jack had gotten a hold of the security footage from behind her building, which showed someone dressed in black climbing the fire escape, then forcing themselves through the narrow, bathroom window in the middle of the night.

A shudder ripped through her. Knowing someone had broken into her apartment—and loft—was one thing. Watching it happen on video was another.

After someone came in and dusted for prints, and Jack had collected the shredded orchid leaves for evidence, she'd finally been told that she'd have access to her loft tomorrow. Which meant she had twenty-four hours to figure out how to pay for and install a new security system. She'd taken enough charity from Jason, and her dad never had an extra dollar in his pocket, which meant piling the debt on her credit card.

But what choice did she have? No one would choose to stay at the site of a recent murder if she couldn't prove she'd taken every precaution necessary to ensure her renters' safety. She just needed to make some extra cash to get her through. A new painting to hang in the gallery was just the ticket. But first she had to push past the block that was stifling her creativity and keeping her in such a dark space.

Over the past year, she'd learned the best way to work through whatever was blocking her creative escape was to unleash whatever emotions were brewing inside her. So she stood in front of a large, blank canvas. She closed her eyes, feeling the warmth of the rays on her face, and let all the fear and anger and turmoil boil to the surface.

She gripped her paintbrush in her hand, her fingers tingling. Normally, she'd have an idea of what image she wanted to convey—what picture she wanted to breathe life into. But not today. Today was about using her paints and her talent to purge herself of emotions the only way she knew how.

Swiping the feather-like tip across a swab of paint on the palette beside her, she faced the blank canvas and slashed her brush over the white space. Left. Right. Up. Down. She let the horrors of the past two days slap against her, beating her with their ugliness. Press down upon her with their evil.

Without cleaning her brush, she dunked it into a different color. Splashing the bright red color onto the lines she'd already made. The colors bled together, becoming bolder until it screamed out her pain.

Tears burned in her eyes. Pressure pushed against her sinus cavity. A scream of frustration at an unfair life filled with unwanted twists she never saw coming built inside her until she couldn't contain it any longer.

In a fit of fury, she plunged her brush in another color and another and another. Throwing them on the canvas, blurring the thick lines and contorting the mangle of colors. Her tears fell faster, her breathing came quicker. All the emotion pouring from her lodged in her throat until she gasped for air.

Spent, she dropped her arm to her side, rapid pants raising her chest. She blinked and stared at what she'd created. A ripple of appreciation and awe waded through the tidal wave of feelings still holding her hostage. The deep reds dripped into the creamy whites and thick lines of black until recognition had her pressing a trembling hand to her mouth.

She'd drawn her orchid. The once-beloved flower that she'd carried in her bridal bouquet, then had given her hope when a mourner had sent one to stand beside her husband's coffin. Now the petals in her mind were stained in blood, the meaning behind the flower tarnished by a single act of... What? Vengeance? Anger?

She'd been so wrapped up in her own misery that she hadn't stopped to consider why the person who'd committed murder the night before would chance coming back into her apartment. Never wondered why someone would use something she'd loved to create something sinister where death would always linger.

But isn't that what she'd just done? Taken the dark and twisted parts inside her and used them to create beauty?

Guilt crushed her windpipe, and she grabbed the palette of paints and threw it at the canvas. Never would she use such a horrible tragedy for her own gain.

A sharp gasp whirled her around, her heart galloping in her chest.

Christine stood in the doorway. Her wide-eyed stare on the canvas. "Why'd you do that?"

Relief sagged her shoulders and she set her brush on the long table that lined the wall. Snagging a rag from the pocket of the old jeans she'd thrown on, she wiped the paint from her hands. "It's nothing," she said, flicking her wrist toward the painting. "Just a way to get some of my emotions out so I can focus."

Christine stepped inside with her deep, red lips parted. "You know," she said, her head slightly tilted to the side. "You didn't ruin it. The splash of colors running together and trailing down the petals are mesmerizing."

Olivia watched the thick drips slide down like tears and shuddered. Not wanting to see the beautiful chaos she'd created, she put her back to the canvas. "What are you doing here?"

Her question snapped Christine out of the weird trance-like stare. "Just checking in. I wanted to tell you about my chat with the detectives earlier and see if you've found anything out about what happened to Courtney." She jingled a set of keys at her side.

A sudden thought barreled into her. Christine had a key to her apartment, which meant she could have come in at any time to grab whatever she'd wanted. Or unknowingly allowed someone else in who'd taken the key to the loft. She would never believe her best friend would ever kill someone, but that didn't mean she didn't know someone who would.

Even if she didn't realize it.

Chapter 7

"How did you get in here?" The shock at seeing Christine standing in her doorway melted away, replaced by curiosity. She'd just changed the locks to her apartment yesterday, so the spare her friend kept in case of emergencies would be no good now.

Christine lifted the ring of keys in her hand and gave them a little shake. The metal clanking against each other like chimes. "Jason stopped by the bakery first thing this morning. He told me about what happened and wanted to make sure we could both help keep an eye on things."

Keep an eye on her, is what he meant. Her brother had looked after her this past year, his constant concern over her well-being one of the issues that had driven a wedge between him and his wife, but giving away a key to her apartment was going too far. No matter how good his intentions.

Instead of making her friend feel bad, she smiled. "I hadn't realized he had made copies." She'd have a talk with him later about overstepping.

Christine tipped her chin toward the painting. "Will you take it to the gallery?"

Facing the canvas, she shrugged. "I need the money, and told Edward I'd have some new pieces today, but something feels icky about selling this." She studied the fluid lines that came together to create what her subconscious had dictated. The vivid colors combined into a flurry of unspoken emotions, energy practically leaping from the canvas.

"Don't be silly." Christine stepped into the room and stood beside her. "You're an artist. You take what you're feeling and morph it into something that makes others feel. This…. this evokes sadness and grief and beauty. It shows hope in a place of darkness."

Sighing, Olivia set her brush on the paint-splattered table. "This is different. Someone was murdered. How can I use her tragic end for my personal gain?"

"You're doing no such thing. You're using your talent to help cope with the messed-up shit life has thrown on your doorstep. Again."

The need for money clashed with the guilt swirling inside her like the mixture of paints she'd thrown on the canvas. But the need for quick cash won out. Before she could change her mind, she plucked her phone from the pocket of her denim overalls she preferred to work in and snapped a photo of the orchid that had poured from her soul.

"Want to walk over to the gallery with me? I'll show Edward a picture of the painting and see if he wants to hang it up."

Christine squeezed her hand, the sound of her sniffing back tears fisting her heart. "Sure."

"Are you okay?" she asked, knowing the last couple days had been tough on Christine as well.

She shook her head. "Not really. We can talk about it later."

The constant fear hovering over her refused to leave, even with her best friend at her side. After locking up behind them and reaching the hallway, she broached the subject that had plagued her all day. "I'm sorry you were dragged into this. I saw the detectives in charge of the investigation. I know they came and spoke with you this morning."

A flash of sorrow lit Christine's eyes, widening behind her glasses. "It's not your fault. I figured they'd want to speak with me. It was just so much tougher than I imagined. I've never had to speak with the police before."

A memory of grim-faced officers showing up to discuss Dave's accident slammed against her. So far, her experience with being approached by officers hadn't led to anything positive, but she couldn't dwell on that now. "What did they say?"

Christine led the way down the stairs, waiting until she reached the shabby lobby before responding. "They wanted to know where I was the night Courtney was murdered. They weren't happy when I didn't have anyone to confirm I was home—alone—all night."

Olivia winced and pushed open the door.

"They also asked about my relationship with Jason and Courtney. The dark stubble on Detective Green's face couldn't hide his irritation with my answers."

"What about Detective Stone?" Olivia couldn't help but ask. She hadn't dealt with the other officer. Jack had been the one by her side. Hell, he was the one who had been on her mind way too much since this disaster started.

Christine shrugged and turned down the empty sidewalk toward the gallery next door. "He didn't say much. Wrote everything I said down, though. That made me jumpy. Like he was analyzing every little word I said and searching for some admission of guilt." The normal falsetto of her voice dipped low. "The only thing I'm guilty of is suggesting Courtney stay at the place where she'd meet her death. Trust me, that's enough to tear me up inside for the rest of my life. I spoke with Eli. He's torn to pieces over this. It's just all too much to process."

"I'm sorry." The words were so small and inadequate but all she had to offer with the front door to the gallery in front of her. When they finished here, she could offer ice cream and a shoulder to cry on, but that would have to wait just a little bit longer.

"It is what it is. As much as I wish I could fix it, I can't. But let's not think about it right now. Let's go make you some money." She opened the door wide, waiting for Olivia to step through the doorway before entering, then letting the glass door close.

Olivia inhaled a deep breath, giving herself one moment of happiness. She loved stepping inside the converted warehouse. Its stark white walls stood in contrast to the mahogany floors and the aged brick outside. A door in the back stayed closed, hiding art that had been sold or kept out of rotation. The mess in there always spiked her anxiety so she steered clear unless she needed to use the bathroom, which was inconveniently located in the storage area. Edward Consuelo had changed her life two years ago when he'd given her a chance and housed her first art exhibit. Ever since, he'd worked hard to build her brand and increase her value as an artist.

"Hola, my lovely Olivia!" Edward's booming voice echoed off the high ceiling. He stood outside his office in the front corner of the room, his arms stretched wide and a huge grin on his handsome face. "Your ears must be burning. I was about to call you, my dear."

She greeted him with a kiss on each cheek before noting a twinkle in his brown eyes. "No burning ears. Just a new piece I wanted to show you to see if you had space for it." She pulled out her phone and scrolled to the photo. Handing the device over, she bit into her bottom lip as she waited for his response. No matter how many pieces she sold, her nerves always danced the first time she showed him something new.

Leaning forward, Edward squinted at the photo. "Oh dios mio. This is powerful. Even on a tiny image on your phone. I can only image the full impact in person."

Christine bumped her with her shoulder. "Told you."

"Do you have space for it?" she asked, her stomach in knots. She hated being so dependent on selling her art to make ends meet. As if pieces of her actual soul were for sale to the highest bidder. But gone were the days when her husband's salary supported her needs while her passion was something that provided her with a creative outlet—any money she earned put toward the fun extras. "I could bring it in tomorrow. Today even, if you want it."

Grinning, Edward clapped his hands, then rubbed his palms together. "Perfect. Because I just sold every one of your pieces to one very special buyer."

Olivia's head reared back. "What?"

He clamped his hands on her shoulders, giving her a little shake as if to pump up her enthusiasm. "Sold! Every single one! I need more work if you want me to make you more money."

A statement that would have set her on cloud nine mere days before had her swallowing bile that crept up her throat. Uneasiness settled in the pit of her stomach. A nagging sensation told her that whoever had cleared out her art was interested in more than just her paintings.

The tinkle of laughter and the cheerful clinking of glasses stood in direct opposition to the teary-eyed man hunched over his beer in the dark corner of the hotel bar. Jack inwardly cringed. Interviewing a victim's ex-husband over a drink wasn't something he relished. But after Brock Bailey's flight had been delayed, he'd agreed to meet the man at his hotel instead of making him come down to the station in the evening rush hour traffic.

A decision he now regretted. Not just because the man sitting in front of him was on his second drink, but because after a long ass day with zero answers, he'd give anything to drown his bad mood in a glass of whiskey.

Brock skirted his gaze around the bar, a scowl on his thin lips. Blond scruff lined his jaw in a disheveled way that matched his messy hair. "How can people still be happy and carefree when my world just crashed down at my feet?"

A beat of confusion thudded along with the tempo of piano keys in the distance. Usually, a man recently divorced held more contempt than concern for their ex-wife. "I'm sorry for your loss. I understand you and Mrs. Bailey had just finalized your divorce."

"Biggest mistake of my life. Now I can never make things right."

The misery etching itself on the other man's face mirrored what Jack carried inside him every day since Mary's death. Life had kept moving forward even after he'd let feelings for a woman he had no business falling for cloud his judgment. He'd never fix that mistake, a fact that haunted him nightly when he lay in bed and chased after sleep.

But he'd loved Mary. Hadn't left her in search of a new life.

"I spoke with your in-laws," Jack said, needing to get the interview back on track so he could go home and wash off this awful day. "They said you two had a loving marriage until Courtney found out you'd cheated on her."

Brock winced and downed the rest of his beer, swiping the back of his hand over his mouth to wipe away the lingering droplets of liquid. "I was stupid. I let my guard down one night when out with my buddies. I told her what happened. Promised it'd never happen again. She said I lost her trust. That she couldn't forgive me and wanted a divorce."

His opinion didn't matter, but he couldn't blame the young woman for wanting her freedom from a man who didn't respect her enough to stay faithful. "Were you angry that she wouldn't take you back?"

With his gaze fixed on some faraway space, Brock nodded. "It was easier to be mad than admit I'd messed up. To realize it wasn't just the cheating that pushed her away. But, man, I loved her so damn much. I'd vowed to win her back."

"Is that why you went to Vegas?" Jack asked, fighting to keep an edge of sarcasm from his voice. If he planned to fight to keep the love of his life around, flying to Vegas with his buddies was the last place he'd be. Unless he needed to be out of town—far away with lots of witnesses.

Brock hung his head. "I was giving her space. Figured if she had some time, she might be more open to talking to me. Now I know if I'd stayed, she wouldn't have been in New York. Wouldn't have called Christine about a place to get away. If I'd stayed and fought for her, she'd still be alive."

So he knew where she was and who had given the recommendation to the victim. "Are you acquainted with Christine Roberts?"

Brock lifted a finger to signal to the server. "A little. Her and my brother-in-law are friends. She'd be around sometimes. Nice lady."

Jack settled back in his chair, keeping attuned to any signs of lying from the other man. "What about Olivia Hickman?"

He shook his head. "Never heard of her."

That jibed with Olivia's claim to have never met

Courtney. "Did your ex-wife have any disagreements with anyone you're aware of in her last days? Weeks?"

"Just me. And maybe the downstairs neighbor. Mrs. Hench's dog always barks in the middle of the night. Drives Courtney nuts because it always wakes her up." Brock's face crumpled. "Drove her nuts."

Jack scribbled a few notes on the notepad he'd flipped open and left on the table. Clearly, Brock Bailey hadn't killed his wife, but that didn't mean he didn't know who had. "That's all I have for you now. Thanks for speaking with me. I'll be in contact if I have any more questions."

Wide, remorseful eyes stared up at him as he stood and slid his notepad in his back pocket. "That's it? Four years of marriage and you only have a handful of questions to ask me about the woman I loved? The woman who was murdered because I couldn't keep her safe? There must be more I can tell you. More I can help with. Please. I have to help find out who did this."

Jack tossed a business card on the table. "Call me if you think of anything else I need to know. In the meantime, the best thing you can do is be better. Don't make the same mistake next time." The unsolicited advice slipped out before he could stop it.

The server brought over another drink, taking the empty glass with her when she walked away.

Brock stared at the white foam frothing at the top of the tall glass. "There will never be a next for me."

With nothing more to say, Jack dipped his head in goodbye and left the grieving man to nurse his pain in the dark corner of the crowded bar. The alcohol might help numb his heartbreak for the night, but it'd be back in full force the next morning, along with a splitting headache.

Jack's shoes slapped against the marble floor as he passed under the opulent chandelier in the lobby. Clusters of people waited in line to check in or perched on seating with their luggage nearby. Nice hotel. Probably cost a pretty penny for a night's stay. He'd poked around in the Baileys' finances before talking with Brock. Not filthy rich, but they did well. Well enough to pay someone to head into the city and get their hands messy for an upset husband who was pissed his wife refused to take him back.

The theory didn't sit well with him, but his gut had been wrong before. Besides, he didn't have any other leads to follow. Irritation hung around him like a cloud of a dust as he bypassed the revolving door and pushed out the side exit.

The sun had set, leaving the air chilled and lights splashing around him. He merged into the stream of pedestrians toward the garage he'd parked his car in, a few blocks away. His phone vibrated in his pocket, and he debated letting it go to voice mail. His shift had ended an hour ago, and he wasn't expecting any calls. Conversation was the last thing on his list of wants at the moment, but an open case meant any call could be important.

Digging out his phone, he saw Max's number flash across the screen and tightened his stomach muscles. "Hey, man. I'm just leaving my interview with Brock Bailey. What's up?"

"I need you to get to Olivia Hickman's loft. Another renter's been murdered."

Chapter 8

Jack inhaled a deep breath, preparing himself for a conversation he didn't want to have, and coughed out stray bits of dust that burned his lungs. The dim lights hung high on the walls cast an eerie glow over the shabby hallway outside of Olivia's apartment. He'd told his partner he'd deliver the news of the murdered renter to Olivia while Max started looking into the life of the newest victim—Priscilla Abbington.

Not like either he or Max expected to find much that would lead to her murderer. Even her boyfriend—the person who'd called in the crime—wasn't high on their list of suspects at this time. The odds that the killer was someone connected with Olivia climbed higher than the Empire State Building with each passing second.

Not being able to put off the inevitable any longer,

Jack waited for a young couple to pass by, then knocked on the warped green door.

The door swung open, as if she was waiting on the other side for him. Her hair was tied back in a low ponytail and not a trace of makeup covered her face. Splatters of paint dotted her overalls, and a streak of blue paint spread across her cheek. The combination charming as hell.

She kept her grip on the round knob and blocked his way into the apartment—as if only placing her slight frame in his path would keep the bad news in the hallway with him. "I'm surprised to see you so late. Do you have news? Did you catch the person who killed Courtney?"

He'd learned over the years the best way to deliver bad news was to just rip off the Band-Aid, but the way she stared up at him with hope shining from her hazel eyes made his chest burn. "Unfortunately, I don't have good news. There's been another murder."

She reared back, and her knees buckled.

Jack swept inside, hooking an arm around the small of her back to keep her on her feet. "You're okay. I got ya."

She blinked up at him as if not understanding what was happening. With one hand still on the doorknob, she gripped the neck of his shirt with the other. "I don't understand. Who? Who was killed?"

"Priscilla Abbington."

Olivia closed her eyes and hung her head. Her body went lax. "No, no, no. This can't be happening."

"Let's get you inside." He loosened her grip from

the door, closing it before leading her to the sofa and sitting beside her.

She stared ahead with her lips trembling. "She had her boyfriend with her. I thought she'd be safe. I didn't think someone could hurt her if she wasn't alone."

He fought the urge to fidget, or worse, lay a reassuring hand on her and offer comfort. "Her boyfriend called it in. It appears he went down to the gym. When he came back to the loft, he found Ms. Abbington dead by the door. Security footage from the building shows someone knocking, the door opening, then the same person turning and walking quickly toward the exit."

A sharp inhale of breath drew his attention to her full lips, and he shifted away so their knees weren't touching. Being this close messed with his head. Something he couldn't afford.

"Are you sure it wasn't the boyfriend?" She cringed. "Is that horrible?"

He lifted the corner of his mouth in an attempt to make her feel better. "No, that's not horrible. But we checked the footage in the gym. The boyfriend was running on the treadmill when Ms. Abbington opened the door."

"Then this isn't about her. Or Courtney Bailey. It's about me." She pressed her hands to her stomach. "I don't understand. How could killing two innocent women have anything to do with me? What's the endgame? What's the point?"

The same questions had kept him up last night and plagued him all day. He'd already asked her the same lineup of questions reserved for victims, but maybe time had shaken a few forgotten things loose. "Can you think of anyone who'd want to hurt you? Who's upset with you?"

She lifted her hands, then let them drop in her lap. "No. I don't even see many people. Most days I spend trapped in my studio. Painting alone. I keep to myself, try to be kind and stay out of people's business. I can't think of anyone who'd want to harm me in any way."

Leaning forward, he tapped his finger against the edge of the coffee table as he worked out a thought spinning in his brain. He'd done some surface level research on her husband, just to get a better understanding of Olivia's situation. He'd read about the accident that had taken his life—a hit-and-run while he'd been out for a jog when on vacation in the Hudson River Valley—the driver never found. Maybe someone with a vendetta against her husband was taking their anger out on Olivia. "What about your husband?"

"Excuse me?" Her body tensed beside him. Her narrowed gaze caused ripples to gather on her brow.

A pinch of unease made him squirm. He hated to bring up something so painful, but he couldn't leave even one stone unturned. No matter how difficult it was for Olivia to discuss. "Someone has an axe to grind. If not against you, who else? The loft was owned by both of you, correct?"

Slowly, she nodded.

"Then maybe your husband pissed someone off before his death, and now they're coming after the only person they can." He felt like he was grasping at straws, but this new theory was better than nothing. Even if it only played as a jumping-off point for more questions.

A sad smile played on her lips. "Everyone loved

Dave. Besides, he died a year ago. What could he have done that someone would let their anger fester for that long, only to go after his widow? It doesn't make sense."

"None of this makes sense, and chances are, it never will to you. Because you aren't the type of person who would take the lives of innocent women. It might be difficult, but you can't look at things logically. Can't be afraid that looking at things in a different way could mean you're a bad person. Nothing you say, even if just thinking out loud, will leave this room if it doesn't have to."

She released a shaky breath. "Okay, but I'm not looking at my husband with rose-colored glasses. He was a great man who people respected and liked. I promise, if I could think of anyone who would come after me because of him, I would tell you."

She paused for a minute, her stare unfocused, and rubbed her thumb against the spot on her left finger where her wedding ring should have been. "What about the person who hit Dave?"

"What about them?" he asked.

"Whoever was driving the car that took his life was never found. I'm sure the police did everything they could to catch the driver, but…" She shrugged and wiped at her eyes. "It never sat right with me. That whoever killed him was still out there, unaffected and going on with life. I've always wondered…" Her voice tailed off, as if she was afraid to speak her mind.

"Wondered what?"

She finally caught his gaze head-on. "If it was really an accident."

Her statement had him sitting on the edge of the

cushion. "Is there a certain reason for you to think it wasn't?"

Again, she shrugged and twisted her mouth to the side. "Just a feeling. But everyone told me it was my grief talking. That as much as it sucked and I didn't get the closure I wanted, I needed to move on because nothing would bring Dave back."

Unable to resist a second longer, he squeezed her knee and offered a reassuring smile. "I'm sorry for what you went through, and if you think something was off, I trust your instincts. I'll call the station and try to get a look at the files. See if anything stands out to me."

She blinked, as if not believing him, her lips parted. "Seriously? That's…that's amazing. Thank you."

He patted her leg, then removed his hand. Not wanting to cross any boundaries. He'd make the call in the morning, but until he could get his hands on Dave Hickman's case files, he had to get his head back on his current case. Switching gears, he considered a different angle. "Maybe someone is trying to scare you away from the loft."

Olivia snorted and flopped against the back of the sofa. "Well then it's working."

Mirroring her body language, he leaned back against the plush cushions. "Can you think of anyone who would want you to sell your property? Anyone that could benefit from you not wanting to live there or rent it to travelers?"

The tightening of her jaw alerted him to something she hadn't yet given voice to. "What is it?"

She twisted her hands in her lap and refused to meet his gaze. "I'm sure it's nothing."

The slight tremble in her words had him sitting straight. "Tell me."

"After Dave died, my brother helped me a lot. Lots of visits and phone calls and sorting out my finances. Dave didn't have any life insurance, so it's been difficult to navigate how to pay my bills and get by on my own."

"Sounds like a nice guy," he said, not following her ramblings or what they had to do with the case.

"He is. This is his apartment, and he's subletting it to me at a crazy low price. Otherwise, I'd never be able to afford it and keep the loft."

He drew his brows together in concentration, trying to understand her train of thought. "Are you saying your brother would want you to sell your property?"

"Not my brother," she said, sandwiching her bottom lip between her teeth. "His wife. Well, soon-to-be-ex-wife, actually. She didn't like how much he helped me financially, and it bothered her that I'd keep the loft instead of just selling it. All the attention and money Jason gave me put a strain on their marriage until it was too much for her. Even though I promised to pay them back, she filed for divorce a month ago."

He mentally flipped through the names and numbers she'd listed of the people who'd been in her apartment. Her brother's wife had been among them. "Clara, right?"

She nodded.

The timing lined up. If her sister-in-law just left her brother, she could have snapped and taken things into her own hands to get money she thought rightfully hers. Selling the loft would get Olivia out of the apartment, which in turn could line the other woman's pockets.

"Have you been in contact with her since she filed for divorce?"

"No. She hasn't wanted anything to do with me. I've reached out, but she never answers," she said, frowning deeply with her lips drawn down.

A beat of anticipation echoed inside him. Finally, a theory that might pan out to be something more. "She's not going to have a choice now. She'll talk to me whether she wants to or not."

Olivia's head spun. How was this her life? Being somehow connected to multiple murders and now the police wanting to speak with Clara, like she was a possible suspect. Her sister-in-law might harbor some ill feelings, but she'd never hurt anyone. Well, anyone else besides Jason, who was still beside himself at the path his marriage had taken—doing whatever he could to win back his wife.

"I noticed you installed a security system in the loft," Jack said, interrupting her thoughts.

"I wish it would have made a difference." A headache brewed inside her, and she pinched the bridge of her nose in an attempt to stop the mounting pressure. She'd been so stressed about the cost of installing the system, as well as the rush order to get it done that afternoon. Even if the influx of money from selling all her paintings to some mysterious buyer had given her the cash she needed, the money felt tainted somehow.

Maybe that was something she should bring up to Jack. "Something else happened today."

Concern clouded Jack's baby blues. "Were you hurt? Did someone threaten you?"

The hitch in his voice pulled at her heartstrings. Instinct moved her hand to rest on his arm, squeezing lightly to reassure him she was fine. "Nothing like that. I went into the gallery that sells my art and someone had purchased every piece."

He dropped his gaze to her hand and flicked his tongue over his lips. "That's impressive. Did you have a lot of pieces there?" he asked, raising his brows.

Heat simmered in her core. Nodding, she slid her palm off his arm. Touching him—hell, being near him—made her stomach do somersaults. She needed to take control of these ridiculous feelings and concentrate on what mattered. "Twelve paintings. Altogether, close to twenty thousand dollars."

He let out a low whistle. "Quite the haul. Has this ever happened before?"

She couldn't help a small laugh. Being an artist, especially at the start of her career, wasn't a lucrative venture. Most people had an idealized notion of how much money she made and the way she spent her time. Her days consisted of too much caffeine and too little sleep just to break even—if that. "No. Definitely not. Even when I've headlined my own shows, I haven't made half of that."

"Did the owner of the gallery give you any details about the buyer?"

"He had the guy's name and number but didn't know much more about him. He called this morning and paid with a credit card. Said he'd send for the paintings soon."

"I can run down a credit card number easy. I'll get a hold of the owner of the gallery tomorrow. What's his name?" Jack scooped up his ever-present pencil, ready to write down whatever she said.

"Edward Consuelo. He'll help you with anything you need." He'd been a good friend over the past couple years, even before Dave's death. His interest in her as an artist had given her confidence and taken her career to the next level.

Jack frowned, his hand paused with the pencil poised over the pad of paper on the coffee table. "Another name from your list. Does he come here, to your apartment, often?"

A bite of something—jealousy maybe—tainted his words, and she hated the giddiness it stirred inside her. Not only was her relationship with Edward strictly professional but causing jealousy in a man she had no business being attracted to shouldn't cause her anything but irritation. "He stops by from time to time to see what I'm working on."

The side of Jack's mouth twitched, as if there was more he wanted to ask but wasn't sure how. "Does he take an interest in you...personally?"

She stifled a chuckle. "No. He's interested in my art and how to sell it. Nothing more."

"Hmm. Well, I have some questions for him tomorrow as well. Maybe our luck has turned, and our culprit slipped up with buying your art." He tossed the pencil down.

A sudden chill made her shiver. It was hard to imagine any sort of luck coming out of this situation. Nothing but death and despair had been at her doorstep lately. She just wanted it to stop.

Ding.

"What's that?" Jack glanced around the room in search of the noise.

"A notification on my laptop." She stood and swiped her computer from the counter in her kitchenette. Flipping open the lid, she brought up her browser window and clicked on the tab for the rental site. "I need to go online anyway. I have to delete the listing for the loft and get a hold of people who've already booked the property. Let them know I'm taking the loft off the site."

"For good?" He anchored his forearms on his knees, stare fixed on her.

She shrugged, even though her mind was made up. "I kept the loft because it was my home with a husband I loved more than anything. Even if I couldn't afford to live there myself, I couldn't part with it. Couldn't say goodbye to one more thing I loved. Especially when it was the one place I could sit and close my eyes and pretend for just a couple of minutes that my life was the way it once was. The way I wish it could be."

A lump lodged in her throat and tears misted in her eyes. Dammit. Why was she always falling apart in front of this man? Wiping at her eyes, she drew in a shuddering breath. "All that is gone now. I'll never feel love or joy or comfort in that place. Dave isn't there, and the loft is stained with the blood of two innocent women. I don't want to hold on to it anymore."

As the words left her mouth, a weight lifted from her shoulders. As though holding on so hard to such a huge part of her past had been holding her back and she hadn't even realized it.

"I can understand that," Jack said, sincerity in his gravelly baritone.

She snorted. "Which part?"

"All of it." A slow smile spread across his mouth, but sadness lingered in his eyes. "I understand wanting to keep something close, even if it won't bring back the person you love. Even if it doesn't make sense to anyone else. I also understand needing to let it go, even if you don't know how."

Glancing up from the screen, she studied the faraway look in his eyes, and it twisted something inside her. She'd bared parts of her soul to help him catch a criminal, but she knew close to nothing about him.

And the fact that she wanted to scared the hell out of her.

Needing to break the strange intimacy of the moment, she shifted her focus back to the computer. A little bell in the corner of the website indicated she had a new review. She clicked on the icon and a flurry or words scattered on her screen and made her blood turn cold.

Jack jumped to his feet and hurried to her side. "What is it?"

Trembling, she handed him the computer.

He squinted at the screen, then swore under his breath before reading the review out loud. "'Stay out of our home or I'll get you, too.'"

Chapter 9

Hours later, anger boiled inside Jack so raw and hot he thought it would burst out of him. He wanted to punch the bright red throw pillows beside him on Olivia's couch. As much as he'd known in his gut the murders were related to Olivia, the new threat written down for all the internet to see was a digital slap in the face.

To make matters worse, he couldn't trace the sonofabitch who'd had the balls to leave the threat on the website. A major hit to his pride. As a former Cybercrimes detective, this was his specialty. But a conversation with the representative from the rental company had led nowhere, as the information given to create the profile was all a bunch of bullshit. All he was left with was a bogus name and phone number to a pizza shop in Queens.

He'd tossed the information over to Max, who was wading through the muck of false leads and scattered bread crumbs at his own place. Jack was stuck in his own personal hell. He set up shop in Olivia's apartment, her fear so great she'd asked him to stay for a little while.

Now Olivia sat on the edge of her bed, one bare foot dangling with the other tucked beneath her, and her computer on her lap. She stretched her arms high above her head, and he fought to keep his attention on the laptop he'd secured from his car.

Frustration had him raking his palms down his face. Pointy whiskers scratched his skin. Damn, he needed to head home to shower, shave, and regroup. All things he couldn't do with Olivia so close. "I'm getting nowhere," he admitted as much to himself as her.

She perked up, hazel eyes wide with worry. "Are you leaving?"

Indecision weighted his words. A part of him wanted to run for the hills and put as much distance between him and Olivia as possible. He could do the little research he had on his plate anywhere. He'd gotten all the information he needed from her at the moment.

But the aura of fear wrapped around her made leaving difficult. "I need to take a break. I've hit a wall. All the words on my computer are starting to run together."

"Are you hungry?" she asked, jumping to her feet. "I hadn't eaten dinner before you arrived, and with everything that's happened, I kind of forgot about it until now."

Hope lifted the lines of her face. He moved his hand to the back of his neck and refused to meet her eager stare. Sharing a late meal with her wasn't exactly what he had in mind. He needed space, distance until their paths were forced to meet again.

As if his body rebelled against logic, his stomach growled.

"Dinner it is." She crossed to the ridiculously small fridge and searched inside. "I don't have much. Cooking isn't really my thing."

He couldn't exactly refuse her now, so he stood and stretched the stiff muscles in his legs. "You know, I could use a little air. How about we grab a bite somewhere close before I head home?"

Nodding, she swallowed hard. "Okay. Do you like Mexican? There's a place down the street that's pretty decent."

"Perfect." Grabbing his stuff, he met her at the door, then followed her down the hall after she'd locked up.

She stepped outside and pointed over her shoulder. "The gallery that sells my art is right there, by the way."

He peered behind him at the warehouse. The lights were off inside the building, but the streetlights illuminated bold, black letters on a white sign that read A Peculiar Sight. "What time does Edward get to work in the morning?" The man hadn't answered his or Olivia's calls earlier. He planned to show up in the morning and get the information he needed regarding the mysterious buyer of Olivia's artwork.

Olivia shoved her hands in the pockets of her jean jacket and huddled against the chilly air barreling down the street. "He's usually there pretty early. By 8:00 a.m. at the latest."

"Is it normal for him to dodge your calls?" He was

used to people ignoring him, the number coming through as unknown, but he was surprised the man orchestrating Olivia's career had sent her to voice mail. Not bothering to call her back after she'd explained in a message why she'd called.

She lifted one shoulder, then turned toward the restaurant with bright red and green banners hanging from the window. "Not really. But he's probably busy."

"Hmm," he grunted, not willing to share his real thoughts about the gallery owner. A quick background check of Edward Consuelo had red flags flying at warp speed. The man had bankrupted two galleries before moving to the Meatpacking District of Manhattan. Both in Queens, not far from the pizza shop he'd tracked down with the bogus number left with the vacation rental site. Add the fact that Edward had been in Olivia's apartment, and that he was the only one who knew who'd bought her paintings, and Jack had his first real suspect.

Needing to let all the information he'd collected percolate, as well as needing to end the sudden starvation gripping his stomach, he opened the door and a blast of live mariachi music slammed against his eardrums. He waited for Olivia to precede him before entering the restaurant. Orange vinyl booths lined the walls, most of them empty. The scent of fried tortillas and grilled meat made his mouth water.

A hostess stood behind a wooden podium. She grabbed two menus and smiled. "Two?"

"Yes, please," he answered, following Olivia to a booth in the back.

A server hurried over with a basket full of chips and

two small bowls filled with salsa. He scurried away before Jack could ask for a glass of water.

Olivia grabbed a chip and broke it in half before dipping part of it in the salsa and popping it in her mouth. "Everything is good here."

"Smells amazing." He searched the menu for the same dish he ordered at every Mexican restaurant, then closed it and laid it beside him. "How are you holding up?" He shouldn't ask—shouldn't care as much as he did—but she'd been through hell the last couple of days. If she needed someone to vent to, he was as good as anyone to take on that burden. At least for the time being.

She shrugged. "Nothing feels real right now. Like, this can't be my life. But I've been in this place before."

He arched a brow and snagged a chip from the plastic basket.

She snorted out a laugh. "Not exactly like this. But I've been in that place where every waking moment is more like a weird, unbelievable dream than reality. It was the same after Dave died. And just like before, as much as I hope to wake up and have everything back to normal, that will never happen. I just have to keep moving, keep figuring out the next step, until things get better."

He bit into the crispy chip and took in her words. "I understand what you mean."

She tilted her head, eyes narrowed, as if trying to see inside his head. "I'm sure as an officer you've experienced things I've never even imagined."

The intensity of her stare made him squirm. The plastic cushion underneath him crinkled.

The server returned, order pad in hand, before he

was forced to delve into the unspoken question she'd thrown his way. "Would you like something to drink?"

"Margarita on the rocks with no salt," Olivia said. "And I'll have a taco salad for dinner."

His mouth watered at the idea of tequila, but as much as he wanted to soothe his quaking nerves with liquor, it wasn't a good idea. "Water and chicken fajitas, please."

The server dipped his chin and scurried away.

Olivia leaned back and placed her clasped hands on the table. A hint of interest lightened the amber in her eyes. "Enough about me and the hell I've gone through. I want to know something about you."

He swallowed hard. In his line of work, he'd sat across from a lot of really bad people. The anxiety nestled in his gut told him sitting across from Olivia, answering personal questions, just might be the scariest thing he'd ever done.

The cool splash of lime and tequila warmed Olivia's veins. She took another sip, gaze fixed over her large glass at Jack. She'd meant what she'd said. She had no desire to tell this man any more information about herself—personal or otherwise. Like him, she needed a break from thinking about who could be tormenting her, and she'd spilled enough emotions over Detective Jack Stone to last a lifetime. It was his turn to confide in her a little bit.

Whether he wanted to or not.

"Tell me, Jack, how long have you been a homicide detective for the great city of New York?"

"A few months." He took a sip of his water.

She lowered her glass to the table and her jaw

dropped. The man—or at least one of them—who was responsible for finding the killer out to get her had only been on the job a few months? A buzz of anxiety mixed with the alcohol in her blood. "Oh."

He chuckled. "I've been a detective for the last five years. I worked for the Cybercrimes unit until a short while ago. I transferred over to Homicide."

She sagged against the plush booth in relief. Homicide might be different than what'd he'd done before, but he had experience as a detective—understood how to work a case and get to the bottom of things. "Why the change? I'd imagine you'd see some pretty grisly things working homicides."

A flicker of emotion crossed over his chiseled features. Regret? Sadness? "I'm sorry. I shouldn't assume one area would be worse than the other." She rushed to cover her comment, hoping to erase the look from his face. She wanted to know more about him, but she hadn't wanted to make him uncomfortable.

The server approached the table with a plate in each hand. He set her salad in the fried tortilla bowl in front of her, then slid the platter of sizzling meat and vegetables in front of Jack.

"Thank you," she said, then grabbed her fork. She speared a bite of tomato and ground beef but waited for the server to leave before taking a bite.

Jack opened the foil pack of flour tortillas. A beat of silence wove between them with the sound of maracas and guitars strumming in the corner. Finally, Jack said, "I've learned that some of the worst crimes are orchestrated behind a computer screen. For years, I sat at a desk and tracked the moves of monsters. It took a toll in a way I never thought possible."

"Is that toll different than what you're doing now?" She forced herself not to ask specifics, but she found it difficult to believe it was harder to sit behind a screen searching for bad guys than staring death in the face every day.

He twisted his lips to the side, as if really giving a lot of thought to the question. "Yes and no. I have a partner now. Someone I trust and respect who I can share the burden with. Who can keep an eye on me."

She took another sip of her drink and considered his words. "That's nice. I miss having a partner. Knowing someone is always there when I need them. Having someone who can ease the burdens of life from my shoulders." A sudden bolt of realization struck her. "Are you married?"

Shaking his head, he took a bite of the taco he'd assembled. He closed his eyes on a moan. "No wife."

"Ever? What about a girlfriend?" He was sexy, smart, and kind. A killer combination that would be hard for any woman to resist. She found it hard to believe he was off the market.

He opened his eyes and amusement lifted his lips. "No to both."

Heat burned her cheeks. She shouldn't have asked such a personal question, but she couldn't help herself. "Well, at least you have a partner at work."

His smile faltered. "My job takes a lot of time and energy. Most women I've known aren't very accepting of that."

"Maybe you just haven't found the right woman."

Oh my God. Had she just said that? She dropped her gaze to her salad and pushed the lettuce around with her fork. It was the tequila talking. She was sure of it.

He chuckled, but a sadness weighed down the sound. "You might be right, but my job is complicated. It's gotten in the way of a relationship more than once. The outcome worse than just a broken heart."

She wanted to ask more, to dig deeper, but she fixed her attention on her dinner instead, allowing Jack to do the same. When her stomach ached, she settled against the seat back and focused on finishing her margarita. Her body warmed as she watched him finish his meal, and she considered ordering another drink.

No, one was enough. More than enough based on the questions she'd brazenly asked this virtual stranger after practically begging him to have dinner with her. As much as she wanted to believe asking him to stay with her for a while longer was based on fear of being alone, a part of her knew she just liked being around him.

"This was a good idea. Thanks," he said, scraping up the last bits of food and shoveling them in his mouth. "I was hungrier than I realized."

She smiled, glad he was satisfied. "Told you." She drained the rest of her drink. "Ready? They keep the checks up at the register."

Nodding, he stood, then grabbed his wallet from his back pocket. He plucked out a few bills and tossed them on the table.

Not wanting him to pay for her dinner, she hurried to the front counter and handed over the credit card she had tucked in her jacket.

"What are you doing?" he asked, coming to stop beside her.

"I asked you to come here, so I'll pay." She mentally cringed at the charge to come. The payment she'd be getting for her artwork should be in her bank account tomorrow, the day after at the latest, but she'd be a nervous wreck about finances until then.

He frowned. "You shouldn't have done that, but thanks."

"No problem." She took back her card, then led the way back to her apartment. The cool air fanned the alcohol-induced heat creeping up her neck.

Jack fell into step beside her. The feel of his body so close had her heart racing. The tips of her fingers tingled, and the sudden desire to grab hold of his hand and take comfort in his strength had her shoving her fists in her jacket pockets.

A sudden wave of guilt crashed against her and had her picking up her pace. She must be lonelier and more confused by her circumstances than she'd realized to have such a strong reaction to Jack. She needed to get away from him and get her head on straight before facing another long, hard day tomorrow.

At the door to the building, she faced him with a tight smile. "Thanks for spending so much time with me this evening. I know that's not part of your job description. I feel better now. You don't have to walk me up. I'll be fine."

He lingered beside her, and her pulse picked up. Maybe he'd wanted to spend time with her as much as she had him. Maybe this weird connection wasn't just because of her harebrained emotional state. She held her breath, waiting for his response.

"My computer's still up there," he said, scrunching up his nose.

Humiliation crushed her windpipe. She busied herself opening the door and leading the way up the stairs so he couldn't see the battle for composure she was losing. She should have known better than to have a drink with dinner. The alcohol was making her stupid. Next time she'd do the smart thing and wait until she was alone to crack open a bottle of wine to numb her fear. At her apartment, she turned the lock and threw the door open wide, letting Jack shimmy past her to grab his things.

With his computer tucked under his arm, he faced her with concern etched on his tanned brow. "You sure you'll be okay?"

Not trusting her voice, she nodded.

"You have my number. Call if you need me. Even if you think it's something small. I'll be here as fast as I can."

"Thanks."

He blew out a long breath and darted his gaze around the apartment as if searching for a reason to stay longer. He finally held her stare. "I'll be in touch."

She molded herself against the door and gave him a wide berth as he stepped into the hallway. "Thanks again. For everything." She didn't wait for a response before shutting the door and turning all the locks. She rolled their conversation over in her mind. He'd mentioned heartbreak, and the ending of a relationship being worse than that.

She understood. The ending of her relationship with Dave had been worse than heartbreaking—it had been soul shattering. As she tidied her space and got ready for bed, the weight and questions of the last few days were far from her mind. Instead, she couldn't help wondering about Jack. Who had broken his heart, or had he broken someone else's? Because the only thing she had learned tonight was that if she let him, Jack could surely hurt her. Not only was she attracted to him, but he fascinated her. She wanted to know more, get to the bottom of what made him tick. If she were honest with herself, she hadn't felt so drawn to someone since she'd met Dave.

And after everything she'd been through, even a tiny tap on her taped-together heart could destroy her.

Chapter 10

The morning sun had yet to break through the night sky and the street around him still buzzed with life. Jack had planned on stopping by to question Edward Consuelo first thing this morning, but he hadn't expected a call from Max to force him from bed to meet him at A Peculiar Sight so damn early.

The cup of coffee he'd grabbed on his way over was still half-full, but he chucked the paper cup into the trash as he approached the storefront. There wasn't enough caffeine in the world to clear the cobwebs from his exhausted mind. He'd spent half the night tossing and turning in an attempt to forget about his evening with Olivia.

An evening that had been far more enjoyable than it should have been. He shouldn't have spent so much time with her. Not when he couldn't get a grip on the growing attraction that intensified every time he saw her. But that was an issue he'd have to handle another time. Now he needed to focus on what waited for him at the art gallery.

Max stood in front of the converted warehouse, hands plunged deep in his jacket pockets, and huddled against the biting wind. Noticing Jack, he dipped his chin. "Morning."

Jack couldn't help but cast a quick glance toward the third-floor windows of Olivia's building before addressing his partner. "Have you spoken with Edward?"

"Nope," Max said, rocking back on his heels. "Just got here a second ago. I wanted to wait for you to head in. Dispatch said things were vandalized last night. An officer is here taking the owner's statement. Thought it'd be best if we arrive together so we can both get a read on him from the start."

"I have a whole list of questions for this guy. Let's see what he has to say."

Jack followed Max inside, blinking at the glare of the bright lights against white walls. Yellow crime-scene tape stretched across paintings hanging in thick black frames. Slashes cut through the bright colors like gaping wounds on the canvas. He crossed over the gleaming dark wood floors and read the gold plaque mounted beside the ruined artwork.

Olivia Hickman.

His pulse picked up speed, but he kept his questions to himself as he led the way to the office, where an officer stood guard outside the opened door.

Max flashed his badge. "I'm Detective Green. This

is my partner, Detective Stone. We're here to speak with Edward Consuelo."

"He's inside the office, sir. He's speaking with Officer Peterman. The first on scene this morning after the break-in was reported."

Jack followed Max into the cramped space. Clutter collected on the floor and stacked boxes reached waist-high. Papers scattered along the top of a narrow desk. A man with a thick head of dark hair and hipster glasses sat behind the desk with a dazed look on his pinched face.

A policeman in a well-pressed uniform stood in the corner and jotted down notes. "I have everything I need, Mr. Consuelo. I'll write up my report, but you'll need to speak with these detectives. Tell them everything you told me. They'll be handling the case from here."

"Thank you, Officer," Jack said, waiting until the man left before focusing on Edward. "I'm Detective Jack Stone, and this is my partner, Detective Green."

A flash of recognition lit his brown eyes. "You called me last night."

"I did, yes, and you didn't return my call. I am curious, though. Did you call Olivia back?" Olivia had told Edward her reason for calling when she'd left a message the night before. A dealer who wanted to keep his artists happy would have called back and given her the information she'd asked for—the information Jack needed regarding the mystery art buyer. The fact he hadn't heard from Olivia told him Edward hadn't bothered to contact Olivia, which was another strike against him in Jack's book.

"Excuse me?" Confusion knit his brow. "I thought

you were here about the break-in. How do you know Olivia called me last night, and why do you care?"

Jack took note of the defensive hint in his tone. "You didn't answer the question." Not like it really mattered, but the guy rubbed him the wrong way. He wouldn't let the gallery owner weasel his way out of any questions, even if his business was a current crime scene.

Edward worked his jaw back and forth. "No. Not like it's your concern. I thought you were here to figure out what the hell happened. It's a mess out there." He flicked his wrist toward the doorway. "I need you to find the asshole who ruined my paintings."

"That is why we're here." Max folded his hands in front of him and widened his stance.

Jack hadn't confided in his partner about his instincts regarding the gallery owner; he wanted Max to make his own assessment of Mr. Consuelo. "Why don't you start by telling us exactly what happened?" Making himself at home, he scooped up files from a chair in the corner and placed them on the floor before taking a seat.

Edward threw his weight against the back of his chair like an overwhelmed child. "I came in early this morning. I had a big sale yesterday and the buyer planned to send movers over to handle transporting the paintings. I came in to finish the paperwork and get everything ready. When I got here, the door was smashed. A whole wall of paintings was vandalized."

"I noticed one of the paintings was Olivia Hickman's," Jack said.

"They all were." Edward snorted, then rubbed his forehead as if to smooth out the wrinkles given to him by either age or too much time in the sun. "My buyer's going to be pissed."

Jack straightened, then met Max's curious stare, his mind spinning.

"Were other artists' work damaged as well?" Max asked.

Edward shook his head. "Just Olivia's."

"What about your possessions? Anything stolen or tampered with?" Max pressed.

"Doesn't look like anything else was touched," Edward said. "Except the security system. The video feed is garbage, and the alarm system was deactivated. An alarm should have gone off when the door was broken, but the company who monitors my system wasn't notified there was a break-in."

Dread curled in Jack's stomach. Anger pushed him to his feet. "Are you saying someone broke into your gallery, had access to everything inside, and chose to only cut up Mrs. Hickman's paintings?"

"Yes," Edward snapped. "What about this is so hard for you cops to understand? But whoever ruined her paintings didn't just slash the canvases."

"I think it's time you show us what the burglar *did* do." He clenched his jaw, waiting for Mr. Consuelo to rise and march out of the office.

He followed close behind with Max at his heels, sweeping his gaze around the room. Hurried footsteps echoed off the high ceiling. Bright lights shone down between metal beams that stretched above them, highlighting the framed displays on the walls.

Mr. Consuelo stopped in front of a small alcove and swept a hand in front of him.

A large canvas depicting a quaint country church sat on an easel. Trees in full bloom surrounded the brick structure. Colorful flowers dotted the flower bed bent around the stone stairway that led up to wooden, double doors—stained glass towering high on the sides of the building.

And bright red paint scrawled across the picture...

I would have given you everything.

The heavy canvas weighed down Olivia's arms as she bumbled her way to the gallery. A rumble of thunder growled above the thick clouds overhead. A text from Edward the night before told her he'd be in early to make sure her paintings were ready to be shipped off to the mysterious buyer. Since he'd already given her the green light on her new piece, she hoped to bring it in and show it to whoever came by to pick up the work he or she had already bought. Maybe she could make another sale with her newest painting. She just needed to get it inside before the skies opened and the impending rain came.

Her gait slowed as she approached the familiar brick building. Yellow crime-scene tape stretched across the shattered door screamed a silent warning. Her blood turned colder than the early morning wind. She might not know what happened, but it couldn't be good. And a nagging sensation in the pit of her stomach told her she couldn't just hurry home and ignore whatever had happened at A Peculiar Sight.

Inhaling a deep breath, she steadied her nerves as much as possible and knocked on the broken barrier that blocked whatever crimes had been committed inside. A few seconds passed before footsteps came forward and the door swung open. The same piercing blue eyes and full, red lips that had kept her up all night stood in front of her. "Jack. What are you doing here?"

His gaze dipped to the painting in her arms. Heat crept along the back of her neck as he quietly studied the splash of emotion that had poured out of her the day before. She should have covered the canvas with a sheet or something, but she hadn't expected anyone to see it during the brief trip to the gallery. Especially not Jack.

Gosh, she hated how his silent scrutiny tightened the muscles in her core, as though his approval mattered.

He cleared his throat before meeting her eye. "Did you paint this?"

She nodded.

"It's amazing."

His praise lifted her lips. "Thanks, but it's also really heavy. Do you mind letting me in?"

The look of awe vanished from his face, replaced with concern. He cast a quick glance over his shoulder before easing the painting from her hands. "You might as well see this."

His words tightened her insides like a vise. She trod lightly over the broken glass and followed him inside. Another slash of yellow tape caught her attention on the wall. "Oh my God," she said, covering her mouth with her hand. "Someone broke in and ruined the artwork?"

Jack tilted her painting against the wall, then ushered her away from the vandalized art. "Correction. Someone broke in and ruined *your* artwork."

She swiveled around to face him. "What?"

He urged her forward. "Please. I'll explain, or at least

let Mr. Consuelo explain. But there's something more important for you to see."

Dread slowed her steps, but she continued in the direction until she approached Detective Green standing beside a scowling Edward.

They both turned at the sound of her footsteps.

"I stopped by to drop something off." She pushed the words out of her suddenly dry throat, fear keeping her from turning toward whatever the two men had been looking at.

"Mrs. Hickman," said Detective Green. "I'm afraid what's happened here involves you." He dipped his head toward the indent in the alcove. "Now we just need to figure out why."

She sent her gaze in the direction he indicated, and crushed her eyes closed at the message scrawled across the image of the church she'd been married in. Her legs wobbled, and the spike of her blood pressure made dizziness swim in her head. Her body swayed, her muscles refusing to keep her upright.

A sturdy hand settled on her lower back and the heat of a large body invaded her senses. A hint of orange peel and spice, a scent that had taken hold of her and refused to leave the last few days, told her exactly who kept her steady on her feet.

Jack.

"Take it easy," he whispered, his breath warm on her cheek. "I got you."

Three simple words that meant so damn much right now. Not a flurry of questions or even a hint of pity. Just a promise to keep her on her feet and be there. Even if only for a second until she found her bearings. Opening her eyes, she stared at the shocking words: *I would have given you everything.*

"I guess this threat isn't any worse than the one left on the website. I shouldn't find it so shocking. But I do." Her voice cracked, and she rubbed her palm over the base of her throat.

"What other threat?" Edward asked, eyes wide.

"That's none of your concern," Max cut in before she could open her mouth to offer an answer.

She swallowed her response, understanding there were things that needed to be held back from the public. Although she didn't understand why Edward had to be kept in the dark about anything, especially now that he too was a victim of whoever was behind this.

Realization struck down on her like a blow to the temple. "Were these the paintings that had been sold? The ones that were to be packed up today?"

"Yes," Edward said. "Every single one of them. Ruined."

"Were they insured?" Jack asked, somehow giving voice to the question she hadn't quite formed.

Edward nodded. "We'll get reimbursed for some of what they're worth. I'll need to figure out numbers and payments. Call the buyer." He shoved his hand through his perfectly coiffed hair, giving him an unkempt appearance she'd never witnessed.

She pinched the bridge of her nose as her reality grew grimmer by the second. Hopefully the insurance money could keep her going until she sold her loft. Because her decision had been cemented after stepping onto another crime scene. She needed as much distance as she could get from this entire situation. Selling the loft would set her up for her future—open the next chapter that lay ahead of her. All she needed was enough money to see her through.

"Is it normal for one buyer to purchase all of an artist's work from a gallery at one time?" Jack asked.

He had asked her the same question the night before, but she was interested to hear Edward's answer.

Edward shrugged. "Not necessarily, but it's not unheard of. If a serious buyer wanders into a place and has the means to buy whatever they'd like, it's happened before. Sometimes people want to snatch everything up before anyone else has a chance."

The word *snatch* made chills dance down her spine. The threats left for her on the rental site and on her painting made it clear that someone wanted to do a lot more than just snatch her up.

"We'll need the contact information of the person who bought Olivia's work, as well as access to the video feed from your security system." Max pointed at a camera hoisted in the corner, near the ceiling.

"Anything else?" A hard edge clipped the words.

Edward's sour attitude made her bristle with irritation. She sympathized that his property had been vandalized—hell, she'd experienced the same thing multiple times in the past two days—but the detectives were here to help.

Help find a killer before he slashed her like he'd slashed her paintings.

Chapter 11

A paleness swept over Olivia's smooth complexion, making the pink of her lips stand out like a beacon. Hell, who was he kidding, her mouth always stood out to him. But at this moment, he wasn't tempted to erase the space between them and taste those lips.

Now the urge to protect her had him positioning himself between her and Edward. She shouldn't have to be here, staring at her mutilated painting with a message aimed at her while the gallery owner was being questioned. Something didn't sit well with him where this guy was concerned, and it was time to figure out why. And while Max talked to Edward and tried to get to the bottom of what had happened at the gallery, he'd press Olivia for details only she could give. "How about we step outside for some fresh air?"

Olivia nodded. "Okay."

"I'll see that she makes it home safely while you finish speaking with Mr. Consuelo," Jack said.

"Shouldn't take me long," Max said. "I'll text you when I have everything I need."

With his hand still on the small of her back, he led Olivia out to the sidewalk. "You all right?" What a stupid question. Of course she wasn't all right. How could she be?

Leaning forward, she inhaled deeply. "When is this going to end?"

Jack waited for two young mothers to pass by with their strollers, a large umbrella shielding them, before coming to Olivia's side. "I wish I could tell you. All I can say is we're doing everything we can to catch the person responsible."

"Poor Edward," she said, straightening. She hooked a lock of hair behind her ear and stared through the window into the gallery. "This place is his entire life's work. He was shaken up. I could tell just by the way he spoke. He's usually not so defensive."

So she'd noticed it, too. Jack had spoken with a lot of people who had been victimized. Although it was true everyone responded differently—had a whole host of defense mechanisms—he'd found that the ones who were defensive usually had something to hide. "So his asshole behavior in there wasn't just his shining personality?"

Olivia huffed out a sharp laugh. "Not usually. He can have a bite sometimes, but he's one who resorts to honey more than vinegar to attract flies."

Her description of the man didn't quell Jack's suspicions. He didn't trust someone who could ooze charm when necessary, then switch to a rude jerk when the chips were down. "How did you meet Edward?"

"A friend of a friend kind of thing." She flicked her wrist as if to connect one person to another, but hesitancy flickered behind her eyes.

"How so?" A gust of wind barreled against him, bringing with it a smattering of raindrops.

Sighing, she turned to face him head-on—eyebrows hooked high and lips pursed. "He saw my work at Christine's bakery. I made some custom pieces for her when she opened."

He rocked back on his heels and digested the information. Her good pal had crossed paths with a lot of people in his investigation. And guessing from the look on Olivia's face, she understood the suspicion swimming around in his brain. But he'd deal with his questions regarding Christine later. Now he needed to focus on Edward. "So he sought you out? Then what?"

"He told me he had a gallery and wanted to display my work," she said with a small shrug. "It was a big break for me. I was selling pieces from our home before that. Trying to get noticed as best I could."

"What did your husband think of him?"

"He was happy for me. Dave was always my biggest cheerleader." A sad smile stretched her lips.

Cheerleader or not, it was clear neither of them had done their due diligence as far as Edward and his past business ventures were concerned. "But nothing seemed off about the guy to either of you?" He watched her carefully, searching for any signs she was keeping anything from him.

"Nothing." She threw up her hands. "Edward has been gracious and helpful. He's promoted me and taken my career to a whole new level."

A horn blasted, and he searched for the obnoxious driver—tensing when a college-aged man jaywalked across the busy street. "Were you aware that he previously owned two galleries that went bankrupt?" Jack asked, refocusing on her.

She blinked, long and slow. "No. He never mentioned that. But then again, why would he?"

"Maybe so you'd know who you were trusting your career with? He's managing your sales. Taking a part of your earnings to finance his gallery. Transparency is important. Someone who hasn't had success with two different businesses might not be trustworthy with a third."

A flash of lightning sliced through the gray clouds, drawing Olivia's attention overhead. She rubbed her hand across her forehead, then wiped away the rain from her face. "Listen, I understand where your concern is coming from, but I don't have the information you're looking for. If I had any inkling that Edward was involved with any of this, I'd tell you. But I don't. And honestly, doesn't this show that he's a victim as well?" She swept an arm toward the busted door.

Moisture coasted down the back of his neck, and he shivered. He weighed his words carefully before responding. "Possibly."

"Possibly? Seriously? How can you even say that?" She took a step back as if the word assaulted her, nearly stumbling into a passing jogger.

"Listen. I get you know this guy and he's been good

to you, but I have to look at all the facts. The facts right now are telling me I need to be wary of him."

"His gallery was just broken into. How does that make you wary of him?" A heaviness weighed down her words as though she struggled to understand his logic, no matter how hard she tried.

Jack blew out a long breath and tried to calm his frustration. "And his security system just happens to be down with no video footage or indication someone broke in. All we have is a vandalized studio, where he can now collect insurance money on your artwork."

"Those pieces were sold. Why would he need insurance money when he'd get commission?"

"I don't know," he said, suddenly exhausted from the morning. Damn, he needed a second cup of coffee to push him through the rest of this day. "But once I have the name of the person who bought the artwork, I'll know a lot more."

Her head fell forward. "I can't think about this anymore. I just want to go home."

Sympathy pulsed inside him, increasing with each steady beat of his heart. "I'll walk you back."

She offered a weak smile, then fell in step beside him to close the short distance to her apartment building. The sounds of the city rang between them, and he stayed by her side as she opened the door and entered the lobby. She might be inside the building, but he wouldn't be satisfied she was okay until he saw her safely tucked into her apartment.

He walked behind her up the three floors. When they reached the landing to her hallway, she came to a quick stop, and he bumped into her. Instinct had him latch-

ing his hand to her hips to steady her. His chest heaved
with the feel of her pressed against him, but warning
bells went off in his head. "What's wrong?"

She shifted her head to the side and kept her voice
low. "There's a man standing in front of my door."

Urgency propelled him into action, and he swept
her behind him. He rested his palm on the butt of his
sidearm secured at his hip, hidden behind his jacket.
He stared at the broad back of a man who stood in front
of Olivia's door with something in his hands. A box?

Without moving, he yelled, "Whoever the hell you
are, take a step away from the door and put your hands
in the air."

Olivia hid behind Jack's back. Fear expanded her
lungs. A man had made it into her building without
being buzzed inside and now stood in front of her door.
She tightened her muscles and stayed on the balls of her
feet, ready to run in a second's notice.

"I said hands in the air," Jack repeated, authority
clear in his gravelly tone.

She stayed hidden, not wanting to come face-to-face
with the man on the other side of her protector.

"Now slowly turn toward me." He barked out his
command. "Place the box on the ground, then put your
hands right back up."

Olivia held her breath. The sound of her rapidly beating heart hammered against her eardrums. She fisted
the back of Jack's jacket in her hand, the soft material
damp from the rain.

"I don't understand what's going on. I'm just here
to see a friend."

The familiar voice sagged her shoulders. Staying behind Jack, she peeked around him. A squeak of relief escaped her mouth. "Mason!"

Jack lowered his weapon, but his frown stayed firmly on his face. "You know this guy?"

"Olivia, what's going on?" Concern furrowed Mason's brow, his light eyebrows dipping low above his green eyes. "Are you okay?"

"Of course she's okay," Jack snapped.

Stepping to Jack's side, she smoothed her palm over his bicep. His tight jaw told her that she needed to defuse this situation as soon as possible. She couldn't tell if it was jealousy or lingering suspicion that made him look like he was about to explode. "Jack, this is Mason Shaffer. He's an accountant at the firm where my husband used to work."

Mason dropped his arms to his sides. "And who are you, Jack?" He smiled, but it fell way short of a friendly offering.

Jack tucked away his gun. "Detective Jack Stone. I work for the NYPD."

Mason's smile fell. "Police? What's going on?"

"It's a long story," Olivia said. One she hoped not to retell. She'd wanted to escape everything, not relive it. "Did I know you were stopping by this morning? I've had a lot going on the last couple of days. I'm sorry if it slipped my mind."

He cut his narrowed gaze to Jack before aiming a sheepish grin her way. "Nah. I was just in the neighborhood and wondered if you wanted to grab some breakfast or something. Haven't seen you in a while. Just wondered how you're doing."

Jack cleared his throat, and a weird tension hung heavy in the hallway. She didn't want to hurry either of the men away, but it was clear some kind of unspoken challenge had been exchanged between the two of them.

"I'd love to catch up." She felt Jack tense beside her, and she fought the urge to keep him close. She needed some space before she did something stupid. "Jack, thank you for walking me home. If you or Detective Green uncover anything else, please let me know."

He worked his mouth back and forth, pivoting to block her view of Mason. "I'll call you later. Be careful." He shot a hard look Mason's way, then hurried down the stairs.

She watched him go and ignored the regret that dotted her heart like tiny pinpricks. These feelings were so new and raw and complicated. Hell, her world had been turned upside down. Chances were whatever she felt was just some weird attachment to the man who offered her protection and security.

"Olivia?"

She turned back toward Mason. "Sorry. It's been a day." A forced laugh lifted the last word, making it come out pitchy and cracked.

"And it's only 8:00 am." He lifted the side of his mouth, making one of his dimples more prominent through the rough patch of whiskers.

Securing her keys, she made her way to the door and opened it. "What'd you bring with you?" She dipped her head to the package at his feet.

"Nothing. This was sitting here when I came up." He scooped up the brown box and followed her inside. He placed the package on the coffee table. "Want to talk about what happened?"

Mentally beaten down, she flopped on the couch and shrugged out of her wet jacket. She tossed it on the floor and sighed. "Not really."

"Fair enough." He sat beside her and rested his palms on his thighs. "With the exception of whatever it is that's going on, how've you been? I've been so busy lately I haven't checked in. I'm sorry about that."

"You never have to apologize for being busy." Mason had showed up to support her in a more subtle way than her brother. Where Jason was a bit overbearing and had stepped in to do whatever he thought she needed, Mason had sent texts of support or had meals delivered so she didn't have to leave her apartment. He was never pushy—never crossed boundaries. Just been a friend at a time when she desperately needed one.

Those texts had dwindled, as had the amount of times he'd stopped by for a quick hello. But that was to be expected. Life went on for everyone, those left grieving usually forgotten.

"After that unfortunate introduction to the good detective, I'm afraid to ask what's new," he said, a glint of interest in his eyes.

She sighed, wanting to answer his question without divulging too many details. "All I'll say for now is that what's happened has forced me to put the loft on the market."

"I'm sorry. I know how much that place means to you."

"I remember the first time he took me there. He was so excited when you two went looking for places and he stumbled across it. Said it was meant to be." She wiped at her eyes. "Saying goodbye will be hard."

Mason rested a hand on her arm and gave a light squeeze. "You and I both know Dave would want you to be happy, no matter what that means. Even if it's selling the place you loved."

She blinked away unwanted tears. As much as she knew selling was the best option, the idea of losing another piece of her husband was so damn hard. "It's for the best. But enough about that. Let's find out what someone sent me. Maybe it'll lift my spirits."

Mason grabbed the box and used his keys to slice through the thick tape before handing it to her.

Flipping open the cardboard flaps, she found herself staring at stacks of loose-leaf paper. She grabbed a few pieces and read a jumble of words smashed together in smudged ink. Praise for her work and talent. Replicas of her art made with colored pencils. Questions about her and her life.

"What is it?" Mason asked, peering over her shoulder.

"Looks like fan mail. I don't usually get this much." She shuffled to the next page, and her pulse picked up. "Did Edward forward this over? All the handwriting looks the same."

Mason shrugged. "Maybe it's from a really big fan."

Trepidation shook her hand as she snatched another stack of papers. The same small, loopy letters smudged the page. "Your art is so inspiring. I want to be just like you. You're so talented." Each page heaped more and more praise on her tense shoulders.

She reached for the last sheet of paper at the bottom

of the box and gasped. A pencil sketch of herself stared up at her. The detail in the picture was so unnerving, as though someone had studied every single line of her face. "Oh my God."

She tossed the sheet back in the box, then shut the lid. She scanned the brown cardboard and gasped.

"What?" Mason asked.

She tapped on the top of the package. "There's no address on the box. This wasn't sent in the mail. Someone left it at my doorstep."

Chapter 12

The constant tap of Jack's foot against the tile floor bounced around his office. The package from Olivia's apartment occupied the space on his desk where his laptop usually was. Olivia and Mason sat across from him, and it took way too much effort not to throw the slick sonofabitch out the door. His boy-next-door charm might work on Olivia, but Jack saw right through the thoughtful friend pretense.

He saw a man who was biding his time until it was appropriate to tell Olivia what he was really after. And the hungry look in Mason's eyes told him that the prize wasn't an innocent friendship—it was Olivia.

"I wish you would have called me right away," he said, choosing to ignore Mason and focus on Olivia. "I was right next door. I could have been back to your apartment five minutes after you opened the box."

Mason hooked an arm over the back of his chair and let his hand dangle next to Olivia's shoulder. The forest green stripes in his tie matched his eyes—his black suit well tailored and oozing with money. "She was scared and shocked. She needed a few minutes to gain her bearings."

Jack stilled his foot and met Mason's stare head-on. A quiet confidence surrounded the other man in a way that suggested he was used to getting his way. That might be true in his corner office of some stuffy downtown building, but not here. Not in Jack's office.

Here, he was in charge. And he'd make sure Mason understood that. "I wasn't talking to you. Olivia is more than capable of speaking for herself."

Mason inched closer to Olivia. A wolf in sheep's clothing moving in on his prey. "I'm only trying to help. She shouldn't have to handle this alone."

"I agree. That's why I'm here." Jack folded his hands on top of his desk, sitting straight. He wouldn't back down from this uptight intruder.

"Both of your help is welcome." Olivia slid her gaze from Mason to Jack. "And I didn't call right away because I wanted to go through each piece of mail to make sure I wasn't overreacting. You have enough on your plate. I didn't want to add more if it wasn't necessary."

Her logic made sense. Even if he hated that she'd been fine to depend on someone else to help her with any issue before reaching out to him. Damn, he was losing his shit where she was concerned. He should be relieved someone else had been around when she needed them. Someone she knew and trusted. Instead, he was acting like a jealous teenager.

He cleared his throat, pushing down all his unwanted emotions. "I'm glad you brought it in now. I just hope we can still find prints on the evidence after you both touched everything."

Olivia winced, and Mason smoothed his hand over her shoulder. "We can give you copies of our prints so you know which ones to rule out," he said.

He fought to keep his gaze from lingering on Mason's hand as anger heated his blood. The bastard didn't need to be touching her. Running his tongue over his top row of teeth, he focused on the reason Olivia was here and not on the ridiculous jealousy he had no right experiencing. "That'd be appreciated. Olivia, did you notice the box when you left this morning and headed for the gallery?"

She shook her head. "No, but the painting I carried blocked my sight line. The box could have been left on one side of the door and I wouldn't have seen it."

Which meant he couldn't count out Edward placing the box in the hall before he'd called the police regarding the break-in at the gallery.

Or Mason. There was no way to eliminate the man who was caught carrying the box outside of Olivia's apartment.

Wanting to get a better idea of what they were dealing with, he slipped on a pair of rubber gloves and lifted out the top sheet of paper. "Did you look at every piece of paper?" he asked as he read the messy writing.

"I think so. Not every word, though," she said. "At first, it just seemed like normal fan mail. But something rang a little off. Then I saw the picture. Someone put a lot of detail into that drawing. And when I realized there was no address on the box…" She wrapped her arms around her middle and shuddered.

He shuffled through the papers until he reached the sketch. He whistled, long and low, while taking in the delicate shading and precision that someone used to create almost an exact copy of Olivia's face. "Do you know anyone who specializes in this type of art?"

"It's hard to tell. I know a lot of people in the art community. Most artists specialize in one medium but are skilled in many."

He threw the picture back in the box. "What about Edward? He obviously appreciates art. Does he create his own?"

Olivia bit into her bottom lip and nodded. "He mostly focuses on photography. Black and whites. He has a few hanging in the gallery."

"Who's Edward?" Mason finally dropped his hand to the arm of the chair.

"That's none of your concern," Jack said.

Olivia quirked a brow, berating him without saying a single word. "He owns the gallery next to my apartment."

"Where your art hangs?" Mason asked.

"Yes. The gallery was broken into last night."

"Well, shit." Mason widened his eyes.

Jack kept his mouth shut. If Olivia wanted to give out details to an ongoing investigation, that was her business. But he wouldn't tell Mason anything he didn't need to know. Which, at this point, was jack shit.

A low rumble vibrated, and Mason shifted to glance

at his smartwatch. "I'm sorry. I need to step out and take this call."

"Yes. Please. Go," Olivia said.

Jack couldn't have said it better himself. Except maybe to add *and stay the hell away*, but he kept quiet and waited until Mason left the room before addressing Olivia. "You trust him?"

She rolled her eyes. "I already told you I don't think Edward is the guy we're after."

"Not Edward. Mason." He was self-aware enough to admit he couldn't trust his gut reaction to her friend. His dislike of Mason had more to do with hating the way the guy looked at Olivia than having a reason to assume he was capable of murder.

She nodded. "I've known Mason for years. He worked with Dave—the two of them were good friends—and has been nothing but kind and respectful of me since Dave's death. Yes, I trust him."

He rubbed at the tension tightening the muscles at the back of his neck. "I don't know. This guy shows up out of the blue with a package that contains mail from what looks like an obsessed fan. I have to make sure he didn't orchestrate the whole thing."

"Oh, come on," she said. "He planned for me to show up at that very moment and catch him holding a package he brought with crazy mail?"

Jack shrugged. "The package has no address. He's found carrying the box. You don't remember seeing it when you left, although you admit you could have missed it. Now he's with you at the police station and volunteers to give us his fingerprints. Prints that we all expect to find on the box because he conveniently carried the damn thing around."

Sighing, she stood. "It must be sad to always be forced to see the bad in everything. Even when it's not there."

Her statement knocked against him with the force of a hurricane. Is that what she saw when she looked at him? A sad man who just looked at the negative? Is that what he'd become?

If it was, then he had good reasons for it. "I don't have a choice. When I don't open my eyes to what's in front of me, people die. I can't let anyone hurt you. I couldn't live with myself if I let that happen."

Pity pooled in her eyes. "Sometimes what's in front of you is good. You just have to be open to the possibility."

Mason popped his head in. "I need to get to the office. Do you want a ride back home?"

"That'd be great." She aimed a smile back at Jack. "Thanks for seeing us."

A flurry of words lodged in his throat. So he set his mouth in a firm line and watched her walk out the door.

Olivia opted to pay a visit to Edward at the gallery instead of heading up to her empty apartment. Mason had wanted to walk her to her door, but the idea of just sitting alone with her thoughts and questions made her skin itch.

With her head down, she hustled through the sheets of rain and entered the gallery. A thin piece of plywood had been stretched across the shattered door. The yellow crime-scene tape was gone. The destroyed paintings had been taken off the wall, leaving them bare. A sight that was somehow more jarring than the bright colored tape that had greeted her that morning.

"Edward?" She called his name, not wanting to startle him. After the morning he'd had, she didn't need to give him another shock. "It's Olivia."

Edward stepped out of his office with an exhausted set to his shoulders and a deep frown. "What are you doing here?"

"Just checking on you," she said, brushing away a droplet of rain from her cheek.

He sighed and leaned against the doorframe. "What a mess. After speaking with the police, I've been on the phone with the insurance company all day. They won't make it easy, but I'll get what's owed."

She wanted to ask if the amount the artwork was insured for matched the sales prices, but it didn't seem like the right time. "And what about the buyer? Did you give his name and information to Detective Green?"

He crossed his arms over his chest and snorted. "I did, for what good it was."

The hairs on her arm stood at attention. "What do you mean by that?"

Red clashed against the bronze skin of his cheeks, and he glanced away as if unable to meet her eyes. "I don't know who was behind it, but the whole thing was some sort of scheme. When I called the number I was given, there was no answer. I ran the credit card, and it was rejected. I explained that to the one officer who stayed behind, then gave him everything I had on the guy."

His words attacked her like physical blows. "You

didn't check any of this out before you told me you'd sold the pieces? This doesn't make any sense."

Edward squeezed his eyes shut. "I'm so sorry. I've never had this happen before. Never been duped so badly."

She hated the suspicion that crept up the back of her neck. If Jack was right, and she had no reason to doubt him, Edward had found himself in several situations where deals must have gone south. Maybe he'd been tricked and that's what had forced his previous businesses to close.

Or maybe he'd pulled a stunt or two to collect money that hadn't been earned. That wasn't his to collect. And someone had caught on and made him pay the price.

Another thought tensed her muscles. If she was wrong about Edward's business practices, what else had she been wrong about? Maybe she'd been too hard on Jack earlier. Maybe she needed to start being more of a cynic if she were to ever get to the bottom of this mess.

"Olivia?"

She blinked her way back to the present.

"Can you ever forgive me?" His eyes were wide and pleading.

Not wanting him to realize her image of him and who he was had shifted, she nodded. "You did nothing wrong. You're as much a victim in some con man's game as I am. But if you'll excuse me, I need to rest a bit. I'm afraid everything that's happened has left me a little overwhelmed."

He took a step toward her.

She peddled her feet backward, an urgency to get away from him seizing her vocal cords.

"You're awfully pale. Do you want to have a seat and catch your breath before you leave?"

She held up a palm to stop him. "No thank you. I'll see you later."

Fleeing the suddenly suffocating space with as much dignity as she could manage, she welcomed the cool rain on her heated skin. Confusion and a sense of dread tightened her chest. She'd traveled the short distance between her apartment and the gallery countless times, but now her home seemed so far away. The exposed skin on her neck prickled with unease, as if she were being watched. She gritted her teeth and ran. She didn't care if she looked like an idiot. She needed to escape the maddening sensation that made her feel as if she were falling over the edge of a cliff with nothing to cushion the fall.

Nothing and no one. As life crashed down around her, who could she trust? Who didn't have an air of suspicion dancing around them, waiting to be dissected?

Jack.

In this upside-down world, he'd come out as the one person who stood beside her and offered comfort. He wanted nothing from her. He didn't push or demand, pry or come with expectations. Because she was the one who hadn't opened her eyes to what was right in front of her. And now she wasn't the only one who was paying the price for her ignorance. Courtney and Priscilla had, too.

Reaching her building, she flung herself inside and sprinted up the steps to her apartment. Her lungs burned as she unlocked the door and rushed inside. She shut the door, turning the locks, when a familiar scent invaded her senses.

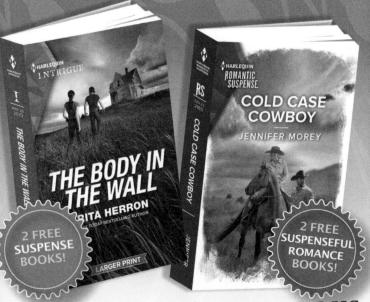

YOU pick your books –
WE pay for everything.
You get up to FOUR New Books and
TWO Mystery Gifts...absolutely FREE!

Dear Reader,

I am writing to announce the launch of a huge **FREE BOOKS GIVEAWAY**... and to let you know that YOU are entitled to choose up to FOUR fantastic books that WE pay for.

Try **Harlequin® Romantic Suspense** books featuring heart-racing page-turners with unexpected plot twists and irresistible chemistry that will keep you guessing to the very end.

Try **Harlequin Intrigue® Larger-Print** books featuring action-packed stories that will keep you on the edge of your seat. Solve the crime and deliver justice at all costs.

Or TRY BOTH!

In return, we ask just one favor: Would you please participate in our brief Reader Survey? We'd love to hear from you.

This FREE BOOKS GIVEAWAY means that your introductory shipment is completely free, <u>even the shipping</u>! If you decide to continue, you can look forward to curated monthly shipments of brand-new books from your selected series, always at a discount off the cover price! <u>Plus you can cancel any time</u>. Who could pass up a deal like that?

Sincerely

Pam Powers

Pam Powers
For Harlequin Reader Service

Complete the survey below and return it today to receive up to 4 FREE BOOKS and FREE GIFTS guaranteed!

FREE BOOKS GIVEAWAY
Reader Survey

1

Do you prefer stories with suspensful storylines?

◯ YES ◯ NO

2

Do you share your favorite books with friends?

◯ YES ◯ NO

3

Do you often choose to read instead of watching TV?

◯ YES ◯ NO

YES! Please send me my Free Rewards, consisting of **2 Free Books from each series I select** and **Free Mystery Gifts**. I understand that I am under no obligation to buy anything, no purchase necessary see terms and conditions for details.

❑ **Harlequin® Romantic Suspense** (240/340 HDL GRPH)
❑ **Harlequin Intrigue® Larger-Print** (199/399 HDL GRPH)
❑ **Try Both** (240/340 & 199/399 HDL GRPV)

FIRST NAME | LAST NAME

ADDRESS

APT.# | CITY

STATE/PROV. | ZIP/POSTAL CODE

EMAIL ❑ Please check this box if you would like to receive newsletters and promotional emails from Harlequin Enterprises ULC and its affiliates. You can unsubscribe anytime.

Fear hitched her breath. Her normally soft, floral fragrance was thick and pungent in the air, as if someone had doused every fabric in the place. She darted her gaze around the room until she spotted something on top of her colorful comforter. She stayed on high alert as she made her way to the bed. A red card laid on the bed with big, black letters:

"We'll be together soon."

Chapter 13

A bell rang in the quiet hallway of the junior high. Doors swung open and a sea of teenagers flooded the scuffed-up linoleum floor. Barn-red lockers opened and shut as kids shoved books in bags and hurried toward the exit.

Jack would rather face down a murderer than be back in middle school. With a face full of acne and a whole host of insecurities. Hell, he'd rather be in front of a handful of killers than be responsible for teaching any of the students rushing around him with irritated eye rolls and muttering under their breaths.

With any luck, he'd be in and out quickly after he and Max spoke with Clara Searing—Olivia's soon-to-be ex-sister-in-law and current substitute teacher for afternoon classes at the swanky private school.

Max pivoted out of the way of a flock of giggling girls. "We should have waited until all these kids were gone before coming inside."

Jack snorted in response, strolling toward the classroom at the end of the hall. As much as he wished they could have, Jack hadn't wanted to give Mrs. Searing a chance to leave before nailing down their interview. A quick call to the principal had assured him the young teacher would be in the classroom in the afternoon until the end of the school day. "Let's just get this over with."

At the open door, Jack knocked and waited for the brunette sitting behind the desk to glance up.

Mrs. Searing held up a finger, signaling for them to wait, as she wrote on a piece of paper. After a few seconds, she looked up with a tired smile, which quickly dropped into a confused frown. "Can I help you?"

"We're here to speak with you about an ongoing investigation." Max lifted his badge.

Low whispers came from behind Jack, and he whipped around to stare down two gawky boys. He waited for them to scurry away before turning back around.

Mrs. Searing sighed. "This is about Olivia, right? Jason filled me in on what's been going on."

"Do you mind if we step in, Mrs. Searing?" Jack asked.

"Please, call me Clara." She stood, showcasing long legs in her slim-cut black pants. "Close the door. I'll grab a few chairs from the back of the room so you don't have to sit at one of the students' desks."

"No need," Max said. "We won't take much of your time."

"Good. It's been a long day." Clara perched on the front edge of her desk. She anchored her arms behind her, leaning slightly backward. "If I'm being honest, it's been a long few months."

The fine lines along the gentle dip between her brow revealed an exhaustion that went beyond a hard afternoon of work. But that didn't surprise him, knowing she was going through a divorce. "Care to elaborate?"

She twisted her lips, as if attempting to rein in her emotions. "Something tells me you already know."

"I'm sure divorce can't be easy," Jack said, testing the waters.

Max cut him a look that told him he didn't understand where he was heading.

Jack ignored his partner. The video feed they'd recovered from Priscilla Abbington's murder showed what appeared to be a man. Clara might be tall, but her slender frame didn't match what they'd seen on-screen.

But just like with Courtney Bailey's ex-husband, that didn't eliminate the possibility she was aware of who was responsible for two murders and stalking Olivia. Not to mention she knew a lot of the different players that he had his eye on. He didn't want to throw the same routine questions her way—he already knew those answers. If he was a betting man, he'd place a month's wages she had a solid alibi for all the times in question. He wanted to go a little deeper with Olivia's sister-in-law.

"It's definitely not," Clara said. "Unfortunately, it couldn't be avoided."

The low tone and faraway look in her eyes told Jack that divorce wasn't what she wanted. That didn't fit the narrative Olivia gave him. "I understand your husband has devoted a lot of time to his sister."

Clara tucked in her lips. "He can be very devoted… when he wants to be."

Maybe he was missing something. He could putter around the questioning, try to be tactful and respect her position, or he could come right out with what he wanted to know. Something told him Clara was the type of woman who'd rather just get down to business. "Did it upset you that Jason spent so much time—so much money—on Olivia after the death of her husband?"

She tilted her head to the side, lips turned down. "Yes and no."

Max shifted on his feet beside him as if her answer surprised him enough to knock him off-balance. "Did all the attention your husband spent on Olivia make you angry? Do you hold a grudge against her because of it?"

"Goodness no." The statement came out on a huff of outrage. She straightened, standing tall and flushed with indignation. "Olivia is the last one I'd blame for the issues Jason and I have had in our marriage."

"And what exactly are those issues?" His guess had been Clara was upset that Jason was helping Olivia financially, but maybe there was more to the breakdown of their marriage. Issues that Olivia wasn't aware of.

She dropped her head and rested a hand on her flat stomach. "We wanted to start a family. Funny how something that was supposed to bring us closer together is what tore us apart." She looked up, her heartbreak written all over her face. "We had trouble getting pregnant, so we didn't tell anyone we were trying. Hell, it was fun for a while. But when it didn't happen…" She shrugged. "We started to worry, which caused a lot of tension."

Sympathy pulled at his chest, but he didn't understand what her fertility issues had to do with Olivia. "Did your husband turn to his sister, which upset you?"

She shook her head, then sucked in a deep breath. "Sorry. This is difficult to talk to about."

"Take all the time you need," Max said.

"After months of tests and tears and worry, we finally got pregnant. Last year. We planned to tell Olivia and Dave first, because we were so close with them. We all went away together, and the night before we planned to tell them, I lost the baby. We were devastated."

Snippets of her story clicked together. "Was this around the same time Dave Hickman was killed?"

She locked her gaze on him. A world of sorrow swam in her light brown eyes. "The same weekend. Dave was hit by a car the next day."

Max tucked his chin. "I'm sorry for your loss. I'm sure losing the baby and your brother-in-law so close together was very difficult."

"It was impossible. For both of us," Clara said. "Jason buried his grief over the baby and losing his friend and focused on helping Olivia. I understood, of course— she'd lost her husband. But I'd lost something, too. And it felt like Jason chose to ignore my loss—our loss—because it was too much. Over time, I just couldn't look at him the same. Couldn't forgive him for turning his back on me and our lost child. So yes, I'm resentful. I'm angry about the time he's spent with Olivia, but that has nothing to do with her. It has everything to do with my husband abandoning me when I needed him most."

"Have you spoken with Olivia about any of this?" Olivia blamed herself for a situation that had nothing to do with her beyond being caught in the middle. If these women had been close, she deserved to understand what had really happened.

Clara shook her head. "I don't want to upset her. She's had a rough go of things. Adding to her heartbreak is the last thing I want to do. Besides," she said with a shrug, "she's Jason's sister. How does that even work in a divorce? If I'm the one walking away, shouldn't I walk away from both of them?"

Jack considered her words. "I don't have the answer. All I know is that both you and Olivia have lost a lot this year. If you two were as close as you said, do you need to lose each other, too?"

"Maybe you're right," she said.

"What about Christine Roberts?" Max asked, cutting in and bringing the questioning back on track. "Are you friends with her at all?"

A weird expression crinkled the lines of her face. "Not really. She and Olivia have been best friends. She didn't like anyone else getting too close to Olivia. Whenever I was around, she wasn't very pleasant. So, I kept my distance."

Interesting. Olivia's best friend had been in shock when they'd spoken with her but had seemed friendly enough. Was that all an act, or was Clara Searing purposely planting seeds of doubt because of some personal grudge against the other woman? Either way, the teacher had given him a lot to think about.

His phone rumbled in his pocket, vibrating against

his thigh. "Sorry. I need to take this. Thank you for your time."

Answering the phone, he hurried into the hall. "Detective Stone."

"Jack, it's Olivia. Someone was in my apartment. I need you to come. Now."

Olivia sat at the counter in the diner across the street from her apartment. She couldn't stay in her home, knowing someone had been inside. Hell, this person could be watching and waiting for her to return before cornering her and doing whatever sick things they'd planned. After reading the note, she'd run, fleeing to the safety of the busy restaurant before calling the police.

"Olivia!"

She turned toward the frantic sound of her name. "Jason? What are you doing here?" After giving her statement to the officer on scene, she'd called Jack. He'd need to be filled in on the newest part of her nightmare, and she wasn't too proud to admit she needed his comforting presence. But she'd never reached out to her brother.

"Clara called me and told me something happened. Are you okay?" He settled onto the stool beside her, then gave a quick shake of his head when the waitress behind the counter glanced his way.

"How did Clara know?" She lifted her glass of water with a trembling hand and took a long sip. The cool liquid helped calm her jumbled nerves.

Jason moved his lips in a small circle, a tick he'd had since childhood whenever he was irritated. "Apparently the detectives who should be chasing down whoever is responsible for all this thought it was important to interview my wife at her work. One of the detectives got your call while they were there, and he brought it up to his partner. She overheard. She called me, and I rushed over."

She wasn't surprised Jack wanted to speak to Clara, but she wouldn't tell Jason why. He had been wounded enough when seeing the list of names she'd provided the police. If she confided that she'd told Jack Clara had been upset with Jason because of her, he'd be furious. And to be honest, Clara's and Jason's issues were low on her lists of concerns.

Pushing away thoughts of her sister-in-law, she rested a hand on Jason's. "I'm glad you're here. I'm so scared. I don't know what to do."

"What exactly happened?" The tight lines on his round face announced his anxiety, but his surgeon's hand stayed steady.

"Someone broke into my apartment—again—and left a note on my bed." She dropped her head in her hand. "I just replaced the locks. How could someone bypass them so easily? How can I be sure it won't happen again?"

"You can't stay there. It's not safe." Jason's big brother voice told her that he meant what he said and wouldn't accept any argument from her. "You'll come to my place and stay with me until this is all over."

A part of her wanted to let him swoop in and fix all of her problems the way he always had. But she couldn't let him. Not this time. She needed to stand on her own two feet and help Jack uncover who was out to destroy her life. "No. I can't endanger you."

He puffed up his chest. "I can protect myself. And you. You can't be alone. At least until this person is caught."

She shook her head, refusing to hear his argument. "You have enough going on right now. You're trying to make things right with Clara. Harboring me is the last thing you need to do to help that situation."

Something twisted his face, as if what she said made sense even though he didn't want it to. "Your safety is more important than my marriage. I don't know if I can ever make things right with Clara. I *can* protect you."

His words warmed her, even though she couldn't accept. It was too risky. "I appreciate the offer, but I can't."

He huffed out a frustrated breath. "Okay, then what about leaving the city for a while and staying with Dad? Or maybe Christine."

She hated that he was right. Staying in her apartment alone wasn't an option, and the loft was out of the question. She didn't have the money to stay in a hotel. But she couldn't put anyone she loved at risk. "I can't handle Dad right now, and Christine is in her honeymoon phase still with Paul. Besides, she's a mess over her part in all of this. I can't drop my troubles at her doorstep as well."

"Olivia, are you okay?" A deep, gravelly voice slid over her skin.

She turned and found herself staring into Jack's intent blue eyes. His puckered brow showed off his curiosity. "Jack! I'm so glad you're here."

Jack's gaze traveled to her side. "I see I'm not the only one who came running. It's nice to see you Mr. Searing."

Jason stood and extended a hand. "Call me Jason. My wife called me, and I came over right away."

Nodding, Jack shook his hand. "I didn't realize the two of you still spoke so frequently."

"I'm sure there's a lot you don't realize," Jason said. "Thanks for coming."

A phone rang, and Jason swore under his breath. Leaning to the side, he retrieved his phone from his pocket. "That's the hospital." A clash of emotions brewed on his face. "I can tell them I'm busy. It should be fine."

"Don't be silly," Olivia said. "They need you, so you have to go. I'm okay. I'm with Jack. Nothing will happen." She didn't want to mention it, but this was another reason she couldn't stay with her brother. If someone paged him, he needed to get to the hospital. Which would leave her by herself, defeating the purpose of staying with him to begin with.

Jason gave Jack an assessing stare before standing. "Fine. I'll call you when I can, and we'll finish this conversation." He pressed a quick kiss on her cheek. "Be careful."

She took a swig of water, fanning the turmoil boiling in her gut.

"He's right, you know," Jack said, stealing back her attention. "You can't be alone. Not anymore. It's too risky."

"And what do you suggest?" She circled her hands around the glass and relished the feel of the condensation seeping into her skin.

"What would you say to a trip out of the city? With me?"

Chapter 14

Olivia wasn't sure what she'd expected Jack to say, but asking her to go away with him—when he was in charge of a murder investigation—was the very last thing she'd have guessed. A scorching blush clashed against her cheeks that had to be as red as the bright vinyl covering her stool. She gulped down the rest of her water as her mind raced full steam ahead.

"I… I don't know if that's a good idea." She stammered like a schoolgirl. Offending Jack was the last thing she wanted. She enjoyed spending time with him and wasn't opposed to seeing more of him after the case was closed—maybe, but they couldn't go away together. Not now.

Jack grinned and dipped his chin low, forcing her to catch his eye. "I'm not suggesting anything improper, Olivia." His smile fell. "What I have in mind is something far less fun than whatever put that color on your face."

She squirmed under his gaze. "Okay. Then why don't you explain your intentions before I agree to anything?"

A waitress with a fifties-style apron over a gray fitted uniform swept through the swinging door that led to the kitchen. Bending behind the counter, she found a napkin from an unseen space on the other side and placed it in front of Jack. "Can I get you anything?"

"Do you mind if I eat something?" Jack asked. "The day's gotten away from me. I haven't had anything since a crummy cup of coffee first thing this morning."

"Please. Go ahead."

He placed his order.

"And you, miss?" the waitress asked, after scribbling down Jack's request of water and a cheeseburger with a side of fries. "Anything other than the water?"

She nudged the empty cup forward. "Just a refill."

Jack waited until the server disappeared before swiveling on the stool to face her. "I spoke with the officer who came to your apartment. She filled me in on everything, so there's no need to go over it all again. Unless you want to."

Her stomach churned. Partially from nerves, partially from the lingering floral scent of her perfume that she'd never be able to wear again. "Not really. I've gone over it enough, and I know everything's being done that can be. I'd rather hear what your plan is."

"Well, if you change your mind and want to tell me what happened, any of it, I'm here."

The server set a glass of water on Jack's side, then refilled hers, before hurrying away.

"As for my plan, it's more like an idea. One that you might not like." He took a long sip of water, licking his lips as he set it back down. "Before I dive in, I should lay my thoughts out for you. So you can understand where my mind is."

The whiplash of emotion from humiliated yet excited about the prospect of being with Jack to the unease over whatever was brewing in his mind made the water she'd chugged churn in her stomach.

She swallowed her hesitation. If she wanted to help solve her own problems, stand on her own two feet, she needed to take control. Even if that meant staring down the barrel of information Jack had collected. "That's a good idea."

Two men in suits settled beside Jack at the counter.

"Let's head over to a table. A little more privacy." He signaled to the server, then pointed to an empty table in the corner. "We'll be over there."

Grabbing her water, she followed Jack to the far corner, away from the late lunchers and stragglers who'd come into the diner for a midday reprieve. He pulled out a chair for her, then took a seat at her side.

Jack angled the chair toward her and leaned forward, bracing his forearms on his thighs. "Let me start by saying I agree with your brother. It's not wise for you to stay in your apartment alone."

"I don't see any alternative to that now. Even if the idea of staying there is terrifying." Her lack of options pressed against her chest and made it hard to breathe. How had her once-stable-and-tidy life turned so unpredictable and terrifying?

"If you agree to what I have in mind, it will solve that problem for at least one night."

The server hustled over with Jack's meal. A long lock of brown hair fell across her face. "Here you are. Let me know if there's anything else I can grab either one of you."

"Go on," Olivia said, once the server was out of ear-shot. The smell of melted cheese and greasy meat almost made her change her mind and grab something for herself to munch on.

Almost.

Jack snatched a couple of fries before slipping a note-pad from the inside of his jacket pocket. "Whoever is threatening you is escalating quickly. The messages left behind indicate someone who has some demented claim over you—a desire to finally be with you. Strangers staying at your loft were targeted, as though they were intruding in some sacred space." He couldn't help but think of Mason's obvious infatuation with Olivia, but he'd keep that to himself.

"I've rented the loft for over a year. Why get upset about it now?" The question had nagged her. Nothing new had happened. She hadn't changed anything in her life. None of it made any sense.

"Usually in these cases, there is a catalyst. Some real, or imagined, slight that provokes the criminal into acting. Into believing the time is now to get what they want. Figuring out that catalyst might be the key in finding the killer."

"You make it sound so easy." She swallowed over the anxiety swelling her throat. She wished she could just snap her fingers and make all of her problems disappear.

He flipped open his notebook and slid it her way. "I've written down all my thoughts. All the facts I've gathered. There are a lot of players, and most of them have been in your life for a long time. None of them appear to be murderers out to get you."

She eyed his notebook but didn't reach for it. She knew who he was talking about, and although she appreciated him letting her in, she wasn't ready to take a deep dive into what he really thought about her friends and family. "Maybe it's someone we haven't considered yet."

He lifted a shoulder but didn't look convinced. "Maybe."

"Do you think you've uncovered our catalyst?" She steadied herself as she waited for the answer.

He locked his gaze with hers, not a line moving on his face. "I do."

She sucked in a breath. "Dave's death."

He nodded.

"But why start killing people and making threats now? Dave died over a year ago." Her heartbeat thundered in her ears. She'd suspected Dave's death wasn't an accident like the police claimed, but she'd never dreamed the killer would keep coming for her. Not like this. Not after all this time.

"I'm not sure about the timing yet, but after you confided your suspicions regarding the hit-and-run with your husband, I requested the case files. You're right. Things don't add up."

Validation loosened a knot that had tied up her insides since Dave died. "No one else believed me. They said it was my grief talking."

He rested a hand on top of hers. "I believe you. And I think whoever killed your husband is now back to claim you. The writing on the painting of the church you were married in, referring to the loft as *our* home, scattering the flower petals that were left at your husband's funeral—this person knows a lot about you. Whoever is taunting you appears to believe the two of you are meant to be together. Or, if not you, then someone close to you."

His line of logic made sense until the last sentence. "What do you mean someone close to me?"

"It's very possible someone is obsessed with you. But sometimes, in cases like this, the criminal's mind is so distorted that the person who is targeted isn't an object of affection. It could be jealousy. A case of you having what they want."

She laughed at the absurdity of anyone being willing to kill over what she had. "Who would be jealous of *my* life?"

He shrugged. "A best friend. A sister-in-law. Someone who passed you on the street and thought how wonderful your life was compared to theirs."

She fought not to argue, because deep down, she understood his logic and knew he had a point. Even if she hated to admit it. Wanting to throw out another alternative, she added, "Or revenge, but we already considered that and came up short."

Jack pointed a fry at her before taking a bite. "Exactly."

"Which do you think it is?" Another question she wasn't sure she wanted the answer to.

"I don't know, but I do think I have a way to find out. I want you to show me where your husband died."

She gasped, her stomach revolting at the idea of seeing the gruesome scene where her husband's life had
been cut short. "What? Why?"

"Because either your husband's death might have
pushed someone over the edge, or he was murdered to
get him out of the way. Knowing the truth about what
happened to Dave brings us one step closer to understanding who is out to get you."

An odd sensation swept over Jack as he welcomed
Olivia into his modest apartment. A hint of unease
mixed with anticipation as her gaze flickered around,
taking in the living room and the kitchen, which was
separated by a half wall. His place wasn't much bigger
than hers, boasting two rooms for him and his roommate, but the beige walls and worn furniture must look
awfully sad to her artist's eye.

After she'd agreed to show him around the town
where her husband had died, he'd accompanied her back
to her place so she could pack a bag. A flash of urgency
set him on edge. He needed to grab his things quickly
before she changed her mind.

The hesitation furrowing her brow and the tight line
of Max's mouth told him neither of them were completely comfortable with his plan. But he couldn't doubt
himself now. Not when his gut told him finding out
what really happened to Dave Hickman was the key to
solving this whole damn case.

He tossed his keys on the circular table that took up
most of the space in his tight kitchen. "You can have
a seat wherever you'd like. My roommate, Nolan, is

at work so it's just us. Make yourself at home while I gather my things."

"Thanks." She took a step off the square patch of linoleum flooring in front of the door and lingered behind the sofa.

"I'll join you," Max said, following him down the short hall to his room. Once inside, Max closed the door. "Are you sure about this?"

Rummaging through the closet, Jack yanked a bag from the top shelf and selected a few shirts off the hangers. He didn't want his clothes to scream out his profession. A light jacket to hide his sidearm, jeans to blend in, and sneakers. "What do you mean? You agree. Dave Hickman's death looks suspicious. From what we've seen, the investigation into the accident was shoddy. Hardly any information you'd expect to see in a crime like this was inside the file."

"The files the local force sent over don't show much of an investigation at all." Max leaned against the doorjamb and crossed his arms over his chest. "The local police took the easy way out. Didn't ask enough questions. Never found the person responsible. Even if it was an accident, someone should have been held accountable."

"Agreed," Jack said. "I need to see the scene for myself. Draw my own conclusions."

Max snorted. "That's not the part I'm questioning."

Jack tossed his half-full bag at his feet and aimed arched brows at his partner and best friend. "Then what part don't you agree with?"

"Like you really have to ask. You've been down this path before. Gotten too caught up with a woman close to an investigation. It didn't end well last time, and it might not end well this time. I can't stand back and watch you go through that again, or watch Mrs. Hickman get hurt because you can't see past whatever it is that's going on between you two."

A familiar ache tore through him. His last case in the Cybercrimes division had led to Mary's death and almost destroyed a year-long case to end a sex trafficking ring. He couldn't let the same disaster happen again. Especially not to Olivia, who'd already been through so much in her life.

With his chin lifted, he fisted his hands to his sides as if physically holding on to his composure. He appreciated his friend's concern, but he didn't like Max's lack of confidence in him. "I need Olivia to come with me so she can help me walk the same steps her husband had walked—the same steps she had when she spent a weekend in Cold Spring. Without her, all I have is the shitty case file. That won't get me anywhere."

Max lifted his palms in surrender. "I'm not arguing with your plan. I'm questioning if you being alone with Mrs. Hickman for an extended period of time is smart. You've spent a lot time with her lately. Are you getting too close?"

He rolled his eyes at Max referring to Olivia as Mrs. Hickman for the second time. He didn't need a reminder of who she was or to be chided like a child for his feelings. Feelings he had a firm grasp on. After what happened with Mary, Max couldn't make him feel any more guilty—or guarded—than he already was.

"Like you were smart when you spent so much time with Samantha." His partner had fallen hard for a woman in a previous investigation. Things had worked out for them, which Jack was happy about, but he wasn't stupid enough to think lightning would strike twice.

Max reared back. "Well. Tell me how you really feel."

He scooped up his bag and faced Max with squared shoulders. "Listen, I appreciate your concern but I'm fine. She's fine. Neither one of us is looking for anything beyond finding the person responsible for two murders and terrorizing her. I won't let anyone hurt her."

Max nodded, but he didn't look convinced. "Okay then. I'll stay here and tug all the strings we've already exposed. Hopefully whatever I untangle will aid you, and vice versa."

"Sounds good," Jack said with a nod. "I need to go. Olivia's been waiting out there alone long enough."

Pushing by Max, he stepped into the bathroom and swiped his toiletries into his bag before zipping it up and going out to meet Olivia.

She stood from her spot on the couch and faced him with a tight smile. "You ready?"

"Yep. Let's get going." He hoisted his bag on his shoulder, casting a glance around the room for anything he might have forgotten.

Max met them at the door. "Keep me posted on what you find. Stay safe."

Jack led them all into the hall. His hand shook as he slipped the key in the lock. He had to keep a tight leash on whatever the hell he was feeling. He might not have been 100 percent honest with Max, but he was certain of one thing he'd said. He wouldn't let anyone harm one hair on Olivia's head.

Not even himself.

Chapter 15

Driving away from the noise of the city usually lifted Olivia's burdens from her shoulders. But not this time. As the sun hovered just above the green trees that lined the sprawling mountains, her muscles tensed. A hundred memories of the last time she'd arrived at the quaint town of Cold Spring, New York assaulted her, forcing her to shut her eyes against their crushing blows.

Just over a year ago, she couldn't get enough of the cute little shops and colorful buildings. The charming red brick sprawled over the walkways and the gazebo that sat in front of the river had made the artist in her sing. Now she couldn't stomach the sights. Didn't want to inhale fresh air or remember the last steps she'd walked with her husband before everything in her life changed.

"Are you okay?"

The gentle timbre of Jack's voice turned her toward him. His broad shoulders took up the seat back as he drove with his hands hung loosely on the steering wheel. His gaze was fixed straight ahead, but she had no doubt he could read her energy in the confining space of his car.

"I'm as fine as I can be. I don't really know what to expect." That was true of multiple things. She never expected to be back in the little town nestled in the Hudson River Valley and wasn't sure what kinds of emotions she'd face during their brief stay.

But there was also a thrill running along the edges of her nerve endings. Excitement over being alone with Jack—away from the city with only each other for company. She had no illusion that this trip was anything beyond professional. A fact-finding mission to put a stop to the mess consuming her life. But she'd be lying if she didn't acknowledge a part of her tingled with anticipation.

"We'll make this as fast and painless as possible." He flicked a quick glance her way. "I promise."

A hum of agreement purred from her throat.

"We don't have much daylight left," he said as he turned off the main street. "We can head to the rooms I booked and get a fresh start in the morning. Or, if there's something else you'd rather do, let me know. I don't want to put any pressure on you. Take whatever time you need."

Her thoughts ping-ponged in her head and made her dizzy. A quiet evening in could be nice. Maybe she'd soak in a bath or try to sketch.

A nagging in her gut told her relaxation would be impossible. Jack would be close, probably down a short hall in his own room, and that knowledge would keep her on edge for all kinds of reasons she didn't want to examine right now. Then there was anxiety about what tomorrow held. Her mouth went dry, and she ran her tongue over her teeth. Sleep would be hard to find, knowing what waited for her with the sunrise.

Decision made, she blew out a long breath. "Can we go somewhere before we get to the hotel?"

"Sure. What do you have in mind? We can grab a bite to eat if you're hungry. Or take a walk to calm our nerves."

She smiled. "You're nervous?"

He shrugged, not answering her question.

The idea he was tense somehow put her a little more at ease. "I have something else in mind. I want to head to the place where Dave was hit."

A beat of silence pulsed before he asked, "Are you sure?"

"Yes. Seeing it will be the hardest part of this little trip. I want to get it over with." Then she could grab that bath and maybe a glass of wine and unwind all the tension circling her neck like a noose.

Jack parked the car on the side of the street. He let the engine idle as he fiddled with his phone. "The spot where he was hit is close." He programmed his GPS then pulled back onto the quiet street, following the directions given.

"We stayed a few blocks from downtown, so I figured it was nearby. Dave ran every day, so he set out for his morning jog first thing that morning." Jack hadn't asked her any questions, but the urge to fill the silence had her spewing the horrible details. "We took the train up and didn't have a car, so we wanted to stay close to town."

She chuckled to herself, replaying the quick banter she and Dave had exchanged before their getaway. "He was so annoyed. The train doubled the time it took to get up here. But the scenery was so pretty, and I wanted us all to relax and just enjoy every second. Dave said I was ridiculous but agreed to skip driving on the highway anyway."

"What about your brother and Clara? Were they irritated by the longer travel time?" He spared her a quick glance before returning his attention to the quiet, residential street.

She tilted her head to the side and studied his profile. Nose slightly crooked at the end and a square jaw covered with scruff. He kept his gaze ahead as he traveled the charted course, but his tight grip on the wheel told her he was very interested in what she had to say. "Not at all. They were so happy. It's sad how things unraveled in their marriage. I hate that I could be the reason."

"You should talk to her," he said. "When we only have our own perspective of a situation, it can be hard to see the big picture."

She leaned back against the soft, leather seat—happy to think about something besides their destination for even a few seconds. "I wish she would talk to me. She's always been one of my closest friends. I hate the thought of losing her."

Jack rested a hand on her arm. "I don't think you have to."

The scenery outside her window stopped moving, and Jack put the car in Park. Her heart stopped, and she caught Jack's concerned stare. Sweat moistened the back of her neck, and she struggled to keep the nausea in her gut settled. "I don't know if I can do this."

He slid his hand from her arm down to her palm. "You don't have to do anything you don't want to do."

She nodded, grateful for his support but knowing she owed it to Dave and Courtney and Priscilla to step out of the car and face her demons. Hell, she owed it to herself. She needed to put fear behind her once and for all. And the first step in putting the terror of the past in her rearview mirror was to look it in the eye. "I'm okay."

She turned to stare out the window and black shaded her vision. The world stood still. The spot where Dave had been hit and left for dead was marked with a small, wooden cross. She swallowed hard and clenched her jaw to keep the tears misting her eyes from falling.

"It happened right there," she said, lifting a finger to point at the spot that looked like just an ordinary stretch of sidewalk in a suburban neighborhood.

"I'm so sorry." He squeezed her hand. "We can get out if you want. Or stay in the car. If you need to step outside for a moment to yourself, I'll sit here. You tell me whatever you need."

She tore her gaze from the shabby patch of grass between the sidewalk and road, not wanting to see the sprinkle of yellow dandelions on the lawn beyond. "It's weird. I can see that morning so clearly. When I got the call, I ran down here. I remember the swarm of people milling about, wondering what happened. Police cars and sirens. The torn-up earth where the car had driven. But now…it doesn't even feel like the same place."

"The world keeps moving, keeps changing, even when you wish it wouldn't," he said. He gently swept the pad of his thumb over the back of her wrist. A comfortable silence hung in the air. "How do you feel?"

She shrugged and struggled to put her emotions into words. "Sad. Relieved. Scared. I thought this would be unbearable, but I'm glad I came. Even if nothing else comes from this trip, this is worth it. Because it shows me that even when you don't witness the change, time heals. Heals wounds and ripped-up earth and broken pieces of concrete."

"Do you want to look around?"

She shook her head. "We can come back and do that tomorrow. Now I want to recharge a bit."

With her hand still in his, he merged back onto the road and headed the way they'd come.

She settled against her seat, happy to be lost in her thoughts. In her new sense of peace. Something had shifted inside her. Freed her from a whole host of things holding her back. And for the first time in a long time, even amidst the horrors waiting for her back home, she could finally breathe. Finally believe her future held more than just hurt and pain and grief.

She just had to stay alive long enough to get there.

Jack hadn't spent a lot of time researching places to stay in Cold Spring. He'd hopped online, searched for vacancies, and booked the first place he'd found with good ratings and a central location. A little bed-and-breakfast close enough to town for he and Olivia to walk wherever they went—The Rivers Edge. Standing in the doily-filled room with the lace curtains and floral wallpaper, he wished he'd been a little pickier.

Olivia giggled in the doorway that led to her connected room. "I don't think I've ever seen anything more feminine than this room."

"Me neither." He snorted and plopped his bag on the wheeled chair by the desk. "How the hell am I supposed to sleep when it feels like these flowers are going to come to life and strangle me?"

She laughed, full and loud. A sound he'd never heard from her before, and that made sleeping in this ridiculous room worth it. "Don't worry. Mine's not much better."

He doubted it, but he didn't want to ask to take a look for himself. Knowing she was on the other side of the wall would be torture enough tonight. If he had an image of the bed with her in it, it'd be pure hell. "It's still early. I might order in a pizza and look over some notes. Get a good idea of what's waiting for us tomorrow. You hungry?"

She rubbed her bare foot over her calf, moving the stretchy black fabric up and down. "A little." She nibbled on her bottom lip as if she had something she wanted to say but didn't know how.

He unloaded the files he'd packed, along with his laptop, and placed them on the narrow desk tucked in front of the lone window at the foot of his bed. "Spill it."

"What do you mean?"

"I can see you're chewing over something in your mind. Might as well tell me what it is."

She slunk into the room and plopped on an armchair

adjacent to the bed. Her auburn hair spilled around her face and fell over her shoulders. Most people needed to clean up after a day of travel and emotional upheaval. Not Olivia. She looked even more gorgeous with a slightly disheveled appearance and the glow of the dim lamplight illuminating her pale skin.

He mentally whacked himself on the side of the head. What the hell was he doing? He couldn't get lost in some stupid fantasy. He was here to solve a murder, with a woman who was being stalked. Forgetting any of that, even for a minute, was a dangerous game he had no right playing.

"You've talked a lot about my brother and his wife." She grabbed the frilly pillow behind her back and hugged it tight. "I don't understand why. The video we've seen of the person breaking into my loft is clearly a man. Clara should be off your list of suspects, and I'd rather die than think my brother had anything to do with this."

He mulled over her question as he organized his files on the desk. It was a thin line to walk between keeping her up-to-date on the investigation and divulging too much. She was close to all the people on his suspect list. Confiding too many details could be detrimental to their working relationship. Treading lightly around the subject wasn't an option, so he might as well be as up-front as possible. "I'll be honest. I don't know how much I should tell you. I don't want my thoughts or opinions to upset you. My looking into the lives of people you're close with could be unsettling."

"True. But it's like you said before. Looking at a situation from one perspective isn't usually the best way. I can offer a different perspective."

He chuckled. "Man, I never thought my being right would be such a pain in the ass."

She smiled, but it quickly fell. "Do you think my brother or Clara are involved with this?"

Pushing the bag to the floor, he sat on the chair and sighed. "Are you sure you want to do this?"

"Yes," she said, pulling at the strings on the pillow.

"Fine. I've spoken with your brother and his wife. The end of their marriage is a sad and tragic thing. One that you aren't responsible for."

She straightened and opened her mouth to speak, but he held up a hand. "I won't tell you things you don't need to hear. Their story is for them to share. You aren't to blame, but there were events that led to the demise of their relationship and could have pushed one of them over the edge."

"You can't be serious."

He leaned forward and battled the war inside him. He wanted to be open with her, as much as he could be, but his thoughts on her friends and family might change the way she viewed him. "You said you wanted to hear this."

"You're right. I'm sorry." Her shoulders heaved from her intake of breath. "But if the person after me is showing in some demented way they want to be with me, how could it be one of them?"

"That's what I hope to figure out while we're here."

"Okay," she said, drawing out the syllables. "I won't argue, but I will say I don't think either of them could have anything to do with this."

He smiled at her scolding tone. "You don't think anyone you know could have a hand in this mess."

She wrinkled her nose. "I know you don't like Edward. But it still doesn't make sense to me that he'd ruin my artwork because he was obsessed with me, then settle for less money for the work."

"That's not the only person I don't trust."

"Who else?" Tilting her head to the side, she let her hair spill over her shoulder.

He let his head fall forward and closed his eyes. He was tired and hungry and not prepared for this conversation. But there was no reason to lie. "Mason Shaffer. His prints were found on the box you two brought in, and on the papers inside. He's been in your apartment. Knows where your artwork is hung. Did he know you and Dave were here on vacation?"

Her grip tightened on the pillow and smooshed its edges, making it look more like a circle. "Maybe. I don't know if Dave told him, but it wasn't as if it was a secret. They worked closely together. Mason would cover for Dave when he was out of the office, and vice versa. He'd have no reason to want to hurt Dave. Or come after me. We're friends. Nothing more."

The hard edge to her voice pinched his chest. He didn't like Mason and didn't trust the guy's intentions. But he hated that Olivia jumped to the other man's defense. "Are you sure about that?"

Frowning, she lifted her brows. "Can I be sure about anything?"

"Fair point," he said, not wanting to press her further on her relationship with Mason. "Did anyone else know you were coming to Cold Spring?"

She set her jaw and narrowed her eyes. "Christine. She watered my plants while we were away. My dad, who lives in Jersey. I don't know if any of the others mentioned it to friends or coworkers."

He swallowed hard, steeling his resolve to ask his next question. "Christine's name is mentioned a lot. Clara told me she wasn't a big fan of your friend. That Christine wasn't very nice and often seemed irritated when you were around others. Does she have a temper?"

She stood and paced around the small room, her fist bunching the pillow at her side. "Christine has been my best friend my entire life. She's been there for me for the hardest moments. When I was at my lowest point, she brought me back to life. Is she protective of her friends—of me? Yes. Has she ever hurt anyone? No."

Sympathy turned his stomach. Olivia was in an impossible position. Dissecting all of her closest relationships couldn't be easy, but it had to be done. "She's never been jealous of you or your relationships?"

Olivia laughed, but it morphed into a stifled sob. She sniffed and pressed the back of her hand to her mouth. "Never. She's never been anything but supportive and loyal. She's tangled up in this whole mess through no fault of her own. Just like everyone else. People are hurt or dead or their stores have been broken into because of me. Now if you'll excuse me, it's been a long day and I need some sleep." The tight set of her mouth quivered, and she hurried through the adjoining doorway, disappearing and locking herself away before he could respond.

Jack slumped down in his chair and flipped open the file he'd filled with information on Christine Roberts.

So much for a quiet night in with a good meal. The tension in his gut wouldn't let him consume a damn thing. He longed to break through the door and comfort her, let her know that he trusted her instincts about the people she loved.

But he couldn't do that. Not when he had cold hard facts to look at, and those facts didn't add up when it came to more than one person in her life. So instead of erasing whatever unease brewed between him and Olivia, he'd keep his head down, his emotions in check, and focus on the only thing that mattered. Doing his job.

Chapter 16

A heavy weight pressed down on Olivia's chest, pinning her to the mattress. The morning sun flowed through the gauzy curtains. She stared up at the light pink fabric of the canopy that covered the queen-size bed and groaned. Facing this day was like standing against a slobbering guard dog who was bound to pounce if she made one wrong move. It'd be better if she didn't have to move at all and she could just burrow deep under the down comforter and forget all her troubles.

Unfortunately, the constant repeat of her conversation with Jack made forgetting anything impossible. The glass—or two—of wine the night before had done nothing but give her a light headache and cloud her judgment. She'd tossed and turned, going over all the things she should have said. Regretting some of the things she had.

More than once she'd considered knocking on the thin door that separated their rooms. Explaining that her emotions were boiling at the surface, and she had no right to take her turmoil out on him. Even if she didn't like it, she understood he was doing his job. Trying his hardest to keep her safe and put a criminal behind bars.

Instead, she'd stayed in her own room. Berating herself and praying she hadn't ruined their friendship. Or even worse, made him regret confiding in her.

The sound of her phone buzzing turned her toward the oak nightstand. She lifted it and winced. Christine never called this early, but she was probably concerned, knowing this trip would be difficult. She normally wouldn't hesitate to answer her friend's call, but something inside her had her hitting the silent button, then typing out a quick text message to let her know she was all right before tossing down her phone.

Not wanting to spend any more time going over things she couldn't change, she hopped out of bed. If yesterday was any indication, today would be tough. She needed to have her head on straight. Rummaging through the drawers she'd filled with her clothes, she found what she needed to go for a little run. Running was another love she'd lost over the past year, but something about being back in Cold Spring made her want to do something to bring her closer to Dave. Something they'd loved doing together. And if nothing else, a little exercise could go a long way in getting out some of her pent-up nervous energy.

After dressing and securing her hair into a high ponytail, she stopped in front of the door that led to Jack's room. A part of her wanted to just go, leave everything behind for a small moment in time. Jack and all her problems would be waiting when she returned. But the logical part of her told her that leaving without telling Jack was not only rude, but stupid.

Steeling her resolve, she knocked on the white door and waited.

A few seconds passed, and she doubted her decision to disturb him. Maybe he was still asleep. Dawn had just broken, and most people would want another hour or two before climbing out of bed. "Jack?"

Anticipation shifted her weight from one foot to the other. Straining her ears, she listened for the sound of movement on the other side of the wall but heard nothing. She'd knock once more, then slip a note under the door to let him know she'd be back soon. Fisting her hand, she pulled back to tap again, and the door swung open.

Jack stood in front of her with his hand clenched around the ends of a towel swung low around his hips. His chest was bare, drops of water running along the grooves of his muscles. His hair spiked up in all directions, and the desire to run her fingers through the wild strands had her swallowing the lump of desire lodged in her dry throat.

"What's up? Is everything all right?" His blue eyes were wide and searching.

Unable to speak, she nodded. "Mmm-hmm."

As if suddenly realizing he was half-naked, he took a step backward and winced. "Sorry. I was in the shower when I heard you call for me. I, uh, didn't want to wait to see you if something was wrong."

Dear Lord, there wasn't an ounce of fat on him.

Keeping her gaze locked on his face was the hardest thing she'd ever done. "I'm fine. Just going out for a run and wanted to tell you." The high-pitched quality of her voice made her cringe. She needed to get her act together and quick.

She turned away and yanked on the handle to shut the door.

Jack grabbed the edge. "Hold on a second. You're leaving?"

"I just want to get a run in. I'll be gone fifteen minutes tops." She stumbled over her words, her mind refusing to focus on anything other than the wet man in front of her.

"Give me a second and I'll get dressed and join you. I don't think it's smart for you to be out and about by yourself."

She smiled at his concern but couldn't chance spending another second in his presence. Heat scorched her cheeks, and her mind produced an imaginary highlight reel of all the delicious things she could be doing to burn some calories besides a sweaty jog. All activities that involved Jack as her costar and made her burn with something she hadn't felt in a very long time.

"I'll be fine. I promise. I'll be back before you know it." She backpedaled until her knees bumped up against the bed. She swiped her phone and room key off the stand and slipped them in the little pocket at the side of her pants.

"Please. Give me two minutes. I don't want anything to happen to you."

His earnest plea melted through her desperate need to escape. "Okay. I'll wait."

He disappeared back into his bathroom, re-emerging seconds later sporting a pair of black joggers and a worn T-shirt with a football team's mascot on the front. "Ready?"

Still not trusting herself to speak, she nodded and led the way out the door and down the stairs. Once outside of the two-story bed-and-breakfast, she breathed deeply, trying to calm her racing heart. She stretched her arms high above her head, noting the blue skies that had pushed away the previous day's rain. Swirls of pink clashed against the yellow glow of the sun, but white fluffy clouds already floated by.

"Which way?" Jack asked, bending at the waist and reaching toward the ground.

"Doesn't matter. Let's just head down the street." Choosing a direction, she pounded down the sidewalk. Birds chirped in the flowering trees and squirrels darted across yards. The neighborhood was quiet. Most people probably just starting their mornings in their homes. The air was warm with a lingering crispness grazing her face. The day promised to be a beautiful one, and Olivia focused on each footfall as she increased her pace and pushed herself just a little bit harder.

"Do you run often?" Jack asked, his breathing steady as he kept pace beside her.

"I used to. Dave liked to start our days together with a run, when possible. After he died, I stopped. Today, it just felt right. I forgot how much I miss it." She sent him a quick glance and noted his form. "What about you? You look like a natural."

He managed a small shrug while his arms pumped back and forth. "Working out every day is a given. Run-

ning, sometimes. Cardio isn't my favorite. I'd rather lift
and focus on strength training."

She didn't have a hard time believing that at all. After
seeing him shirtless, she guessed he must spend hours
honing his body like a sculptor chiseled a piece of stone.

They fell silent as they passed house after house.
Parked cars lined the quiet street. The sound of their
shoes slapping the sidewalk competed with her labored
breath. Her lungs burned, but she wouldn't admit she
was winded. Not yet.

Needing to give herself some motivation, she asked,
"Wanna race? Around the block and back to the B and
B?"

He slowed to a stop and doubled over, catching his
breath. "Seriously?"

"Scared you'll lose?" She slowed down and stood a
little in front of him. Grateful for the small break.

"Never." He flashed a wicked grin. "Let me tie my
shoe first."

She waited for him to crouch low, then took off at a
full sprint down the sidewalk.

"Hey!" he called, a laugh engulfing the word. "No
fair!"

She followed the curve of the sidewalk around the
corner and fought back a giggle. It'd been too long since
she'd done something just for the fun of it, and beating
Jack in a race would sure be fun.

The rev of an engine had her glancing over her shoulder. A black SUV roared around the corner.

Her heart rate sped up and she charged forward.

The squeal of brakes and the sound of a car door
opening followed by heavy footsteps hitched her heart

up to her throat. Fear pushed her to lengthen her stride, increase her pace.

A hard yank on her ponytail had her stumbling backward, tripping on the uneven concrete. A rough hand gripped her waist and anchored her to a hard chest. "I finally got you alone. I knew I'd find a way."

She tried to recognize the cadence of the words, the tone of the deep, masculine voice, but panic swallowed up her brain and she struggled to free herself from her captor.

"Get away from her!" Jack's deep, gravelly voice called from the down the street.

The grip fell away, and she crashed to the ground. Pain exploded in her head. She squeezed her eyes closed and stars burst through the darkness. Pushing through the agony, she squinted and curled onto her side. A pair of white sneakers ran in the opposite direction before jumping in the black SUV and driving away.

Adrenaline edged out the terror zipping through Jack's veins. He bolted forward. Olivia had gone down hard and hadn't moved since she hit the pavement. As he ran, he grabbed his phone and snapped a picture of the back of the black SUV as it raced away. No way he could chase down Olivia's attacker, but at least he got a good view of the license plate.

He'd worry about running the plates later. For now, he needed to get to Olivia. Reaching her side, he crouched low and surveyed the damage. She lay curled in a ball by his feet, her eyes closed. "Olivia? Can you hear me?"

She opened her eyes and hissed out a breath. "What

the hell happened?" Her tongue darted from her mouth and wet her lips.

"Someone grabbed you from behind. Darted from an SUV parked on the road." His heart continued galloping in his chest even though the danger was long gone. He'd witnessed a lot of scary things in his line of work, but watching from a distance as Olivia was attacked ranked high on the list.

She braced her hands on the sidewalk and pushed herself up to a seated position. Red scratches ran down the side of her face. Tiny pricks of blood dotted the wounds. "Sonofabitch," she said, cradling the back of her head with her hand.

He settled on the ground beside her and called the police. "Take it easy," he said as the line rang in his ear. "Head injuries are tricky. We need to make sure there's nothing else going on in there before you do too much."

"I'm fine. It's just one hell of a goose egg on the back of my head from where I hit the ground."

She attempted to climb to her feet, but he guided her back down beside him. "I'm serious. Just sit a minute."

The line picked up, and a dispatcher asked for his emergency.

Noting the names of the street signs at the nearby corner, he prattled off details of where they were and what happened. Olivia made a face when he requested a medic to examine her before ending the call. Then he quickly sent Max the photo of the license plate with a request to search for the owner of the vehicle.

"I don't need a medic fussing over me. I told you. I'm fine."

He brushed stray bits of dirt and a few pebbles from

the front of her pants. "Medics don't fuss, they fix. Besides, it's better than me driving you to the emergency room."

"Fine."

Focusing on her bruised face, he lifted a hand and said a silent prayer of thanks he'd made the decision to come with her. Strands of hair slipped from her rubber band. He skimmed his knuckles over her jaw. He let out a long breath and couldn't stop a quiver from shaking the hand cradling her face. "That scared the shit out of me."

She squeezed her eyes shut and grimaced. "Wasn't a picnic for me either."

Her sarcasm loosened the knot in his chest. He didn't plan to let her out of his sight until he knew she'd be safe.

When she opened her eyes, her wide, hazel irises bored into his. "You saved me. If you hadn't yelled and scared the attacker away, I wouldn't have stood a chance." She touched the spot on her head again. "We were followed all the way here. I didn't think that was a possibility. That someone would leave the city and come here." Sadness and fear made her words tremble, and she took a firm hold of his hand.

He dropped his palm from her face and trapped her hand between both of his. He wanted to take her in his arms and vow to protect her. Swear to find the answers to every question she asked. But he didn't want to scare her with the intensity of his emotions or spike her pain with any sudden movements. "We were either followed or someone knew where to find us. Did you tell anyone we were coming here?"

She curled her fingers around his. "Umm, my brother. He was worried about where I'd be tonight, and I wanted to let him know I was okay."

"Anyone else?" He didn't want to press her too hard right now but needed to know what he was working with.

She winced. "Christine called me this morning. I didn't answer but sent her a text letting her know I was out of town and everything was fine."

"After seeing who just tried to grab you, it's safe to say it wasn't Christine. Did you mention our visiting Cold Spring to any other friends? Is it possible someone overheard something, or Jason told someone?"

"I don't know. I can't be sure."

"Well, someone knew. And my guess is that same someone understands why we are here and wants to stop us from digging into your husband's death. Because if we get this case reopened, it's more police looking for them."

Tears filled her eyes. "I hate this so much. I thought losing Dave was bad, but this? The not knowing and the constant fear. I don't know how much more I can take."

His heart twisted at the pain in her voice. "You're strong, Olivia. You can handle anything life throws your way, even if it's unfair that you have to. But I'm right here beside you, and I won't leave until I can promise you that whoever is responsible will never hurt you again."

A wobbly smile lifted one corner of her mouth. "Thank you. I trust you. Even if it didn't sound like it last night. I was overwhelmed and upset, but that was no excuse to snap at you like I did."

The weight of tension that had pressed on his shoulders since their conversation dissipated. "I appreciate the sentiment, but you don't need to apologize. You had a rough night. Hell, you've had a rough few days. Most people would have cracked under the pressure already."

"I'll do better."

Instinct took over and he lifted her hand to his mouth and pressed his lips to the soft skin on the inside of her wrist. "You're already the best woman I've ever met."

A screeching siren wailed into the quiet morning. A squad car and ambulance turned onto the deserted street, dashing the intimacy of the moment.

Jack cleared his throat and stood to welcome the law enforcement. Thankful for the interruptions. He'd already said too much to Olivia. Confessed more than he should. But now he needed to focus. He had to convince the local police this wasn't an isolated incident, and it was all connected to the investigation involving Dave Hickman.

Then he'd get the case reopened. Because it was time to end this, and not only ensure Olivia's safety but finally to get her husband the justice he deserved.

Chapter 17

Each step sent another jolt of pain against the back of Olivia's skull. She had been right. Her dangerous encounter had left her with nothing more than jangled nerves and a giant goose egg at the back of her head. She needed a pain pill and a shower, but the thought of water pounding down on her head sounded about as tempting as jumping in the Hudson River.

Jack kept a steady palm cupped under her elbow as he guided her up the porch steps of the bed-and-breakfast. "One more step. Almost there."

His fretting made her smile. "I told you I'm fine. The paramedic told you I'm fine. Hell, even the old man who poked his nose out the door after the police showed up could tell you I'm fine. I can make it up the porch steps."

He lifted his hands, but his deep scowl and furrowed

brow showcased his concern. "Let me at least get the door." He hurried to pull open the storm door, waiting for her to enter before following close behind.

"Well, my goodness. There you two are." Marta, the owner of The River's Edge, stood beside one of four tables in the dining nook that sat beside the check-in desk. "You're a mess. Your poor, beautiful face. What happened?"

Not wanting to call any more attention to herself, Olivia forced a wide grin, the motion making her head spin. "Just a little fall. I'm always so clumsy. Is there a first aid kit in my room?" Although she'd agreed to let the medic take a closer look at her injuries, she hadn't wanted the young man to mess with the scratches on her face. She could take care of the superficial wounds herself.

"Of course, dear. Should be one in the top drawer in the bathroom. Just holler when you're finished, and I'll make sure breakfast is all ready for you both. My specialty, fresh scones and homemade strawberry jam, for breakfast. Or, like my grandbabies like to call it, Nana jelly."

The idea of food made Olivia's stomach rebel, but she didn't want to be rude. "Sounds delicious."

With a hum of satisfaction, Marta wiped her thick, wrinkled hands on her apron and rushed into the kitchen.

"If we don't watch it, I think she'll force spoonfuls of food down our throat," Jack said with an amused snort as he guided her up the winding staircase.

"I hope not. I couldn't eat a crumb, even if it smells

heavenly down there." Heck, the mouthwatering scent of freshly baked bread was just as strong upstairs.

She stepped slowly on the carpeted floor. A thick, striped border ran along the center of the walls that flanked the hallway, separating the maroon wallpaper above from the—surprise—array of flowers that dotted the bottom portion. Black-and-white pictures of the past were framed and hung wherever Marta could find a spare space.

"This reminds me of my grandmother's house," she said, letting her mind wander back in time. To simple days of sleepovers and baking cookies and playing tag in her grandparents' large yard. "Funny how such simple times sounds so darn good in the middle of a shitstorm."

He chuckled. "I guess. But to me, simple times always sound good. You have your key?"

She swiped the old-fashioned key from the slit at the side of her pants and preceded him into the room. Fatigue and the sharp stings on her face made her want to just fall back into bed. But that wasn't an option. She and Jack were here for a reason, and she needed to see this through. Needed to help jam the pieces of the world's most frustrating puzzle together.

Jack whistled as he crossed the threshold. "You were right. My room's worse."

She choked out a huff of laughter as she passed by the girlie canopy bed and dainty furniture to the bathroom. The sleeping area might have escaped the attack of flowers, but the bathroom more than made up for it. Pale pink and cream blossoms sprouted everywhere, the mirror over the sink multiplying them. At the vanity, she pulled open a drawer and found the first aid kit, right where Marta said it'd be. Zipping open the square, white canvas container, she riffled through the contents.

"Let me help you," Jack said. "Do you want to sit in here or find someplace more comfortable?"

A flash of him in his towel earlier made her face burn. "Bathroom is better. More natural light." That might be a lie, but no way she trusted herself with him in such an intimate setting.

The heat from her face traveled south, and she turned her back to Jack so he couldn't read her wayward thoughts. The brush of his body against hers tightened her muscles.

"Sorry." He leaned around her to the mahogany cabinet. He fished out a washcloth and wet it under the faucet. "Why don't you take a seat?"

She shoved the pretty white shower curtain out of the way and sat on the edge of the porcelain tub. The thin edge wasn't the most comfortable, but she anchored herself with a firm grip on each side of her lap.

Facing her, Jack tucked his thumb under her chin and dabbed the cloth on her cheek.

She hissed in pain and reared back.

"Almost done," he said, staring intently at her wounds. "Gotta make sure all the dirt's out of there."

She sat still as a statue as he dabbed a few more times.

"All clean." He grabbed the kit he'd placed at his feet and found a miniature tube of disinfectant. He squeezed a little on the tip of his index finger then gently slid it on her scratches.

He leaned close, his breath warm on her face. His

singular focus on fixing her up warmed parts inside her that she'd thought died along with Dave. Parts that had nothing to do with the desire he'd already ignited. This was different. Deeper. Scarier.

Dropping his hand, he kept his thumb on her chin and his gaze locked on hers. "How do you feel?"

"Fine," she said, the word nearly caught in her dry, cottony mouth.

"You don't have to be brave. Don't have to swallow whatever it is you're feeling. What happened was terrifying. Anyone would have a hard time coming to terms with being attacked."

He was wrong. She had to work harder than ever to hide how she felt, but her blossoming emotions had nothing to with the killer who'd sent her reeling. But she couldn't admit that, so she cracked a small smile and confided all she was willing to say. "As long as you're near, I'm okay."

His eyes widened, as if her confession was the last thing he'd expected to hear. "I'm not going anywhere." His gaze fell to her mouth.

Leaning forward, she licked her lips and gave in to the raw instinct. Her heart stalled and her breath caught. She closed her eyes. The feel of his lips brushed against hers and sparks ignited inside her. All the air left her lungs and her stomach flipped. She raised her arms and hooked them around his neck, bringing him closer. The scent of his woodsy soap surrounded her, and she curled her toes against the cool tile.

He deepened the kiss, his lips parting her mouth. His arms holding her close. The rough scruff on his jaw moved against the sensitive skin on her chin.

Warmth pooled in her core and her guarded heart soared. A small moan slipped from her mouth.

He pulled back on a gasp and flashed a smile. "See. Head wounds make people do the damnedest things."

A tug of disappointment kick-started her heart, but she forced a smile. No way she'd let him see how badly she wanted that kiss to continue. So instead, she lied. "You're right. Now let's head down for some scones before I do something even more stupid."

Needing to not be alone with Olivia, Jack opted to wait for her downstairs while she changed out of her dirty clothes. There might not be a lot of extra eyes in the dining area to keep him in line, but Marta bustled around the first floor like a bull charging after a red flag.

With his seat facing the door to keep an eye on anyone coming and going, he took a bite of the scone covered with jam and closed his eyes on a moan. The sweet taste of strawberry and the warm pastry was a potent combination. He'd have to see if Marta sold her homemade goodies before they left.

The phone he'd laid on the blue and white gingham tablecloth glowed with the announcement of an incoming call.

Max.

He took a sip of black coffee to wash down his food before answering. "Hey, man. Find anything?"

"Ran the plates from the SUV. The information given to the car rental place just outside the city is the same name and number given to the vacation rental site where Olivia's loft was listed—the one from the user who left the threat. Not the hit we wanted, but my gut tells me not a dead end either."

Although disappointed not to get the real identity of the driver, Jack wasn't surprised. Olivia's attacker wouldn't have planned on getting caught, but history showed this person was clever enough to not take any chances. "Agreed. Renting a car gives high probability whoever drove it doesn't own their own vehicle. Or he had to cover his tracks because Olivia would recognize the car. I'd also bet the alias and information given is sentimental to whoever uses it. We just have to figure out why."

"I'm securing video footage from the vehicle rental as we speak. Maybe we got something on tape we can use," Max said.

Jack circled his hand around his warm mug and kept his attention fixed on the stairs. How long did it take Olivia to change her outfit? The longer she was out of his sight, the higher his anxiety rose. "The address given was in Queens, right? A pizza shop?"

"Yep."

Olivia appeared at the top of the stairs. Her hair now released from the ponytail, the loose strands waving and a little messy. Skinny jeans molded against her shapely legs and the V-neck of her fitted white T-shirt shot up his blood pressure. She flashed a smile at Marta before taking the seat on the other side of the table.

He dipped his chin to acknowledge her before getting back to his conversation "My guess is the person we're after has ties to Queens. Grew up there, family around, something that makes that shop—that neighborhood—feel like a safe place to use."

"Makes sense. Shit like that is almost never random," Max agreed.

Another thought struck him. He'd been so concerned about information on the license plate, he hadn't asked about the driver. "Have you spoken with the local police about finding the SUV and the person driving it?"

Marta sashayed her wide hips and wider grin their way with a full plate and a carafe of coffee. She placed the plate in front of Olivia and waited for her to turn over her dainty, white mug before filling it with coffee. "Let me know if you need anything else," she said, keeping her voice low, throwing a wink his way, then headed back toward the kitchen.

"No sign of it yet. I'll call if I hear anything else."

He said his goodbyes, then disconnected and set his phone on the table beside his now-empty plate. He watched Olivia take a bite of her scone and a drip of jam landed on the side of her mouth. He bit back a groan as well as every urge to wipe the red goop away in a very creative way.

She flicked out her tongue to lick it off herself and his core tightened. Dammit to hell and back. Never would he imagine having a beautiful woman kiss him would make his life miserable. But now that he'd tasted her lips—and seen a softer yet take-charge side of her—he'd never be satisfied until he had more.

And he'd never allow himself that pleasure, so it was best to shove those stupid thoughts and desires all the way down to his toes.

"Was that Detective Green?" Olivia asked, drawing him back from his wayward thoughts.

He took a long sip of coffee and nodded. "He ran the plates. The SUV was a rental."

"And the information was from Queens? Just like the person who started the account and left the threat on the review for the loft?" She wrinkled her nose.

"Yes," he said, drawing out the word.

"Sorry. I overheard." She leaned back in her chair and stared down at the barely touched food. "If I want to help, I need to stop being so sensitive. Clearly, someone I trust—someone I know—is capable of things I never could have imagined."

Her voice was so small and sad, he wanted to forget the idea of staying away from her and gather her in his arms. But he couldn't.

Clearing her throat, she shifted in her seat and finally met his eye. "I've been thinking about yesterday. When we stopped by the site where Dave was killed. The street was similar to the one I was on earlier. A short stretch of road in a quiet neighborhood. Stop signs ridiculously close on a small block."

He pulled the visual back in his mind. The space between stop signs hadn't registered to him earlier, his focus entirely on making sure Olivia was all right. But looking back, she was right. Only a handful of houses lay between one corner of the block and the next. "I guess that's not too uncommon in neighborhoods."

"But how could a car hit Dave so hard, been driving so fast, when there really wasn't enough space to accelerate? Unless it was done on purpose."

Sonofabitch. She was right. He'd trusted her instinct that something wasn't right about her husband's death, but the files he'd been sent by the local force hadn't mentioned anything that pointed at the hit-and-run being anything other than an accident. The reporting officer might have mentioned the torn-up earth and Dave's extensive injuries, but no note was mentioned that the accident could have been intentional. "I can't believe that wasn't noted in the case files." It made him wonder what else had been missed in the initial investigation.

"So you believe me? That my husband's death wasn't an accident?" The worry shining from her wide eyes twisted his insides.

"More than that. I believe that whoever killed your husband is now after you."

She shuddered and squeezed her eyes shut for a beat before refocusing on him with a wobbly smile. "I should have listened to my gut. Everyone told me it was my grief keeping me up at night. That I wasn't thinking straight, and I just needed to accept the truth of what happened—even if the person who'd hit him was never caught. If I would have been more assertive, spoken louder, maybe all of this could have been avoided."

"You can't blame yourself for that," he said. "And now you are being assertive and speaking up. You came here with me, didn't you? And we'll keep checking every angle until we figure this out."

She released a shuddering breath. "Okay. What's the next step?"

"Are you sure you're up for more? You've had a rough morning."

"I'm sure."

"Then we head into town. I want to know every-where you went with your husband when you were here.

Everything you did. Maybe a memory will spark something, or someone, you saw when you were here. And while we look, we talk about your friends. Because as much as it sucks, someone you know is out to hurt you."

Chapter 18

The subtle breeze pushed the water of the Hudson River gently downstream as it cut along the edge of Cold Spring. The tiny ripples lapped along the riverbanks. Not exactly the sound of crashing waves, but a gentle lull of motion that made Olivia sway from her spot on the bench, overlooking the peaceful sight. The day had turned out as beautiful as she'd expected, bookended with an orange glow outlining the distant mountains.

Jack hooked an arm around the back of the bench. "We packed in as much as we could. How you holding up?"

She considered the question. Nothing about this terrifying adventure had panned out the way she'd expected—today's jog down memory lane among them. "You know, I hate what brought me here again, but I'm glad I came. I thought I'd be a mess. Tears and heartbreak weighing me down with every step. But it's been…cathartic."

"I'm glad. Shake anything loose?"

Considering, she twisted her mouth to the side. "I keep thinking about how happy Jason and Clara were. Laughing at the ice cream parlor. Teasing each other about saving their pennies at the antique shops. Snuggling at dinner. Seems strange that things changed so quickly."

He tucked in his lips as if having a hard time keeping things to himself. "I already told you I can't say more on that subject."

"I know. But I will try harder to talk to both of them about it. Beyond that—" she lifted her hands then let them drop on her lap "—just memories of time here with Dave. Nothing I haven't already mentioned. I'm sorry."

He grazed the side of her shoulder with his knuckles. "You already did more than enough with your observation about the spot where Dave was hit. Max spoke with the police. They've reopened the investigation and plan to send over everything they uncover. That's huge."

Relief pushed her back against the hard bench. She'd hate to think this trip had been for nothing. Now more officers were searching for the person who killed her husband. She had to believe Dave's killer would be found and punished for taking his life. A life that might have been cut short because of her.

"You look upset," Jack said.

She turned to him, surprised again at how well he could read her. She wasn't sure if it was because it was his job to get to the bottom of things, or he just knew her so damn well so soon. "If we're right, if someone killed Dave to get him out of the way, then he's dead because of me." Guilt thrummed along with each beat of her heart. Losing Dave was hard. Finding out she had a part in his death was unbearable.

Jack frowned. "No matter what is uncovered, you are not to blame for your husband's death."

She sniffed back tears. "How can you say that? If someone killed him to get to me, I'm the connection. I'm the reason he was targeted." She dropped her gaze to her clasped hands, wringing them to keep herself from falling apart.

"You can't think like that."

"How can I not?" Her voice cracked and she sucked in a shuddering breath.

"Look at me," he said.

She lifted her eyes to his.

"You are not responsible for someone else's actions. Ever. What happened to your husband is tragic. I didn't know him, but I know he wouldn't want you to blame yourself."

"Your words make sense, but it's difficult to believe them." Each new piece of information they'd uncovered the last few days twisted her heart just a little bit more until the pain was almost unbearable.

Jack turned his gaze to the river and a flash of sorrow and regret flickered on his face. "I understand that. More than you realize."

Needing to focus on something else, she studied his sharp profile. The hurt in his voice had her reaching out and grabbing his hand. He'd shown her a glimpse of his past before but hadn't delved deep into what put that haunted look in his eyes. And she'd been so wrapped up in her own drama she hadn't stopped to think the pain he suffered could be just as consuming as what she'd carried with her the last year.

"Do you want to talk about it?" she asked, taking a gamble. He'd been a source of comfort and strength for her when he didn't have to be. That wasn't part of his job description. She could never explain how much that meant to her. If she could give back just a fraction of that patience and empathy, she wanted to.

Lifting his arm from over her shoulders, he scratched the back of his neck. "Liv, I don't know. I mean, this isn't about me, and I don't want to make it about me. I just want to be here for you."

The little nickname made her stomach flip. "And I want to be here for you, too." The truth of that statement set a flame ablaze inside her. It wasn't that long ago she thought she'd never want to let anyone into her life—allow herself to be vulnerable to another man. The thought scared the hell out of her, but also made her hopeful and a little bit excited.

He leaned forward and braced his forearms on his knees. His stare remained forward with a faraway look in his eyes as if he saw something that wasn't really there. "Remember when I told you I used to work in cybercrimes?"

She nodded.

"My last case was a rough one. For many reasons I won't go into. It was a year-long operation to shut down a child sex trafficking ring."

Despite the warm weather, a chill swept over her.

"I had a contact in the operation. A woman who had

spent a lifetime enduring unimaginable abuse. The man in charge kept her in the house with the kids. Her job was to wash them and make them…presentable."

Nausea swam in her gut. She wanted to tell him to stop. These details weren't what she'd expected, and she wasn't sure she could handle hearing more. But sensing he needed to tell his story, she kept her protests to herself.

"We got close. Too close. I wanted to help get her out of this life she'd been forced into."

She winced at the situation, not sure she could feel anything but disgust for a woman in her position. "How was she forced?"

"The leader told her he'd kill her mother and sister. He had pictures of them to prove he could get to them. Mary wanted to protect her family." He rubbed a palm down his face. "The closer we got, the more mistakes I made. I put her ahead of everyone. I didn't want her to risk herself, but the operation needed her. I tried to step in, to get her out, and the leader found out. He…. he…"

Her heart lodged in her throat. She didn't need him to finish his sentence—to know what happened to this woman she'd never met. "I'm so sorry you lost her."

He wiped at his eyes, refusing to glance her way. "Not only did I lose her, but it almost ruined the bust we'd planned for so long. All those kids were almost lost forever because I couldn't keep a lid on my feelings. Because I fell in love with Mary. And even though I'm not the one who put the gun to her head, it felt like I was the one who killed her."

"But you didn't. From the sound of it, you gave her

something special she'd never had before. The love of a good man, and I'm sure that meant more to her than you'll ever realize. You gave her a gift. You didn't kill her."

Still leaning forward, he turned his head to face her. "And you didn't kill Dave."

She swallowed hard, for his sense of peace as well as her own. "Then neither one of us has anything to feel guilty about."

He cracked a weak smile, although he didn't look convinced.

His phone rang, and he dipped a hand into his front pocket for his phone. "It's Max," he said, glancing on the screen. "Give me a second."

While he answered the phone, she reflected on their conversation. Jack had mentioned some things being more painful than a broken heart. She understood now what he meant. In this weird, upside-down world she'd been dumped in, she'd found things she'd never imagined. She'd found an acceptance that her past could be remembered with warmth and even happiness, but she didn't need to carry her grief and hurt with her like some kind of widow's badge.

"Thanks for the heads-up," Jack said into the phone.

She straightened, focus back on her present situation. "What is it?"

"The SUV was found ditched just outside of town. The driver nowhere around. They're dusting for prints, but so far, no luck."

Another chill engulfed her. "Which means whoever left the vehicle could be anywhere, but chances are, they came back here."

* * *

With the sunlight fading and a cloud of paranoia surrounding him, Jack led Olivia through the quaint downtown and back to The River's Edge. Twilight sparkled off the water as they walked along the brick pathway. Away from the quiet moment where he'd laid his soul bare. He wasn't sure what made him confide in her; maybe it was the fact that she had hit such a low point and he wanted her to know he understood.

No matter the reason, a crack had splintered the wall he'd built so high after Mary died. If he wanted Olivia to believe that she was guilt-free in her husband's death, didn't he need to do the same with the part he played with Mary?

No, it wasn't the same. Olivia was an innocent bystander. Caught up in someone else's sick game. He had been responsible for making smart decisions to keep Mary alive and he'd failed. He might not have pulled the trigger, but the gun wouldn't have been on her if he'd made better choices.

Not wanting to go back down that rabbit hole, he focused on the feel of Olivia's body next to his. Even with the rough beginning and reasons for being in Cold Spring, the day had been pleasant. Nice weather, a beautiful woman by his side, and hours spent reviewing the last days Olivia had spent with her husband.

She'd held up much better than he'd expected. Watching her remember details and hearing the stories she told showed him a different side of her. A lighter side, carefree and happy. A side he wished he could know more of. He hoped what she'd told him was true. That this trip was healing in a way she'd never thought possible. Maybe that's what he needed to do. Face his past head-on in order to move forward.

They took a detour around the busy downtown and turned onto the quiet streets of the residential area. He kept on high alert. Streetlamps cast small halos of light on the sidewalk, and the noisy bustle from downtown murmured in the distance.

"How's your head?" he asked, hoping she hadn't overdone it.

"Hurts a little." She touched the spot on the back of her head where her long hair hid the goose egg. "Still tender."

"A good night's sleep before heading back to the city should help." A tug of disappointment slowed his steps. Returning to the city should mean going their separate ways, but he couldn't let her out of his sight until the danger was gone. He just needed to figure out how to make that happen.

"I hope so," she said, smiling. "Lord knows I'm tired enough to fall into bed and sleep till morning."

He rounded the corner and a sea of red and blue lights clashed against the sky. Two police cruisers and an ambulance were parked in front of the bed-and-breakfast.

Olivia slowed to a stop and her palm covered a gasp. "Oh no."

Urgency swept through him, and he grabbed her hand to tug her along. "Come on. We need to find out what happened."

He ran, with Olivia beside him, until he reached the chaotic scene.

Two paramedics carried a stretcher with a motionless

woman out the open door and down the porch steps. A
weathered officer with a heavily lined face and protrud-
ing gut spoke with the man at the front of the gurney
as they moved toward the ambulance.

"What happened?" Dropping Olivia's hand, Jack secured his badge and stormed across the yard. He flashed
his identification to the officer. "I'm Detective Jack
Stone from the NYPD."

The man in the pressed uniform frowned. "The
owner of the inn was attacked. Suspect is unknown
and on the loose."

"Marta!" Olivia squeaked. "Oh no, is she alive?"

Jack glanced down at the woman stretched long on the
gurney. Eyes closed and a piece of white gauze wrapped
around her head. An oxygen mask over her mouth.

"She needs to get to the hospital, or she won't be for
long," the officer said.

Jack took a step back and wrapped an arm over Olivia's shoulders to keep her in place. "Let them get her
in the ambulance and out of here. Then we'll speak to
the police and get the details."

The two young medics slid the gurney inside the ambulance. The man stayed in the back while the woman
with a blond pixie cut and stoic demeanor hopped out,
slammed the door shut, then jumped in the driver's side.

Olivia trembled. "If she dies because we stayed here,
I'll never forgive myself."

"Hey," he said, whispering in her ear. "None of that.
We already discussed this. None of this is your fault.
But Marta is strong. She's too full of piss and vinegar to
let this keep her down." He might not know the owner
of the bed-and-breakfast well, but from what he'd seen,

she was a spitfire who wouldn't give up. She'd fight for her life with everything she had.

Olivia rested her head against his chest and sighed as the ambulance raced out of sight, screaming as it went.

Jack took Olivia's hand again and hurried after the policeman who'd turned back toward the inn. "Can you tell me what happened?" he yelled, getting the man's attention.

The officer lengthened his stride and refused to spare Jack a glance. "It's none of your business. Now leave my crime scene."

Dropping Olivia's hand, Jack jogged around to cut the grumpy cop off before he could enter the house. "That's kind of hard to do when my friend and I are staying here, and all our stuff is inside."

That got his attention. He shifted his substantial weight to his back foot and hiked up his pants. "Well, that does make things a bit different, doesn't it? Now, Detective, what brings you to Cold Spring?"

"Well, Officer—" a quick peek at the name badge revealed his name "—Whitton. I accompanied Olivia Hickman here to investigate the death of her husband. Dave Hickman. Hit-and-run that was concluded an accident."

Officer Whitton bounced his gaze to Olivia then back to Jack. "That case has been reopened. I thought Detective Green was the one heading things up."

"That's my partner. He's managing the communication with your department while Olivia and I were out in the field." Jack widened his stance and crossed his arms over his chest.

"This sheds a different light on things. Figured this

was a bungled burglary. Rare for this area, but not un-heard of. We've had perps come in, rough up the pro-prietor, then go through the rooms and grab whatever a tourist left behind. But this doesn't seem like a random thing. Marta has five guests booked here, but only two rooms were destroyed. If someone was targeting you and your friend, would they know which rooms you were staying in?"

"Someone has eyes on us," Jack said. "I'm sure you heard Mrs. Hickman was attacked this morning when out for a jog."

The officer nodded. "I did."

"So they knew we were here. As far as which rooms are ours…" He shrugged. "Wouldn't take much. This person is smart. We had connecting rooms. That might have clued them in."

"My sketchbook," Olivia said, wrapping her arms around herself.

"What?" Jack snapped his brows low.

"I brought it with me but left it in the room. On my nightstand. I like to keep it near in case I wake up with an idea and need to draw it out. If someone broke in and saw my sketches, they'd know it was my room."

Officer Whitton rocked back on his heels. "That'd explain why both your rooms were tossed. My partner's inside now, bagging up evidence. Marta doesn't have any cameras, but I'm going to canvass the neighbor-hood. Check for cameras on neighbors' houses. Find out if anyone saw anything."

"Can we help?" Olivia asked. "We can knock on doors. I can't just sit in a messed-up room, knowing someone is waiting to strike again."

"Appreciate the offer, but this is a police matter. Better to let me and my partner handle everything. Last thing we need is you roaming the streets in the dark."

Jack respected the man's candor. He didn't want to tell Olivia what to do, and her offer to help was thoughtful, but the tightening in his chest told him he had to hide her out of sight fast before something else happened. Hell, the person responsible for sending Marta to the hospital could be in the bushes now, ready to strike.

"Agreed, but you won't be sitting in a destroyed room," Jack said. "We need to find somewhere else to stay tonight. Do you have any suggestions, Officer?"

Office Whitton rubbed at his double chin. "Most places will be booked. But I can write down a few names."

"Thank you," Jack said, wrapping an arm around Olivia's shoulders. Whoever was after her could be watching and no way in hell he'd give him another opportunity to get his hands on her.

Chapter 19

A dull ache throbbed against the back of Olivia's head. She swiped a bottle of over-the-counter pain medicine from the bathroom sink of the last available hotel room in all of Cold Spring and washed two pills down with a swig of water. The day had been a roller coaster of emotions. Now, thanks to the annual home and garden show and her current luck, she'd be sharing a room with Jack for the night in the upscale boutique on the other side of town.

She braced her hands on the gleaming marble counter and stared at the reflection of the framed picture of a single red flower hung on the wall behind her. The fluorescent light bounced off the marble. She wiped the pad of her finger across the smooth surface. The room was pretty, with its creams and mauves and clawfoot tub, but she'd trade it in a second to be back at The River's Edge, ambushed by floral patterns. A cozy space where she could be alone with her thoughts and reflect on her day.

But that wasn't an option, and she should count her lucky stars they'd found the room they had. Driving into the city after the long day with pain creeping into her head was the last thing she'd wanted. Now she had to gather her courage to go out in the bedroom and spend the night with Jack.

A quick glance in the mirror made her wrinkle her nose. She'd scrubbed the makeup off her face and tied her hair into a braid that she'd flipped over her shoulder. Silly shivers of anticipation zipped down her spine as she left the privacy of the restroom.

Jack sat at the small sofa on the far side of the room with the phone to his ear. He sent her a smile that curled her toes. She considered the best place to sit. The couch would put her right next to Jack, and she didn't want to be invasive while he was on the phone. The single king-size bed seemed like a very bad idea, since it was too early for sleep. A leather ottoman was situated under the window to the side of the sofa, a galvanized tray on top, which held a remote to the television she assumed was inside the cabinet against the wall.

Opting for the ottoman, she crossed the room and set the tray on the end table before sitting cross-legged on the cool leather. She propped a pillow between her back and the wall for support.

Jack disconnected his call. "That was Max. He's been in contact with the chief of police. Too many prints around the B and B to run them all. Even just isolating our rooms."

"Why am I not surprised?" she asked, deflated. "Nothing has been left behind at any crime scene. Guess it shouldn't be different here."

He sighed. "We're bound to catch a break. I know it."

"Until then, what can we do? I meant what I told Officer Whitton. I want to help. Sitting around doing nothing seems like a waste of time."

Jack stared at her, a tiny tick of a smile creeping over his mouth. "What do you propose?"

She squirmed under his scrutiny and fought not to smooth a hand over her shirt. "You told Max you think this location in Queens could mean something. Let's start there."

"Okay," he said. "Do you know if anyone besides Edward has ties to Queens?"

"No, but I know how we might be able to find out. Do you have your computer?"

He leaned to the side and scooped his laptop bag from the carpeted floor. "Glad I remembered to lock it up in the safe before we left. Whoever was in our room might not have taken much, but I'm sure they'd have nabbed this if given the chance."

"Too bad my sketchbook wasn't in the safe." She wrinkled her nose. "Even if all that was in there were half-baked ideas and messy sketches. It creeps me out that someone would steal it. But I guess that's the lesser of the crimes committed recently."

He snorted, then scooted to the far end of the sofa. "Come sit here and show me what you're thinking."

Placing the computer on his lap, he lifted the screen and his fingers pressed on a few keys.

Before she talked herself out of being so close to him, she hurried over and sat. She tucked her bare feet beneath her, and her knee brushed against his leg. "May I?" she asked, dipping her chin toward the computer.

"Be my guest."

She arranged the laptop and opened the internet browser. "You have your list of suspects, all of which I'm friends with. But Christine is the only one I know really well. I would know if she had ties to Queens." She spared him a quick glance. "She doesn't."

Grinning, he held up his palms as if in surrender.

She bit back a laugh. "I am friends on social media with both Edward and Mason. I figured we can poke around on their profiles and see if anything stands out."

"Solid plan. People are always putting stuff on social media that ties them to crimes."

She signed into her account and brought up Edward's profile. Scrolling down his home page, she read his updates and studied his pictures. "Anything stand out to you?"

Jack peered over her shoulder and his breath tickled her ear. "Not really. He hasn't posted in a while. Doesn't seem too active."

She kept scrolling, searching for a hint… Something to scream out *Hey! I'm a killer!*

"You mentioned Edward had failed in his previous businesses. What happened?" Edward might have given her a big break, but she'd been naive to trust him without doing her research. Regardless of where things went, she needed to know more about the man in charge of her career.

"His first art gallery went under because he just couldn't sell anything. Looks pretty straightforward. The second, he took out a loan from an unsavory individual. Not paying wasn't an option. He pulled an insurance scheme. Claimed artwork was stolen and reported it to the insurance company. Got the money, paid off the lender, but couldn't reopen."

"So you know for sure that the break-in at the gallery was a scheme? That no one bought my paintings?" A pang of regret beat through her. For a minute, she'd made the biggest sale of her career. Had it all been fake?

"We can't be sure. The insurance company is looking into things as well. They're wary of Edward. I hope, for your sake, he didn't try the same stunt twice."

"Me, too." Not finding anything of interest on Edward's page, she clicked over to Mason's. Inspirational quotes about never giving up and pictures of what looked like his family littered his feed. "Looks like he spends a lot of time with his grandparents." She smiled as she shifted through the photos. Her grandparents had passed when she was younger. She envied the time Mason seemed to get with his.

"None of the locations are tagged," Jack said. "Any of them look familiar?"

She shook her head. "Most look like they're in someone's home."

"Not Mason's?"

"I wouldn't know," she said with a shrug. "I've never been there."

"Interesting." He drew out the word, annunciating each syllable.

Closing the lid, she narrowed her gaze at Jack. "What's that supposed to mean?"

"Come on, Liv. You don't really buy this guy's 'I want to be your friend' act, do you?"

The hint of jealousy in his voice made her insides quiver. "Of course, I do. Mason has never asked me out. Never even hinted at wanting to be more than friends. Why would I doubt that?"

"Because of the way he looks at you." Jack met her stare head-on, a spark of interest lighting his eyes.

A warm blush settled on her cheeks, but she refused to glance away. "And why would you think Mason looks at me in any special way?"

"Because I saw it with my own eyes. And I hated it. I don't want anyone looking at you that way."

She swallowed hard and forced a tight laugh. "Oh really?" she teased. "Is that why when I kissed you earlier, you blamed my head injury?" The memory of that first kiss was tainted by his reaction. As if instead of outright rejecting her, he came up with some silly excuse to pretend the kiss hadn't happened at all. She'd fought to put that rejection behind her all day, but now, with the soft light around them and words flowing freely, she couldn't let him off the hook so easily.

Wincing, he dropped his gaze. "Not my best moment. You caught me off guard, and I didn't want you to regret it."

"I don't."

He cradled her hand between his. "I regret my response. Do you think I can have a do-over?"

Her heart pounded, and she moistened her lips with her tongue. With her gaze locked on his, she nodded.

He moved forward, eyes closing as his lips brushed against hers.

All the air left her lungs, and she melted against him.

He moved his free hand up the edge of her jaw and settled it on the back of her neck, intensifying the kiss. His tongue parted her lips.

She opened her mouth, letting him in. A fierce hunger came to life inside her. She wanted to taste him, touch him, love him.

The thought was like lighter fluid on a fire, bursting the flames licking inside. Her core throbbed, and for once, her head was in line with the needs of her body. Jack was a man who had stood beside her, protected her, listened to her. He validated all the emotions she'd battled since they'd met. She wanted him in her life, and not just for tonight. And for the first time in a long time, the idea of another man warming her bed filled her with joy and anticipation—leaving no room for guilt.

Moving on impulse, she shifted to straddle his lap. She wanted to erase the distance between them. Wanted to feel every inch of his body against her.

His hands met at the center of her back. One moved up her spine until his fingers loosened her braid. Moving his mouth to her jawline, he pressed kisses over her skin until he reached her neck.

She threw back her head and used her fingers to free the long strands of her hair. His mouth dipped over her collarbone, and a moan of desire purred from her mouth and set her hips in motion. It'd been so long since she'd felt like this—since she'd wanted the feel of a man against her. Inside her. But Jack was special. He'd broken through her heartbreak and grief and showed her that her life still held promise. Even in the midst of turmoil.

Jack entwined his fingers in her mess of hair and moved his other hand to rest on her ass, pressing her against him. Urging her movements harder. Faster.

Pressure built inside her core, flames flying higher and higher. The feel of his rock-hard girth rubbed against her. She grabbed fistfuls of his shirt and yanked it over his head. Her mouth watered at the hard muscles of his chest. Slowing her rhythm, she roamed her palm over his pecks, his abs, dipping her finger into the waistband of his pants.

He hissed out a breath. "Are you sure this is what you want?"

"More than anything." Her voice came out wispy and hoarse. Urgency pushed her to her feet. She didn't want him to question her again. Didn't want him to play the protector role, fearing she was moving fast, acting on impulse. She snatched the hem of her T-shirt and tossed it over her head.

Jack groaned. "My God. You're killing me."

Confidence growing, she hooked up a brow and bit into her plump bottom lip. The way he looked at her— like she was the most beautiful woman in the world— sparked a wickedness she didn't know she had. "You like that?"

Still seated, he anchored his hands on her hips and pulled her to him. "Mmm-hmm." His hands fanned around her waist. He skimmed the pads of his thumbs over her stomach, inching lower until his fingers disappeared inside her little black shorts.

She held her breath and threaded her hands in his hair. Her muscles tightened as she waited for more. Her mind whirled. She'd never been with anyone but Dave. Nerves danced in her belly.

He lifted his chin, moving the lacy pads of her bra to the side with his teeth as his fingers continued their path to her throbbing center. His tongue moving to lick circles around her nipple.

"Oh. My God." Pleasure built inside her, the sensory overload making her crazy and chasing all other thoughts from her head. She wiggled her hips, trying to move his fingers closer to her clit.

He chuckled and moved his coarse whiskers over the sensitive skin on her tummy.

She moaned. "Please. Put me out of my misery."

He moved one hand to cup her soft mound and pressed a finger inside her, making her gasp. "Is this misery?"

She pushed her hips forward. "No. It's so good. More."

A second finger joined the first, moving in and out in a slow, excruciating rhythm. "Your wish is my command." With one smooth motion, he slid his fingers from her warmth and stood, crushing his mouth to hers. His fingers moved inside her as he maneuvered her backward toward the bed.

When her knees hit the mattress, she reached behind her and unclipped her bra, throwing it to the floor. Cool air hit her nipples, and they puckered. Standing at attention, waiting for Jack's touch.

Slipping his fingers back inside her, Jack pumped his

fingers faster as he laid her down on the bed. He used his free hand to slide her shorts and panties down her legs, and she kicked them off. Her mind raced and her heart galloped. Sweat dotted the back of her neck and the sweet feel of ecstasy burst inside her.

Jack moved his hand, and the absence of his touch sent shock waves down her spine. His hand found her breast and he rolled her nipple between his thumb and forefinger.

She pressed his chest, giving her space to pull at his gym shorts. As much as she wanted him inside her, she needed to give as good as she got. Had to show Jack how much she wanted him.

"Want some help?" His voice was rough and husky. His breath coming out in ragged pants.

She nodded, watching him remove his clothing as she propped herself up on her elbows. Desire heated her core, and pressure expanded her chest. She'd waded through a host of emotions and found herself on the other side—lying in front of a beautiful man who filled with her happiness.

"Give me a second," Jack said, crossing the room to his duffel bag.

She didn't mind the show. The muscles of his body moved and flexed like a jungle cat as he grabbed a little foil package and turned toward her with the sexiest grin she'd ever seen.

He flashed the condom. "You sure?"

"Get your sexy ass over here." She'd already had an orgasm, but the anticipation of feeling his body pressed against hers, his dick inside her, had her already craving another.

He crawled over her, and she took the condom from his hand. His mouth found the delicate area behind her ear as she ripped it open. She closed her eyes, getting lost in the pleasure his mouth brought, then closed her fist around his penis.

His body tightened and mouth stilled.

She moved her hand up and down, squeezing lightly.

With his hands on either side of her, he hovered above her. Gaze latched on hers. "I want to be inside you. Now."

His words brought a fresh heat wave over her body. She maneuvered the condom onto the tip of his cock and slid it over his impressive shaft.

He pushed her knees open and pressed the head of his erection to her center, breaking the barrier until her warmth surrounded him.

She let out a cry of pleasure as he filled her. Her arms wrapped around his neck, nails scraping over the flesh of his back as he pumped his hips. She stared into his eyes, the connection never breaking between them as strange magic stirred inside her. Each move, each pump, each mind-numbing motion spiraled her pleasure higher and higher, filled her heart more and more, until another orgasm wracked her body.

He groaned and took her mouth in his. The kiss intensifying as his muscles shook and he pummeled into her faster and faster until he yelled out her name and collapsed. He wiped a sweat-soaked strand of hair from her face, then pressed a kiss to her forehead. "That was amazing."

Unexpected tears filled her eyes and she nodded, words escaping her.

"Hey, now. What's the matter?" He brushed a tear from her cheek.

She smiled up at him. "Not a damn thing." And for the first time in a long time, she absolutely meant it.

Chapter 20

Olivia's warm, soft body cradled against Jack as he drifted out of a deep sleep. He wrapped his arms around her middle and snuggled her close, her delicious bottom nestled against his groin. He kept his eyes shut, because if this was all a dream, he didn't want to wake.

Olivia wiggled against him, causing parts of him to spring to life.

Okay, not a dream.

Grinning, he swept her hair over her shoulder and nuzzled his lips against the back of her neck.

A throaty laugh purred from her throat and desire thickened his blood. His fingers itched to re-explore her body. But an image of her lying under him with tears misting her eyes after making love slammed against him, and he stilled.

When he'd asked if she was okay, she'd assured him she was good. But would she tell him she regretted her decision? Slink away when there was nowhere to escape? He should have pressed her, asked more questions. But after cleaning themselves up, she'd curled against him and fallen asleep while he'd stared up at the ceiling, a multitude of questions keeping his mind awake for far too long.

"'Morning," she said, turning to face him.

"How'd you sleep?" He kept his arm around her, skimming her bare shoulder with his knuckles.

"Pretty good." She stretched her arms above her head and yawned. "I'm not really a morning person. Is there coffee in here?"

A ping of disappointment jabbed his gut. The fancy coffee machine set up in the corner was probably delicious, but it wouldn't hold a candle to the spread Marta had provided for them the day before.

Marta.

He'd have to make some calls and get an update on her status. The fact that's she'd gotten swept up in this mess sat like lead in his gut. "Let me make you a cup." He kissed her forehead, then swung his legs over the edge of the bed.

"Thanks. Just give me a minute." Olivia secured a sage green throw blanket around her naked body and jogged to the bathroom.

He stared at the closed door, wishing she'd throw it open and hop back in bed with him. Start their morning with a little more romance and a little less self-doubt.

Romance? What the hell was wrong with him? He ran a palm over his face. Yesterday he'd laid his soul bare to her, confessing how he couldn't get too close to another woman involved in a case because he'd messed up so badly with Mary. Then he'd fallen into bed with her, a widow who'd been through hell and back the last few days. Now he wanted romance? With a woman who'd cried after having sex. Damn, he needed to get a grip and get back to the city, where things made sense.

His gym shorts lay in a heap on the floor. He scooped them up and slid them on before padding barefoot across the plush carpet and bringing the coffee machine to life. The scent of French roast reached his nose, centering him.

He sucked in a deep breath. Okay. He was overthinking things. All he needed was to get dressed and make a plan for the day. He grabbed a T-shirt and jeans from his bag, keeping one eye on the still-shut bathroom door as he changed out of his gym shorts and into fresh clothes for the day.

His ringing phone had him hustling to where he'd plugged it in by the sofa. "Hey, Max. Got any news?"

"I have a name for the person who sent Olivia the box of fan mail," Max said, urgency in his tone.

The break in the case pushed adrenaline through his veins. He sat on the couch, needing to stay focused on what Max had to say and not fly into action without all the details. "How's that possible? There was no name on the box, and the only prints were from Mason and Olivia."

"I spoke with Edward. He had some mail lying around that had been sent to the gallery for Olivia. Stuff he hadn't gotten around to forwarding to her. The print on the letters matches the handwriting left at her apartment."

"And he put his return address on the envelopes?" He ran a hand through his mess of hair. He'd told Olivia last night they'd catch a break soon. He hadn't expected something so big to fall into their laps.

A stab of guilt penetrated his side. He'd been so wrapped up in his envy over Mason that he hadn't thought to seek out more fan mail. Max asking the owner of the gallery if he had any mail that had been sent to Olivia was the logical next step. A step that he'd bypassed without a second thought. Yet another mistake because his mind wasn't focused entirely on the case.

"No return address on those either. But we did run the prints from the letters inside the envelope."

Jack stilled, not wanting to ask how they'd found a match but needing to know the answer. "The prints were in the database? Did the person have their prints on file for a specific purpose or is he a criminal?" He hoped for the first, but chances were slim.

Max snorted. "What do you think?"

He flopped back against the soft cushions. "Criminal."

The bathroom door creaked open, and Olivia emerged with red, wide eyes and dressed for the day.

The distress on her face clenched his muscles. He wanted to ask what was wrong but needed to get through his conversation with Max first. God, he hoped he hadn't messed things up by moving too fast. Maybe she regretted the step they'd taken last night. He had to find a way to let her know they could slam on the brakes whenever she wanted—move at whatever pace she was comfortable with. Hell, he'd wait a lifetime for her.

"Bingo. The prints belong to a man named Nathanial Cuppio," Max said, drawing Jack's attention back to him. "Previous arrests for indecent exposure and assault. Attended art school before he dropped out. No employment on record."

His stomach dropped. The name didn't ring a bell. Had he missed the mark completely? Olivia's stalker might be someone who wasn't even on his radar. "Have you contacted him?"

"Tried the listed number, but no answer. The address on record is being sublet to a cousin, who doesn't know where he is."

"Shit," he mumbled, gaining Olivia's attention. He held up a finger to signal her to wait.

She flashed a tight smile, then retrieved the now-made cup of coffee. "Do you want some?" She mouthed.

He nodded.

She placed a second paper cup under the carafe and replayed the parade of buttons he'd pressed moments before.

"I'm working on tracking this guy down," Max said. "When are you coming back to the city?"

"Now. We've finished here. Once we have our stuff together, we'll hit the road. It's Sunday morning, so the traffic shouldn't be too bad. My guess, I can meet you in about ninety minutes."

"Sounds good, but if I track this guy down before then, I'm moving in."

The thought of not being the one to nail this bastard made him cringe, but there was no need for Max to wait. The sooner Olivia was safe, the better. No matter who made the arrest. Disconnecting, he accepted the cup Olivia brought over. "Thanks."

She settled beside him, her back straight as a rod. A weird tension simmered in the air between them, but he didn't know how to address it. Hell, he didn't have the time. They had an hour-long car ride ahead of them. Plenty of time to figure out where they should go from here.

"That was Max. He has a suspect, a man named Nathanial Cuppio. You know him?"

Sipping her coffee, she shook her head. "Never heard of him."

"We need to head back. I want to be there when he finds out where this guy is. Can you be ready to leave in ten minutes?"

"I'm ready now. No reason to stay any longer." Her words came out clipped and a little wistful.

He swallowed the lump in his throat. He wanted to take her hand, kiss her mouth, explain how much last night meant to him. But words failed him, and more pressing issues had him jumping to his feet and gathering his things. With his bag packed, he turned toward her, but she'd disappeared behind the closed bathroom door again.

Sighing, he gathered their things and waited. His gut twisted, and a nagging voice inside him told him he'd royally messed things up. He'd taken things too damn far. Let his emotions get the better of him and hadn't stopped to consider how his actions would affect others. He couldn't make the same mistake again. Couldn't keep moving in this dangerous direction when

Olivia's life was on the line. He had to take things one step at a time.

First, make sure to eliminate the danger surrounding Olivia. Then figure out if he could give her what she really needed.

As the quaint little town disappeared behind them, self-consciousness swallowed Olivia up until she wanted to disappear. But that wasn't a choice when she was sitting beside Jack in a compact sedan with nowhere to run. A million words sat at the tip of her tongue, but she held them in.

Besides, if Jack wanted to discuss what happened last night, he would have mentioned it. Instead, while she'd gathered her courage in the restroom back at the hotel, he'd wasted no time getting back to work. Apparently all thoughts of the night they'd spent together nothing but a memory.

"You sure you don't want me to stop on the way to the city and grab some food?" Jack flicked a quick glance her way before returning his focus to the highway.

"I'm fine. I had coffee and can wait to eat. I'd rather get back as soon as we can."

He flashed her a small smile.

Was it her imagination, or did he seem nervous? She sighed. She was so out of the game of dating, she was turning herself inside out with what-ifs and second-guessing everything. It'd only been, what, over a decade since she was at the beginning stages of a relationship? If that's what this even was. Oh my gosh. Had she just had her first one-night stand?

Heat crept up the back of her neck. She needed to talk this out and get another perspective before she drove herself crazy. She sent off a quick text to Christine:

Need to chat. Are you at work?

A few seconds passed before a reply came in:

Here all day. Stop by. Would love to catch up.

She sighed, relief relaxing her muscles. She might not have all her problems worked out, but she was headed in the right direction. A chocolate croissant and her best friend waited for her. Neither had ever let her down. "Before you meet Max, can you drop me off at The Mad Batter? Christine's working. I'd rather not be home alone."

"Sure." He grabbed his coffee cup from the cupholder and took a swig. "Hopefully Max gets a location on this guy soon. His history is concerning."

She shivered and huddled against the leather seat. "How did he get my address? I don't list my personal information. All mail from fans goes to the gallery, then is forwarded to me by Edward."

"Could have seen you at the gallery and followed you," he said with a shrug. "Maybe asked a passing question to someone who thought he knew you. If this is our guy, he's smart. He's gotten a hold of a lot more than just your address. He's managed to fly under our radar as he's killed two women, followed us out of town, attacked you, and sent Marta to the hospital."

Each crime he mentioned was like a blow to the temple, increasing the pain building in her head. "Have you heard more about Marta?" She wished she could have seen the fun-loving inn owner before they left, seen with her own eyes that she was still alive and fighting, but they had to get home.

"She's stable but still not awake. No permanent damage found. Hopefully she'll wake up and can fill in the details on what happened. Max and I can build a solid case, but a good defense attorney will always try to poke holes. A witness who can give a firsthand account always helps."

She watched the scenery fly by, the vibrant trees and scenic landscape giving way to billowing steam pipes on industrial buildings and giant billboards. Another life hung in the balance because of her. And while she'd been sleeping with Jack, Marta lay in a hospital and two families grieved for their loved ones. What was the matter with her?

As if reading her mind, Jack cleared his throat and asked. "How are you today? You know, after last night."

She flinched at the uncertainty in his voice. She wanted to confess all her insecurities and feelings, but something told her that would make him want to run his car into the cement median that divided the highway. Instead of exposing her vulnerabilities, she forced a bright smile. "Tired."

Awkward silence filled the car, and she wanted to slap herself upside the head. She didn't know what to say to make things better. Make them normal. One of her favorite things about Jack was that things between them had always been easy and natural, even with the horrible events that brought them together.

The speakers rang and the information for an incoming call appeared on the screen on the dashboard. Jack pressed a button on the steering wheel. "Hey. We're just getting into the city. Did you find him?"

"I think so." Max's deep, gravelly voice radiated into the car. "Got a couple addresses to check out."

A weird mixture of excitement and nerves expanded in her chest. Her nightmare might be over soon.

"Where are you?" Jack asked.

"At home with Samantha."

"Meet me at The Mad Batter in fifteen minutes. I'm dropping off Olivia so she's not alone. We can take off from there."

"How'd that go?" Max asked. "Did you keep yourself in check? I know you insisted you could handle being alone with Olivia overnight. I hope you didn't cross any lines."

Jack swiped his phone from the center console with bumbling fingers and took the call off Bluetooth. He pressed the phone to his ear. "I'll see you in fifteen."

Humiliation scorched her cheeks, and she squeezed her eyes shut. At this moment, she'd rather try her luck with whoever was out to get her than be trapped in this car another minute. Lowering her guard and sleeping with Jack was a mistake. One she damn well wouldn't make again.

Chapter 21

Needing to be away from the prying eyes of strangers, Olivia opted to enjoy her breakfast in Christine's office. Even though Jack had a solid lead and was on his way to talk to the person who'd left creepy mail at her door, Nathanial Cuppio wasn't under arrest yet. Which meant each man who huddled in a corner or stood in line and cast her a curious glance made her skin crawl.

Not to mention the permanent blush that had to be stained on her face, showcasing her embarrassment to everyone. She'd never forget the words Max had said, or Jack's reaction, as long as she lived.

Pinching off a warm chunk of her croissant, she popped it in her mouth and replayed the awkward good-bye with Jack in her mind. He'd gone in for a hug while she'd turned for the door, resulting in Jack giving her a weird pat on the shoulder. Then she'd all but fallen out of the car and given a little wave before hurrying inside the bakery, feeling the heat of his eyes on her the whole way.

"Stupid, stupid, stupid," she said, leaning forward and lightly tapping her forehead on the edge of Christine's desk. Maybe if she hit her already injured head harder, she could forget the past twenty-four hours entirely.

"Hey, watch how you talk about my best friend." Christine stood in the doorway with her hands planted on her hips. "You look like hell."

Olivia snorted. "I can't say I'm stupid, but you can comment on how bad I look?"

Shrugging, Christine swung the door closed enough to give them privacy while still listening to the sounds of the bakery, then sat on the chair across the desk. "What can I say? I come from a place of love, not self-loathing. Now. Tell me what happened."

"Ugh, do I have to?"

"We both know that's why you're here, so spill it."

She was right. Part of Olivia hadn't wanted to be alone while waiting for word on what was happening with Nathanial, but the other part desperately needed her friend—her sounding board. "I don't even know where to begin."

Christine reached across the desk and patted her hand before settling back in the chair. "Start at the beginning."

Sucking in a deep breath, she shared every detail of the past forty-eight hours. Beginning with seeing the spot where Dave had died and ending with details of her pleasure-filled night with Jack.

Never one to hide her emotions, Christine's feelings on each new snippet of information were written all over her round face. If Olivia wasn't so on edge, her friend's expressions would have had her rolling on the floor with laughter.

"Wow," Christine said. "You sure packed a lot in two days. But before we get into the Jack stuff, how are you feeling after seeing where Dave was hit? That had to be tough."

Her heart lurched and a plethora of emotions constricted her throat. "Yes and no. Reliving that day was painful, but it also showed me that time goes on. Wounds heal. That I will always love and miss Dave, but it's okay to want to honor his memory by finding love again. I think that's what he'd want."

"Honey, I know that's what he'd want. You've honored him every day. Hell, you're the reason the case to find the person who killed him is opened again. *You* did that. And Jack believed in you. He seems like a hell of a guy. Which brings us to the next, juicy part of your story."

She groaned and hung her head. "Yes, the part where I'm stupid and slept with Jack. What was I thinking?"

"You were thinking you like this sexy, sweet cop who has had your back from the moment you met him. Why is that stupid?" Christine edged forward on her chair, as if not wanting to miss one word.

Memories of the morning flared to life inside her, and she cringed. "This morning was so weird. Like we didn't know how to be around each other. He jumped right back into work mode. Didn't say anything about what had happened. What if he regrets sleeping with me?"

"What if he doesn't? Did you talk about it?"

She twisted her lips, hating the doubt that had clouded her judgment. "No."

"Maybe he's as confused as you. Maybe he thinks you regretted sleeping with him, and he didn't want to upset you."

She crushed her eyes closed against the statement, wishing she had been more assertive. She was so wrapped up in her own head she hadn't considered what he'd been feeling. Something she should have done, considering what he'd confided about Mary.

"Enough about what it all meant," Christine said, breaking into her spiraling thoughts. "How was it?" She grinned and wiggled her eyebrows.

Heat crashed back into her cheeks. "Amazing."

Christine let out a squeal and clapped her hands together.

Olivia laughed. "Stop it. Everything happened so naturally. I was afraid my first time after Dave would be weird. That'd I'd be wracked with guilt the whole time. But it was…beautiful and easy and just made me happy." She smiled thinking back on it. "I even cried at the end."

Oh. My. God.

She pressed her hands to her mouth. "Holy shit! I cried after! He must think I'm crazy."

Christine winced. "Or that having sex with him upset you. That you weren't ready. You really need to talk to him about this."

She went back to banging her head against the desk. "Stupid, stupid, stupid."

"Oh, now. You've been through a lot, and this is all new to you. You're allowed to make some…missteps." Christine hurried around the desk and gave her a reassuring squeeze.

"Quick. Tell me something to distract me. How are you holding up?" Mentally bringing herself back together, she focused on her friend.

"I'm okay. Staying with Paul the last few nights has helped keep my mind off what happened to Courtney. And he's been so supportive. The commute from Queens at 4:30 a.m. every morning has been a bit rough, but a small price to pay for happiness I guess."

Olivia straightened and grabbed her phone from her pocket. "Queens? I didn't know that's where he lived. I want to show you something." She opened her Facebook app and clicked to Mason's profile page again. Jack might be on his way to interview a new suspect, but maybe she could find something on Edward or Mason they'd missed the night before. "Do any of these places look familiar?"

Christine grabbed the phone and flipped through the photos. She enlarged one of the pictures and pointed to a large sculpture of the earth behind a smiling Mason with the woman she assumed was a grandparent. "This looks like Corona Park. Paul and I were just there last weekend."

"Anything else?"

She pointed out a few other places she recognized in Queens, then frowned. "Isn't that the guy who worked with Dave? The one who took over his position after he died?"

Oh God. She'd forgotten about that. In her haze of grief and misery, many of the things that had transpired at Dave's work after his death had barely registered. Why would they? She only knew what Mason revealed, and she'd assumed he'd wanted her to feel included in the world that Dave had spent so much of his time in.

"I need to tell Jack about Mason's connection to Queens." She took back her phone and shot off a text, alerting him to the fact that Mason had posted several pictures in the borough Jack had been interested in.

"Why? What does it mean?"

Her stomach turned and a nervousness hummed around her. "It means that if Nathanial Cuppio is a dead end, Jack might have another suspect."

The ding of a text message broke the silence between him and Max as they walked down the crowded side-walk in search of the right building. His heart leaped to his throat when he saw Olivia's name. The message might have information that could prove useful in his investigation, but her words did nothing to the spider-web of thoughts and emotions clogging his brain after their horrible car ride.

"What is it?" Max asked, slowing to a crawl behind two tourists snapping pictures with every step.

"Olivia. Photos we saw of Mason Shaffer are from Queens. Her friend recognized some of the locations." Irritation at the snail's pace forced on them had him tightening his grip on the phone.

The streets were always packed on Sunday afternoons, especially when the weather was warm and the sun was high. Vendors set up shop on the busy sidewalks, hawking their wares. Tourists loitered on the sidewalks, not wanting to miss any part of the city around them.

"That's the only tie we have to Queens so far," Max said. "But a few pictures still don't amount to much."

"Agreed." The new nugget of information made his head hurt. Nathaniel Cuppio fit the mold of who they were looking for. He had prior arrests, violent tendencies, and had shown an interest in Olivia's art with the fan mail he'd sent her. Now this new detail stuck to him like a burr.

He hurried around the stragglers, his focus still on his phone. "I ran a background check on Mason. He lived with his single mom in Brooklyn. Went to school at Columbia. Now lives downtown. Nothing that ties him to Queens."

"Do you know his address?" Max asked than led them to the elevator at the far side of the lobby and pressed the button for the nineteenth floor.

"Not off the top of my head, but I can find it easy enough. If this little meeting ends up a bust, we need to pay Mason a visit next."

"Maybe we won't need to worry about that. Let's keep our heads straight with this interview."

He sent Olivia a quick note of thanks, stuffed his phone back in his pocket, then stepped out of the elevator when the doors slid open.

The hallway was wide and clean. The scent of lemon in the air. Tasteful art dotted the walls between the windows that let sunlight flood inside. The effect reminded him of Olivia's apartment and the bedroom she'd converted into her studio.

Stopping at the door marked 19B, he knocked and waited. Nervous energy zipped through him, and he jingled spare change in his front pocket.

The door swung open to a balding man with a square face and curious green eyes. Dark smudges stained his white shirt. "Hello?"

Max flashed his badge again. "Nathanial Cuppio?"

He frowned. "Yes."

"I'm Detective Green. This is my partner, Detective Stone. Do you have a moment to speak with us about Olivia Hickman?"

His head reared back and the wrinkles running the length of his forehead deepened. "Oh. My. Why, yes. Please come in." He opened the door wide to let them inside, closing it behind them. "I'm a big fan of her work. Is she all right? Geez, I mean, why would the police be here to talk to me about her if everything was okay? Do you want to sit? Water?" He fluttered like a nervous bird, bopping around the open space.

Jack fought to keep his gaze on the jittery man, but the explosion of colors hung on the walls stole his attention. A dozen canvases were mounted all around the room. There was something familiar about the paintings. He stepped closer, studying the thick lines. "Are these Olivia's paintings?"

Nathanial wrung his hands and nodded. "Yes. I admire her work so much. I've followed her career from the start. Bought some of her earlier pieces before you could even find her in a gallery. And now she's at A

Peculiar Sight. Not a super established gallery, but a good stepping-stone for her."

Jack sucked in a long, steadying breath as he took in the ramblings. If they were looking for someone with an obsession, they'd found him. "Did you send her fan mail?"

"Every month," he said, smiling like it was something to be proud of. "As a fellow artist, I understand how difficult it can get to keep your spirits up. I want her to know she has someone on her side. How she's inspired me to be a better artist. Do you want to see?"

He and Max exchanged a long look as Nathanial nearly ran, disappearing behind a wall, only to re-emerge with a sketchbook. "See," he said, flipping it open. "I draw. Mostly still lifes. But Olivia, wow, she's a sight to behold, isn't she? I can't resist trying to capture her essence on the page."

Sketches like the one found in the box filled the white space, and Jack clenched his jaw. Something was off about this man, but he wasn't convinced he was the one threatening Olivia. "Can you tell me where you were yesterday morning? Around 7:00 a.m.?" He refused to give any praise over the disturbing images of the woman he was falling for. No reason to encourage this creep.

Nathanial swished his mouth to the side. "Hmm, yesterday morning at that time I was getting breakfast before heading into work. I just got a new job at an art supply store. Killer discount and I get a chance to speak with other artists. Not the most exciting job, but it helps pay the bills."

"Where did you get breakfast?" Max asked.

"A little café that's just amazing. I go every morning." He widened his eyes as if letting them in on a special secret.

"Can anyone testify you were there?" Jack asked, his gut sinking. If this guy had an alibi, they were chasing a dead end.

Nathaniel shrugged. "Sure. Diane worked the counter. She knows me. She'll tell you. Or I have the receipt still. I always keep those things. Never know when I'll need them." A nervous laugh bubbled from his throat as he scooped his wallet from his baggy jeans and fished out a receipt. "You can have it if you want it."

Jack double-checked the date and time. Dammit. No way Nathanial was in Cold Spring attacking Olivia when he was buying coffee in the city at 7:23 a.m. "I don't need to keep it, but do you mind if I snap a picture? And I'll need the number of someone at your job who can confirm you were at work yesterday."

"Sure, go ahead. Are you going to tell me why you need to know?" He fiddled with his phone. "I can send you my boss's number. Call anytime."

Jack used his phone to take the picture, then suppressed a sigh. He'd thought this was the guy they were after, when it turned out he was just an overly enthusiastic fan who gave off a very bad vibe. He couldn't do anything to stop Nathaniel from admiring Olivia or her work, but he'd put the fear of God himself in the man while he could. "Someone is trying to hurt her. Has threatened and stalked and scared the shit out of her. If I find out that you have any knowledge of who this is, or that you have harmed her in any way, I'll be back, and I'll haul your ass out of here in handcuffs. Do you understand?"

"Yes." Nathanial swallowed hard, a paleness sweeping over his skin.

Max clapped a hand on Jack's shoulder. "We should go."

Jack shot Nathanial one hard look before walking out the door, leaving him and his unhealthy obsession behind.

Chapter 22

"Explain to me why it's important the man who worked with Dave has pictures on Facebook of him and some old lady in Queens." Christine leaned over her shoulder and studied the computer screen like she was waiting for something to jump out at her and tell her what was going on.

"It's a long story," Olivia said, not wanting to get into all the details. "But basically, the person who bought my art and left a threat on the vacation rental site both gave bogus information. That information leads to a pizza shop in Queens."

A spike of pain jabbed against the tender spot at the back of her head. She needed sleep, but since that wasn't an option, more coffee was the next best thing. She lifted her paper cup and cringed at the cool liquid.

"And that's connected to this park because...?" Christine left the end of her question hanging and raised her brows.

"Jack thinks false information given is significant. Not a random place just thrown out." Olivia pushed away her crappy coffee and rubbed at the back of her neck, hoping to relieve some of the tension. The bright lights of the computer screen screamed at her, and she fiddled with the buttons to dim the brightness. "But there has to be something more. Something that really ties him—or whoever used the address—to Queens for it to matter."

"I agree. Let's dig around a little. How deep did you go when looking at Mason's profile last night?"

"We got a little distracted." Images of last night's activities clashed inside her head and heated her core.

Christine laughed and dragged the chair around to sit beside her. "Yeah, you did."

She bumped her friend with her shoulder and rolled her eyes. "Shut up."

"Fine. Click on that picture of Mason at the park again."

She did as instructed. Mason smiled his boyish grin with his arm looped around an older woman with gray hair pulled into a bun at the nape of her neck. "No one else is tagged, but there are some comments." She skimmed through them.

"There." Christine pointed at the screen. "That profile picture looks like the same woman. Click on her and see what pops up."

She clicked and was surprised when the older woman's profile took over the screen. "She must not understand how to make her profile private. And look, she lives in Queens."

"I'd say that's a big connection depending on how she knows Mason. Look at her About Info where relatives are listed."

She navigated to the page and skimmed the long list of names, her gaze landing on the name Mason Shaffer: Grandson. Nausea churned in her gut. "I figured that was his grandmother, but knowing it, and that she lives in Queens, gives me a bad feeling. Does that really mean something? Is that enough to condemn a man who has been nothing but nice to me?"

"It's enough to call and tell your boyfriend," Christine shot back. "Any little detail could be important."

Olivia wadded up her empty pastry bag and threw it at Christine. "He's not my boyfriend. But you're right. If he has to speak with Mason, the more information he has the better. Do you mind getting me another coffee while I call him?"

"Trying to get rid of me?" Christine pressed her mouth into an exaggerated pout.

She flashed her sweetest smile. "Maybe."

"Fine, but only because I need to check on my employees and make sure everything's running smoothly."

Once Christine left, she found Jack's contact information in her phone and pressed Send. Her heart pounded as she waited to hear his voice.

"Olivia? Is everything all right?" His urgent tone boomed through the speaker.

"I'm fine. Did you get my text about Mason?" She slid a pencil from a little jar shaped like a cupcake on the desk and rubbed it between her fingers. Anxiety danced in her belly, her throat suddenly dry. Her reaction was beyond ridiculous. She liked Jack, really liked him, and acting like a nervous Nellie was the worst way to show him she was serious about him and a possible future together.

"I did. Good work. Max and I are on our way to speak with him now." What sounded like wind rumbled and muffled his voice.

Disappointment pressed against her lungs. "What about Nathanial Cuppio?"

Jack sighed. "I don't like the guy, but he's not the stalker. He has an alibi for the time you were attacked yesterday. He gave me a receipt, and a quick call to the café he was at confirmed it. I also spoke with his boss. He worked all day yesterday. If I need more information from him about the nights of the murders, I know where to find him. But he's not our man."

Dammit. Things would have been so much easier if he was. Now the eye of suspicion shifted back to Mason. "You should know, Christine and I found out that Mason's grandma, the woman in the photos, lives in Queens."

A beat of silence pulsed through the phone. "Shit. I did a background check on Mason. He was raised by a single mother. How much you want to bet he spent a lot of time with his grandma? Probably in her home. In Queens."

She brought her free hand up to her neck and rubbed her collarbone. The implication of what she'd uncovered hiking up her blood pressure. "How could I be so wrong about him? How could I not see it?"

"Sometimes the things right in front of us are the hardest things to see. But don't jump to conclusions yet. We can't know for sure until we talk to Mason, and

Max just lucked out with a parking spot right outside the guy's building. Stay with Christine. Don't go home. I'll call and fill you in as soon as I can. Even pick you up after...if you want."

The hesitancy in his voice made her smile and loosened the knots twisting up her insides by a fraction. Christine was right. She wasn't the only one who was on edge after last night. Now wasn't the time to have the conversation, but she could at least let him know the direction her heart was leading her. "That'd be nice. We have a lot to talk about. Be safe. I'll be waiting for you."

When Christine came back with her fresh coffee, she couldn't hide her smile. The idea that Mason might be the one behind shattering her world made her heartsick, but knowing Jack would be with her at the end of the day lifted her spirits. She'd push aside all her fears and tell him exactly how she felt.

Her phone dinged in her hand.

Christine set the hot to-go cup in front of her. "He miss you already?"

She laughed and glanced at the text. "It's not Jack. It's Edward. He got a check from the insurance company for my artwork that was destroyed and needs me to come by before noon to pick it up."

"That's great news."

"Yeah, but I don't want to go alone, and Jack might be busy for a while. Will you go with me?"

"Sure, just let me tell the manager she's in charge until I get back."

Standing, Olivia considered calling Jack back to let him know her change of plans. She didn't want to bother him when he was busy. She'd send him a text to let him know what was happening, grab her check, then be back to The Mad Batter before he was even finished with Mason. Hope bounced around like a buoy inside her chest. The storm she'd weathered had been fierce, nearly destroying her, but she'd made it through. And finally, she was starting to see the rainbow on the other end.

"Here we go again," Jack said as he and Max stood side by side, waiting for the door to open. Mason Shaffer's building wasn't as upscale as he'd expected, but the hallway had a fresh coat of tan paint, and the carpet was clean. "Hopefully this time we have a better outcome."

His phone dinged, alerting him to an incoming text message, but the door opened before he could look at it.

A man with a crisp part in his gelled hair greeted them. "Can I help you?"

The man had the same green eyes and boyish looks as Mason, but it wasn't him. Jack flashed his badge. "We're looking for Mason Shaffer. Is he home?"

"Not here. Sorry." The man took a step back and made a motion of shutting them out.

Max took a step forward before the door swung in their faces. "I'm Detective Green and this is my partner, Detective Stone. We just have a few questions. Is this Mason Shaffer's place of residence?"

"Yes. But he's not here. Hasn't been in a few days, actually. Haven't seen him either, so I'm not sure how I can help you. Now if you'll excuse me, I was on my way out to meet my girl for brunch."

Jack stood his ground. "Just a few more questions Mr…"

"Shaffer. Chip Shaffer," he said with a dramatic sigh.

"You've got two minutes or Whitney will kill me if I'm late."

"You and Mason look alike," Jack said. "Are you related?"

Chip ran a hand over his hair, as if smoothing back the perfectly manicured strands. "He's my big brother. Not like he's acted like it lately. I swear. One thing goes off the rails in his structured little world, and bam! He's a hot mess."

Every muscle in Jack's body tightened. The urge to grab the prick by the neck and squeeze more information out of him had him fisting his hands into tight balls at his sides. "Care to elaborate?"

"Dude, seriously," Chip said with an exaggerated eye roll. He tapped a finger to his watch. "We're down to one minute. I don't have time to go over everything."

Jack couldn't stop the low growl bubbling up his throat. He took a step forward, pressing into Chip's personal space, when a hard hand on his shoulder kept him in place.

"Listen, Buddy," Max cut in. "We don't care about your brunch or your girlfriend. We need to know what's going on with your brother. Now. Either answer our questions here or we'll drag your punk ass down to the station. Then Whitney will really be pissed."

"Geez, fine," Chip said, lifting his palms in front of him. "Mason lost his job last week. It really messed with his head. The guy's like a well-oiled machine. Always has been. He likes things done a certain way and works his ass off. But if something doesn't go the way he planned, he doesn't handle it well. Throws him all out of whack. Not like I blame the guy. Lucked out when some dude died, and he stepped into his shoes. Now he's been tossed out on his ass."

Last week. Right before Courtney Bailey was murdered. The timing lined up. "And by not handling it well, what exactly do you mean?" Jack hadn't found any dings on Mason's record to indicate a temper or criminal tendencies.

"He blows off steam, I guess. Disappears for days. My guess is he's out drinking or gambling. Maybe banging some chick." Chip chuckled, and the slimy sound grated against Jack's eardrums. "*Hopefully* banging some chick."

God, this guy was the worst. Not really wanting to hear the details, but needing to know, Jack asked, "Why would you hope he was with a woman?"

"He doesn't date. I try to set him up, get him to hang out with me and my crew, but he's never interested. Always talks about how he's waiting for the right woman. But, what about Ms. Right Now, you know what I mean." He extended a closed fist toward Max as if wanting a fist bump, like he was in on the joke. When Max didn't make a move to comply, Chip shrugged and let his hand drop to his side.

Max ground his teeth together. "No. I don't know what you mean. So you're saying you haven't seen your brother in a few days, and that he was upset about losing his job? Does that about cover it?"

"Pretty much."

"Do you have any idea where he is? Is there a place he goes when he's upset? Friends he leans on?" Jack asked.

Matt shrugged. "Don't know. Can I leave now?"

"Just one more question. Did you and your brother spend a lot of time with your grandmother?" After everything he'd learned, how much time Mason did or didn't spend with his grandma didn't really matter. Chip had spilled enough information on Mason to shoot him to the top of Jack's most wanted list. But he wanted to get as much information as he could while this idiot was talking.

The first genuine smile lifted Chip's lips. "We did. Mom worked nights, so we'd stay with Nana. She was always so fun. Spoiled us in whatever way she could. Took us to the park, bought our favorite pizza for dinner, always had glass dishes of candy around her apartment."

"Do you still see her often?" Max asked.

Chip's smile fall. "Nah. She died a little over a year ago." He cleared his throat. "I have to go."

Jack dug in his pocket for a business card and handed it over. "We really need to speak with your brother. If you see him, or find out where he is, it's very important that you call me."

For the first time, concern clouded the stupid look on Chip's face. "Umm. All right. Is he in some kind of trouble?"

Jack considered how to answer the question. He didn't want to say too much in case Chip was lying and ran to tell Mason about their conversation. But he also didn't want to downplay how important it was Mason was found. "The sooner we're able to talk to him, the sooner we'll know the answer to that for sure."

They left Chip standing in the doorway and hurried back to Max's car.

Once inside, Jack checked his phone for messages. The one from Olivia made uneasiness settle on his shoulders.

"What is it?" Max asked, checking the road before merging into traffic.

"Olivia went to get a check at the gallery."

"Alone?"

"No, Christine went with her. I still don't like it, though. Not with Mason unaccounted for, and not knowing for certain he's our guy. Will you take me to my car? I want to head there and make sure they're okay."

"Yeah. I'm sure everything's fine, though. Mason is looking sketchier and sketchier. While you get Olivia, I'll start looking for places he could be hiding."

The unease tightened, smothering him and making it hard to breathe. They were closing in on a killer, but with Olivia out of his sight, he hadn't felt further from resolving the case.

Chapter 23

All the lights were off in the gallery, and the thin sheet of plywood still stood in place of the busted door. Edward mentioned getting insurance money for her paintings but hadn't mentioned if he'd received payment to cover the destruction. Hopefully he'd get what was owed for the renovations. Olivia hated that she'd doubted him, and now, she wanted to see him get back on his feet. But that wouldn't happen if he couldn't reopen the gallery soon.

"Wow. You told me this place was vandalized, but I didn't expect this," Christine said, pushing open the flimsy barrier and crossing over the threshold.

Olivia scrunched her nose. "I know. I feel so bad. But if he got the insurance company to reimburse him so quickly, he can get this mess cleaned in no time."

"Olivia? Is that you?" Edward's nasal voice bounced out to the front of the room, echoing off the high ceiling.

"Yes," she answered. "Are you in your office?"

"Sure am. Come on back. I'll give you the check really quick. Then I have to get going."

She gestured for Christine to follow and made her way to the office that took up the right side of the room. She tried to avert her gaze from the bare walls but couldn't manage not to peek. The white walls couldn't have been more depressing if they'd been painted black. "That's where my pieces were that were ruined. Plus one on an easel in the back," she explained.

"Did Edward tell you how much the check is worth?" Christine asked, walking slowly as she took in the damage.

"No. Fingers crossed it's close to what they would have sold for." She'd fretted over the payment amount. Money was tight, and there was no telling how long it'd take to sell the loft. And as much as she appreciated her brother subletting her his rental property, that apartment was tainted. She'd never be comfortable there alone.

Hurrying over the dusty wood floor, she braced herself for what waited. She'd be grateful for whatever she was handed. "I can't believe the insurance company came through so fast," she said, swinging into the office.

Her feet turned to lead, and her stomach dropped down. She blinked, not understanding what she was seeing and wishing it wasn't real. Edward sat at the desk. Tears ran down his face, his red-rimmed eyes wide with fear. Mason stood beside him with the barrel of a gun pressed against Edward's temple.

A sneer twisted Mason's lips. "You're finally here,

Olivia. I thought I'd have to make my new friend Edward here call you again."

"I'm so sorry. I hate myself for telling you to come. But he said he'd kill me. He pulled out the gun. I didn't have a choice." Edward's words tumbled out of his mouth between sobs. His shoulders shook as if he couldn't control his erratic breathing.

Her mind struggled to make sense of his words—of Mason's presence. Of the gun. *Oh God, the gun.*

Footsteps approached the office. "So what's the magic number?" Christine asked, stepping inside.

Bang!

The blast of the gun rang in Olivia's ears, and she tensed, waiting for pain to erupt.

Christine fell to the ground face-first, her head bouncing off the ground, blood pooling underneath her from some unseen wound.

"No! Christine!" She turned to rush for her friend.

"Don't move," Mason said, voice low and calm.

Bile crept up her throat, burning her esophagus. Her entire body trembled, and she couldn't tear her gaze from the sight of her best friend in a bloody heap on the floor. She needed to get to her, to help her. But one wrong move put them all in even more danger.

"You shouldn't have brought anyone with you." Mason clucked his tongue as if scolding her. "I can't have your friend running off and telling that damn cop what's going on. That'd ruin everything—everything I've planned for us for so long."

She tried her hardest to calm her racing pulse and think clearly. Sweat coated her palms and her mind was stuck in a sea of quicksand—all her thoughts emerging slow and muddled. She had to figure out how to get them all out of this mess. But for the life of her, she had no clue how. Except to do whatever Mason wanted. Get him out of here so Edward could call the police and get help for Christine. When she had only herself to worry about, then she could plan her escape.

Needing to make Mason believe her, she faced him and tried to force a smile. But her quivering lips made it impossible. "I won't move. I promise. But can't we get help for Christine? There's a lot of blood. She needs medical attention now." Her voice broke and moisture blurred her vision.

Don't fall apart. Keep it together. You won't save anyone if you lose it.

"Do you think I'm stupid?" Mason asked, a mixture of amusement and irritation clipping his words. "If you call for help, they'll try to stop me. Try to stop us from living the life we were meant to have."

"What's your plan? It can't be to hang out with me and Edward in the office of the gallery. If we call para-medics to take care of Christine, we can leave before they get here. No one will know where we are. No one will ruin your plan." Her knees trembled, and she inched her fingers to her phone nestled in the side pocket of her leggings. If she could hit the call button, just call anyone who could hear what was going on, someone could come and get them out of this mess.

"Of course my plan isn't to hang out here with him." He twisted the gun harder against Edward's skull. "This is just the beginning. The beginning of a wonderful life together. I needed to get you alone, away from that damn detective who keeps sniffing around."

"Please. Stop." Edward said, his voice small and childlike. He hunched his shoulders to his ears, as if bracing for the worst.

"You've got me." She cleared the fear and panic from her throat. The croissant she'd eaten rebelled in her stomach. Every instinct in her body screamed at her to check on Christine and make sure she was alive. But one wrong move, one wrong word, and Christine might not be the only one who ended up with a bullet in them. "Now what?"

He dipped his chin toward her hand. "Now you keep moving toward your phone, then give it here," he said, lifting his palm.

Her heart sank, but she did as instructed. Now wasn't the time to test him. Not with Edward near his breaking point and Christine possibly bleeding to death on the floor. She tossed her phone, the weight of it leaving her grasp like the loss of a limb—or a lifeline.

Mason snatched the phone from the air, threw it on the floor, and stomped his heel on it—twisting his foot for good measure as the device splintered into pieces, then kicked the debris across the floor. "Good girl. Now we don't have to worry about any pesky interruptions."

A small groan alerted her to Christine, who slithered slightly on the ground. Hope rose inside her, only to be snuffed out by the realization that if Mason noticed her waking up, he might take aim a second time and finish her off. She needed to get him out of here. Now.

"Okay. No more phone. Just me and you. Now tell me what's next."

A sickening smile lifted his lips. "Now it's time to start the rest of our lives together. I've been so patient.

Made so many plans. And now it's all coming together. I can't tell you how happy I am." He rounded the corner and extended a hand to her.

She stared at his long, slender fingers. The bile from before coated her tongue and panic tightened her muscles. Ignoring every instinct yelling not to go with him, she took a step forward and grabbed his hand.

"Oops. One more thing." Mason lifted the gun, then brought the butt of the weapon down hard on the side of Edward's head.

Edward's body went limp, his face slamming down on the desk.

Olivia swallowed a scream and sent a silent plea for help into the universe.

Mason gave a tug on her hand and led her out of the office, the gun still in his hand, but tucked into his jacket pocket. "All right, my love. It's time to go home."

Once in his car, Jack called Olivia again. He cursed when the call went straight to voice mail. He'd already tried her line three times on the way to grab his vehicle parked outside the town house Max shared with his fiancé. Now he peeled onto the quiet street, a sense of dread causing him to push the gas pedal to the floor.

His phone rang, and hope soared only to come to a screeching halt when Max's information appeared on the touch screen on the dashboard. "Hear anything?" he asked after accepting the call. "I'm losing my mind. I called the gallery and there was no answer. If we were off the mark and Edward is the one behind this, if I let my emotions and jealousy sway me into sinking my hooks in Mason, and Olivia winds up hurt… I'll never forgive myself. Tell me you've heard something."

"I just got off the phone with Officer Whitton."

"From Cold Spring? What did he want?" A yellow taxi swerved in front of him, cutting him off. He blasted the horn.

"Marta woke up."

A ribbon of relief wove through the terror tightening his insides. "Oh thank God. Did she see who attacked her?"

"She told Whitton that a well-dressed man in his late twenties, early thirties strolled into the inn. All smiles. Blond hair. Green eyes. Boy next door charm pouring from him in waves."

"Mason." A beat of validation strummed through him, but the elation didn't last long. Although it was nice to know he hadn't let his feelings for Olivia mess with his judgment, that didn't mean shit with Mason on the loose and Olivia not answering his calls.

"Yep. The smug asshole even gave her his name. He claimed Olivia was his wife. That she was in Cold Spring with a coworker, and he'd come by unexpectedly to surprise her. Marta was so impressed by his romantic gesture, she told him which room to find Olivia in."

"That's how he knew which rooms we were staying in. Olivia's sketchbook only confirmed it." He blew out a frustrated breath. He couldn't blame Marta for believing Mason's story. The man understood how to lay on the charm and win people over. He'd read Mason like a book from the first time they'd met. Besides, Mason would have found another way to get to Olivia if Marta hadn't confided the room number.

He turned toward the gallery. The old, converted warehouse was visible down the congested street. "What happened after she gave Mason the room information?"

"When she turned her back, he attacked her from behind. It's surprising he didn't kill her. Having her as a witness will be crucial."

"It won't matter if we have a witness or not if we can't find the bastard." A small miracle occurred, and a spot opened up on the street a few buildings away from A Peculiar Sight. He signaled his intention to slide into the spot.

"I'm working on that. I called the captain about securing a warrant for his apartment. I'm on my way to talk to the brother again. Just in case the weasel lied about knowing where Mason might be. If those are dead ends, we'll brainstorm more ideas of where he could be. We'll find him, Jack."

He jammed his car into the tight space and shut off the engine. "I'll grab Olivia and call you back. Reach out if you hear anything." Disconnecting, he yanked his keys from the ignition. He shoved the keys and phone in his pocket and jumped out of his car before pushing past pedestrians to get to the gallery. He hadn't spoken with Olivia in a little over an hour, and the screaming siren inside him told him something wasn't right. With everything going on, there was no way she wouldn't answer his calls. He just prayed he got to her before something bad happened that he wouldn't be able to fix.

A million thoughts zipped through his head as he stormed into the gallery. "Olivia!"

Nothing but the sound of his own voice echoed back to him.

He moved farther into the room. No one was in the showroom, so he jogged over to the office. "It's Jack. Are you in here?" He called out.

He caught sight of the bottoms of a pair of sneakers on the floor, and terror fisted his heart. He broke into a run, catapulting across the threshold. But it wasn't Olivia who lay motionless on the floor. Christine. He fell to his knees to check her pulse, and something sticky and wet on the floor coated his hand. "Shit. Christine. Can you hear me?" He didn't dare shake her—move her—for fear of making her injures worse.

No reply.

A quick glance at the desk showed Edward face-down.

Grabbing his phone, he called 911 and hurried to the injured man. Blood trickled down the side of his face. His pulse was strong, but he made no show of waking up or being alert to Jack's presence.

"Nine-one-one. What's your emergency?" a smooth, feminine voice asked.

"This is Detective Stone. I'm at A Peculiar Sight. The art gallery in the Meatpacking District. I need a couple ambulances immediately. Have two unconscious victims. A man, Edward Consuelo appears to have a head wound, blunt trauma to the temple. The woman, Christine Roberts, is bleeding from a gunshot wound to her leg. Her pulse is weak and thready."

"I'm sending help now. Are you able to find the source of the bleeding?"

"I'll try but get someone here quick. Also send officers. Suspect has fled with possible hostage." He gave the dispatcher the details than disconnected to focus on Christine.

He may have first aid training under his belt, but he still listened as the woman talked him through the best way to move Christine to find the bullet hole on her leg and create a tourniquet with his belt. Once he'd tightened the belt in place, all that was left to do was wait and wonder where Olivia was.

With shaking hands, he stood and circled the room. Every muscle in his body coiled tighter than a spring, yelling at him to move. To act. To get the hell out of here and find her. His mind spun. Where could she be? No way she'd have left her friend to bleed on the floor and Edward passed out on his desk with blood dripping down his face. He wasn't sure exactly what happened, but it was clear Mason lured Olivia to the gallery, then injured her friends. Either as a way to get her to leave, or to keep them from talking.

But where was she now? Mason wasn't at his apartment. Maybe he'd taken her to hers. He wavered between the urge to run to her place and pound on her door or stay with two injured civilians until help arrived.

He couldn't do anything to help Edward and Christine, but Olivia was still in trouble. He had to move, and fast. Chances were Mason had taken Olivia somewhere, but Jack had to make sure the building was clear before he left.

Decision made, he turned to the door and his foot came down on something hard. He stared down at the debris he'd kicked aside. A phone?

He bent low, and anger burned bright inside him. A broken phone with a colorful case was scattered on the ground. Olivia's phone. Determination steeled his resolve and he rose. He had to find Olivia.

Chapter 24

Casting one more glance at the motionless bodies of Christine and Edward, Jack swore under his breath and ran out of the messy office. He wished he could do more for them, but now he needed to focus on finding Olivia. He'd only been inside A Peculiar Sight once before, and even then hadn't spent much time there, but there had to be more than just a showroom and office. Mason might have thought it too risky to drag Olivia outside in broad daylight. Maybe there was a room he'd taken her to inside the warehouse.

He grabbed his weapon and held it at his side, his finger on the trigger. Natural light from the late morning sun swept across the dusty floor. The hum of electricity filled the air. He trained his ears to listen for any other sound that would indicate someone else was still here.

Noting a door at the back of the room, he crept over the floorboards and kept his eyes peeled for any movement. He slowly pulled open the door and found himself in some kind of giant storage closet. Hell, he could fit most of his apartment inside. Multiple stacks of large canvases nestled one on top of the other against the walls, cream-colored sheets draped over them. Two filing cabinets were shoved in a corner. Papers spilled out of one of the partially opened drawers, as if someone had been in a hurry and shoved them inside. Sculptures sat on wooden pedestals and framed sketches hung on the walls.

He peeked around anything large enough for someone to hide behind, surveying every inch. A musty, mothball scent hung in the air. No indication that anyone had been back here jumped out at him. Hell, the thick layer of dust on top of the pieces of art screamed that no one had been in the room in a while.

Another door caught his attention, and he made his way through the discarded artwork and random crap. He steadied his bouncing nerves as he swung open the door, weapon aimed in front of him, and disappointment weighed him down. A tiny bathroom with a toilet and sink had no hiding places for Mason or Olivia.

Shit. They weren't here. And he'd just wasted ten minutes creeping around in a dark, dusty room for nothing. But if Mason didn't keep Olivia at the gallery, and he wasn't home, Olivia's apartment made the most sense.

Jack stuffed his gun back in its place. He erupted from the storage room and ran for the door, desperation to find Olivia nearly strangling him. The sound of sirens hit his ears as the squad cars and two ambulances rushed down the street toward the gallery. Not having the time or patience to wait for the officer, he sprinted to the driver's side and whipped open the door.

"The two injured civilians are in the office. The woman is bleeding from a bullet wound on her right thigh. I've applied a tourniquet to slow the bleeding. The man is unconscious, sitting at the desk. I suspect a head injury so tread lightly." He rattled off the situation as quickly as he could, needing to check Olivia's apartment.

The female officer stepped out of the car, yelling out what she'd just been told to the EMTs who ran by, arms loaded down with medical equipment.

"And the suspect?" She slammed the door closed and fell in step beside him.

He wanted to give her all the details she needed but didn't have time to waste. Picking up the pace, he stopped for a second at the entrance. Panicked energy zipped around his body, demanding him to move. To run. "No other persons on the premises. Suspect is a late-twenties male. Mason Shaffer. Most likely won't be back but stay on alert. Call in the situation. I need as many eyes on the lookout for him as possible. If found, approach with caution. Likely has a hostage. Olivia Hickman. Long, red hair. Hazel eyes."

He threw the last words over his shoulder as he sprinted to Olivia's apartment. For once, he was grateful for the lack of security on the building. A couple of quick, hard yanks opened the main door to the lobby. He darted for the stairs, taking them two at a time, then bolted to Olivia's place.

Fisting his hand, he pounded on the door. "Olivia! It's Jack."

When no one answered, he tried the doorknob. Locked. He pounded on the door again and pain shot up his arm. "Olivia! Are you in there?"

Again, no answer.

Not wanting to waste another second, he took a few steps back, then took a running start before ramming his shoulder against the thin wood. The barrier bent and the hinges groaned from the pressure. He repeated his efforts, again and again, until the door burst open. He stumbled forward, gaining his footing as he fell into the living room.

The pungent stench of strong perfume attacked him. God, it was like the flowers from The River's Edge showed up and exploded everywhere. A quick glance showed him Olivia wasn't there. He ran down the hall and poked his head into the bathroom before pivoting to her studio.

Blinding sunlight showcased the vivid colors of her paintings. The narrow table against the wall held a multitude of paintbrushes and empty palettes. But no Olivia.

"Dammit, Olivia. Where are you?" He retrieved his phone and called Max. As soon as the line picked up, he prattled off the details of what had happened. "Have you found Mason? He has Olivia. I know it. Any idea where he could have taken her?"

"The brother still had nothing to offer, but the warrant came through. I'm on my way there now," Max said. "I called his mother and left a message to call me immediately."

"I'm scared, man. If he hurts her. If he…" He couldn't

finish the thought. Couldn't allow himself to picture Olivia injured and frightened. If he did, he'd crack. And then he couldn't help anyone.

"We'll find them. He has to be somewhere. Had a place ready for this moment. He wouldn't have taken her with no destination in mind."

Jack threaded his hand through his hair, frustration curling his fingers around the strands. Max was right, but how could they figure out Mason's twisted plan? Circling the room, his gaze landed on the painting Olivia had brought to the gallery a few mornings before, hoping to sell, but finding a crime scene instead. The painting she'd created to purge herself of her fear and grief and sadness after the murders in her loft.

A beat of excitement pressed against his chest. "I know where he took her."

"Where?" Max asked.

"He took her back to the place he thinks of as their home. Mason took Olivia to the loft."

Olivia pressed a damp palm to her churning stomach and prayed she wouldn't throw up. Mason had one hand on the steering wheel, driving methodically through traffic, while the other held the gun in place on the center console…aimed right at her.

All the moisture evaporated from her mouth, making her tongue dry. She searched for the right thing to say to defuse the situation, but how did she talk to a man who was so clearly unhinged? She wanted to squeeze her eyes shut and pretend this wasn't happening, but the moment her lids slid closed, images of Christine and Edward invaded her mind. Were they dead? How long would it take for someone to find them? She needed to get help not only for herself, but for her friends.

Mason pulled in a deep breath, puffing out his chest. "It's a beautiful day, isn't? I love when a plan finally comes together. Don't you?"

Maybe if she understood what was going on in his brain, she could figure a way out of this mess. "I do, yes." She swallowed hard over the agreeable words. The last thing she wanted was to be nice and chitchat, but arguing or making him mad wouldn't do her any good. "Can you tell me the rest of your plan? I'd love to hear it." She braced herself, not really wanting to hear anything from him, but needing to know what she was working with.

He shrugged; gaze fixed straight ahead. "Not much to tell. I knew after the night we met that I had to find a way for us to be together. So I did."

"The night we met?" She tried to recall the first time Dave had introduced her to Mason, but all of her memories were a big blur of cooperate events and fancy fundraisers. Nothing stood out as being a pivotal moment. Or one that would encourage him to pursue her in any way.

He chuckled and patted the gun against her knee.

She tensed as the metal touched the thin cotton of her leggings. Pressure filled her torso, squeezing the air from her lungs. She struggled to keep her composure—to remember the night Mason alluded to.

"Come on," he said. "You remember. At the gala. You were sitting alone at your table, something that never should have happened, and I asked you to dance. You smiled that beautiful smile of yours, and you were about to say yes. I know you were. It was like one of those movie moments you dream about. Then Dave showed up." A storm of emotions contorted his face. "Made some comment about how you were already taken and pulled you out on the dance floor. I could tell you felt bad for me. Even apologized as he dragged you away."

Oh my God. Mason had conjured up an entire meet-cute in his head when all she'd done was be polite with a stranger at her husband's work event. She struggled not to squirm or show her disgust. Her mind whirled, trying to come up with a response he'd find acceptable. "I do remember that night and meeting you. You were always so nice to me." She wanted to add *and Dave* but couldn't risk provoking him.

"Of course I was," he said. "We're meant to be to-gether. I've always known that. I just needed to remove some obstacles."

She swallowed hard. "Remove obstacles?"

He flicked her a mischievous grin and wiggled his eyebrows. "You know. Get rid of Dave. He was just in the way. And those people who were in *our* home. I mean, the nerve, right? I had to make sure they'd never come back." He snapped his fingers, the sudden noise making her jump. "Easy."

His nonchalant statement crushed her soul. "Our home?" she echoed, not understanding how he'd come to believe he had any claim on the loft.

"I picked it out. Didn't Dave tell you that?" He frowned, a flash of irritation clouding his face. "Or did he take credit for that, too? That's what he did best. Took credit for my work, kept the love of my life from me, and then swooped in and bought the loft *I'd* shown him. I wanted the loft. For me and you. Knowing he kept you there, pretended like it was his home..." His grip tightened on the wheel, and she leaned against the door, gaining as much distance from him as she could.

Her mind spun. This man had pretended to be a friend to her—to her husband—then slithered like a snake behind their backs to get his way. He'd murdered Dave. Killed two innocent women. And why? Because of some off-the-wall notion that she was his destiny?

She kept her mouth shut as her mind worked. She couldn't handle listening to anymore of his bullshit. Instead, she tried to figure out how to get the hell away from Mason. She needed distance to make any moves. In the confining space of the moving vehicle, any shot could be deadly.

"We're almost there," Mason said, his light and cheerful voice in direct opposition to the turmoil boiling in her gut.

The tree-lined street with the upscale buildings and polished windows was a crushing blow to her psyche. "Where are we going?" she asked, already knowing the answer.

He tossed a wide grin her way before turning into a parking garage attached to the building she used to love so much. "We're going home." He swung into an empty space and shut off the engine.

Her heart raced so fast it made her head spin. She'd hoped to flag down a pedestrian on the street, even just alert someone she was in danger, but the chances of running into anyone in the parking garage were low.

Her only chance to get away was to run. As soon as

he opened his door, she needed to get her ass out of the car and get as far away as possible. The exit was close—three cars down, tops. If she could get outside, she could scream for help. Someone would have to hear her.

Before opening his door, Mason circled his hand around her neck and twisted her toward him. Her insides quivered and unshed tears burned the backs of her eyes.

Don't let him see your fear. Don't give him any idea you're about to run.

"I know I can make you happy. Happier than you've been in your whole life." He crushed his mouth on hers.

She fought the urge to bite down on his lip. His mouth moved against hers and nausea swam in her stomach.

Grinning, he pulled away. "Tonight will be magical."

She forced a smile and nodded. She tightened her muscles, gripping the door handle, and waited for him to gather his phone and keys and step out of the car.

Praying for courage, she pushed open her door and hit the hard pavement running.

"What the hell?"

Mason's angry voice boomed off the low, concrete ceiling, but she didn't turn around. She sprinted toward the exit, weaving back and forth like she'd read in books to make herself a more difficult target.

"Get back here. Now!" Heavy footsteps pounded after her.

She didn't turn around. The door was so close. Her freedom within reach.

Bang!

A scream poured from her open mouth, and she

hunched her shoulders forward. A bullet slammed into the car beside her, and the car alarm screeched, echoing off the cement walls. She kept moving. "Help! Somebody! Please! Call the police!"

Her lungs burned and her tennis shoes slapped against the hard floor. She searched for signs that anyone had heard her. That anyone was in the garage. The exit was a few feet away. If she could get through the door, the stairwell on the first floor spilled onto the sidewalk. Being outside increased her chances of being seen—of being heard. She had to make it.

Extending her arm, she lunged for the metal handle. *Bang!*

A bullet lodged into the steel door, inches from her head. She shrieked, adrenaline pushing away every other thought except escape.

An arm latched around her waist and the rough feel of the barrel of a gun twisted against her side.

She yelped, pain erupting against the tender dip of her flesh above her hip.

Mason griped her bicep, pinching it until she squirmed against his hold. He held her tight against his chest. "Don't do that again. Next time, when I shoot, I won't miss." He nuzzled his nose against the side of her neck, his breath warm and sticky.

Defeat crashed over her as he guided her through the parking garage and into the building. The truth of the moment made her knees buckle, but Mason's grip kept her on her feet—moving forward.

If she disappeared inside the loft with Mason, she'd never make it out alive.

Chapter 25

Olivia darted her gaze around the wide hallway, willing someone to step out of their apartment. She'd always
loved the quietness of the building—the way people kept
to themselves. But not now. Now she'd give anything
for a crowd of noisy people to pour into the hallway.
She wanted to scream, to yell, to throw a toddler-sized
tantrum to alert her neighbors to her plight. But the
gun still wedged against her side kept her mouth shut.

Mason retrieved a key ring from the front pocket of
his jeans and plunged the key in the lock.

Confusion broke through the fog of fear layering her
brain. "How did you get a key?"

"I stole it," he said it in an offhanded, easy way that
made her skin crawl. "The last lady who stayed here
put the key ring on the hook by the door. But is it really
stealing when this place is ours anyway?"

Dread weighed her down as Mason opened the door to the loft with a flourish and ushered her inside.

"Ta-da!" Mason said, sweeping an arm in front of them.

Her jaw dropped, and she wrapped her arms around her middle. But nothing she could do would shield her from what waited for her. The scent of her perfume hung heavy in the air like a weighted cloud ready to burst. Curtains shielded the windows, making the dozens of flickering candles around the living room glow. Printed photos of Olivia were taped to the walls, and a fire roared in the hearth.

"Go in and look," Mason said, excitement lifting each word. "Don't you love it? I mean, I knew if we were going to make this our home, there'd have to be some changes. I couldn't get rid of the furniture, or it might have drawn attention. But I added a few special touches. I really want you to see how much you are always on my mind. Even when we couldn't be together."

He pressed his hand against the small of her back, urging her forward.

She took another step inside, each spot her gaze landing on increasing her anxiety. Her head spun as she ran though her limited options. She had no phone, no one knew where she was, and an obsessed man with zero grasp on reality held her at gunpoint in some creepy little love nest he'd set up.

But Jack was out there. She'd sent him a message that would lead him to the gallery. He'd search for her, put together enough of the pieces to understand what had happened. And when he did, she would put away all her stupid doubts and tell him exactly how she felt.

Because if nothing else, Mason tearing apart each and every piece of her life and attempting to shove them together to fit some twisted image in his head showed her life was short. Spending even one second of her life sitting with doubts and insecurities was a silly waste of time. She'd lay her soul bare, then give Jack the space he needed to figure out his own heart.

If she made it out alive.

Not knowing what to say or do, she stared at the dancing flames in the hearth. A part of her wanted to switch over to survivor mode. To shut off her brain and just give in to whatever Mason demanded. He said he loved her, and even though she was certain he didn't know what love really was, she was fairly positive he wouldn't hurt her. As long as she didn't run or struggle or fight.

A flash of metal snagged her attention, and she caught sight of the fire poker next to the decorative grate. Fight. That's what she had to do, and now she had a weapon. She just needed to get to it.

Doing her best to quiet the flurry of aggressive butterflies in her stomach, she placed a hand on Mason's arm. She struggled to keep her expression from broadcasting her disgust. "I like the candles. Gives everything a…romantic glow."

Fluttering his eyes closed for a beat, he thumped his free hand over his heart. "Oh good. I was a little nervous. I mean, I know this place has some *other* memories for you. But I really do think we can make it exactly what we both want."

She clenched her jaw at his mention of *other*. Meaning Dave. The man she'd shared this home with, her heart with. Anger swirled inside it, building up momentum with each passing second. She held on to the new emotion for dear life. Anger would fuel her desire for escape.

"I'm a little overwhelmed," she said. "Today has been a lot. Can we sit?"

His brow crinkled with concern. "Sure. Whatever you need. Can I get you anything?"

The suggestion had her holding her breath. If she could convince him to get her a glass of water, she might have enough time to grab the poker. She cleared her throat. "I'm a little thirsty."

His eyes lit up. "I have just the thing." He grabbed her hand and pulled her to the dining room. An ice bucket with a bottle of champagne sat in the middle of the table. The crystal flutes she and Dave had used at their wedding beside it.

Fury boiled her blood. How dare this man destroy her life. Kill her husband. Terrorize innocent people. She had no doubt Jack would find his way to her, but there was no telling how long it would take. She couldn't hold herself together much longer. Not when she was drowning in a tsunami of emotions and grasping wildly for something to hold on to in a desperate attempt to stay afloat.

And the one thing she needed to hold on to was the fireplace poker.

She gauged the distance between her and her intended weapon. The thick metal was no match for the gun Mason still held. If she could only get him to set it down for a minute. An idea formed. He'd need two hands to open the bottle. "Champagne sounds lovely."

He hurried ahead, glancing over his shoulder with the boyish smile she used to admire. Now it made her stomach queasy. "Come on. It's all chilled and ready to go."

As soon as his attention went back to the ice bucket, she passed by the fireplace and circled the handle of the poker with her palm. She put her hands behind her back as she walked, keeping the slender weapon hidden. She stopped beside one of the dining room chairs, leaning against it to create a barrier.

Mason cast her a curious glance. "Why did you run from me? You ran and yelled for help. You hurt my feelings. I just want to love you like you deserve."

The switch of emotions softened his face and made him look like a sad child. What happened to this man to twist him into something so dangerous? She couldn't dwell on that now. She needed to answer his question in a way that made sense.

She drew in a shuddering breath. "Coming here threw me. I haven't been inside the loft since a woman was killed. The thought of coming back inside scared me. I was confused…with the gun you had pointed at me and what happened at the gallery…" Her bottom lip trembled, and tears threatened to fall from her eyes. "I didn't know what to expect. If you'd hurt me like you hurt everyone else."

His face fell and he reached out to graze her jawline with his knuckles.

She tensed and her sweat-slicked palm slid against the handle. If he noticed it, she was screwed.

"The only way I'd ever hurt you is if you pushed me to. Everyone else?" He shrugged. "They had to be dealt with. Those people staying here, in our place. It was an invasion of privacy I couldn't tolerate. And I couldn't let your friends call the police. Please try to understand."

She sniffed back her tears and tightened her grip on the poker. "I do. I really do. Now let's pop that champagne. You even bought my favorite brand." She hadn't looked at the label to know if that was true, but the way his face lit up told her she'd pushed the right button.

"I *knew* it! Let's not wait another second to celebrate." He placed the gun on the table and scooped the dark green bottle from the bucket.

She tightened her grip on the poker until her tendons screamed with pain.

Mason wrapped one hand along the neck of the bottle and gripped the top with his other. "This might be loud," he said with a grin.

She swung the poker in the air like a baseball bat and aimed for his head. The pointy edge whacked against his cheek, the impact vibrating up her arms and turning her stomach inside out.

A hiss of pain came from his mouth and the bottle crashed to the table. Mason fell forward.

A rush of adrenaline made her heart pound in her ears. She wanted to run but had to ensure he couldn't follow. Her stomach rebelled at the blood oozing from his face, and the acidic taste of fear flooded her mouth. Steeling her nerve, she thrust the poker above her head and brought it down as hard as she could.

Before it hit his head, he snapped his arm up and caught the steel rod in his hand. Anger contorted his face into a mask of hate. Red invaded his cheeks clashing with the drops of blood dripping down to the floor.

Her breath caught in her throat. She dropped the poker and ran for the door. If she didn't get away, he'd kill her. Terror clawed at her chest, but she raced ahead.

A feral growl from behind her clutched at her heart and moved her faster. "You bitch. You should have just let me love you. I told you I wouldn't miss the next time I took a shot."

Jack swerved onto the sidewalk and slammed his car in Park. Max hadn't found anything yet in Mason's apartment but urged Jack to wait for backup before barging into the loft.

Not an option. His gut told him exactly where Olivia was, and he needed to get to the apartment as fast as possible. Backup would be there soon, but Jack couldn't wait.

Jumping from the car, he ignored the protests of annoyed pedestrians and an angry doorman as he muscled his way into the building. "Police are on their way. There's a situation in Olivia Hickman's loft. Don't get in the way."

Bypassing the elevator, he ran up the stairs and rounded the corner of Olivia's hallway. His lungs burned and expanded in his chest with each labored breath. His heart pounded.

Bang!

The sound of a gunshot had him sprinting to Olivia's apartment. As he ran, he fumbled with his phone and managed to send out a text to Max.

Gunshots fired at the loft. Get here now. Send medical help.

Shoving his phone back in his pocket as he approached Olivia's door, he tested the doorknob, relieved to find it unlocked. He wanted to burst through, guns blazing, but his training demanded he needed to be more discreet. Olivia was in a perilous situation. He couldn't make it worse by charging in without knowing exactly what he'd find.

With a firm grip on his anxiety, he steeled his nerves and crept inside. He had his gun trained in front of him, ready for whatever he found. The same overwhelming scent from her apartment smacked him in the face, and dozens of candles illuminated the quiet room. Taped-up photos of Olivia littered the walls—pictures of her laughing with Christine and walking down the sidewalk. Cleary unaware she was being photographed. Sweat dotted the back of his neck.

He left the door ajar and crept inside. The open space made finding a place to hide difficult. He crouched low, making himself as small as possible. He stepped forward, casting a glance toward the sofa in the living area.

No one was there.

The sound of crying caught his attention and made his blood boil. A white pillar separated the entryway from the dining room—the edge of the long table in view. Mason skirted around the end of the table, his back to Jack and holding Olivia in his arms like a groom carrying a bride. Blood dripped down to the cream-colored rug.

"Stop right there." Jack commanded, gun trained high. He fought the urge to pull the trigger and take the bastard down now. He didn't know the extent of Olivia's

injuries, and if Mason dropped her after getting shot—
or worse, Jack accidently shot Olivia—it could kill her.

Mason spun to face him, and Jack's heart fell to his
feet. Tears leaked from Olivia's eyes, blood blossoming from a spot on her shirt. Her body was lax and her
glassy stare listless and unfocused. She needed medical attention. Now.

The boy next door looks Jack associated with Mason
were twisted into something else entirely. A long gash
sliced down the side of his face. His hand that held the
gun was tucked around Olivia's shoulders, the weapon
lying against her bicep. His hair was messy, and a manic
look dominated his eyes and made Jack's core tighten. A
desperate man was unpredictable. A desperate man who
had a tentative grip on reality was downright terrifying.

Mason met Jack's eye. "She made me do it. I just
wanted to love her. Wanted to give her everything. I
told her not to run. I warned her I wouldn't miss." His
voice cracked and shoulders shook on shallow sobs.
Olivia's body bounced in his firm grip.

Jack fought not to glance at Olivia. He kept his focus
entirely on Mason. As much as he wanted to run across
the room and tackle the asshole, he couldn't. He had
to find another way to get Mason away from Olivia.
"If you love her, you need to put her down. Let me get
her help."

Mason shook his head. "No. I can't let her go. I won't.
She's mine."

"Do you want her to die?" The question wedged in
his throat and squeezed his heart like a vise. Olivia had
a bullet hole in her flesh, just like Mary. And might not
survive another minute, because yet again, he didn't get

to her in time. But at least Mary knew how he felt about her. At least he'd confessed his love. He'd been an idiot not to tell Olivia exactly what she meant to him—exactly what he wanted for their future.

"No," Mason said, his lips trembling. "But if I can't have her, no one else can. And she's shown she's not ready to accept everything I can give her."

Adrenaline spiked through Jack with each heartbeat. It shouldn't be too long before backup showed up, but he didn't know how much time Olivia had. If he shot Mason in the leg, and he dropped her, would that outweigh the risk of waiting for help to arrive? Or what if Mason had the forethought to use his weapon on her again? Finish what he started while Jack could do nothing but stand by helplessly and watch.

Mason sniffed, then used the sleeve of his arm to wipe a mixture of tears and blood from his face. The guy was falling apart. Jack had to move fast.

A slight movement from Olivia tensed Jack's muscles. He didn't want to alert Mason to any changes in her, so he stayed still. Gun trained on Mason. If he so much as moved the arm that gripped his weapon, Jack would pull the trigger.

Olivia turned her head just enough to make eye contact with Jack.

Fear made his palms sweat. He didn't know what was going on in her mind, but something told him she refused to lie still and be a pawn for Mason. He took a steadying breath. Whatever she did, he'd be ready to jump in.

Olivia slowly moved one finger and placed it on her forearm, then two, then three... With lightning speed she grabbed Mason's hand that held the gun and bit hard.

"Sonofa—" Mason jerked his hand away and stumbled backward. The gun fell to the ground. His grip loosened on Olivia, who thrashed in his arms.

He couldn't get off a shot without endangering her, but without Mason's weapon, the threat decreased.

Jack charged.

Mason tossed Olivia to the ground and scooped his gun from the floor. He aimed it at Olivia, who lay in a motionless heap.

"No!" Jack lunged forward. His arms wrapping around Mason's waist and driving him to the floor as the sound of a gunshot rang in his ears. He slammed his fist against Mason's jaw—then again—until Mason's head flopped back. Jack circled Mason's wrist with his hand, pounding his knuckles against the ground until he released the gun.

Mason grunted and swore. "Get off me! I won't let you ruin this! I won't let you take her from me!"

With his body weight pinning Mason down, Jack reached behind his back and found his handcuffs. He shifted enough to spin Mason to his stomach then slapped the cuffs on him. "Stay down, asshole."

Raising to his feet, he hurried to Olivia. He longed to hold her but didn't want to hurt her more than she already was. "Olivia. Can you hear me?"

Her eyelids fluttered open. "Did you get him?"

"Yes. He can't hurt you anymore."

A small smile barely lifted her lips and she reached for his hand. "You promised you'd stop him. I... I'm really cold. And my chest hurts. So bad." Her teeth chattered and her hand was like ice in his.

No. He couldn't lose her now. Not while Mason lay

in handcuffs and the threat to Olivia was over. Needing to be close to her—to comfort her—he cradled her head in his lap. He swept away a matted lock of hair with shaking fingers. "Help will be here soon. Everything's going to be fine."

Her eyes slid closed, and her body went limp.

"Police!" A familiar voice shouted.

Tears clouded his vision as Max led a handful of officers and paramedics into the loft.

Jack dropped his head, panic tightening his hold on Olivia. "Help's here. Please. Please don't leave me. I love you."

Chapter 26

I love you.

Jack's choked-up voice whispering those words waded through the fog of pain keeping Olivia from opening her eyes. Every inch of her body hurt. The weight of an anvil sat on her chest. She wiggled her fingers, but the feel of calloused skin against hers kept her hand still.

She creaked open one eye then the other. She blinked against the bright fluorescent light beating down on her. The astringent scent of disinfectant and sickness permeated her nose. The beep of machines kept pace with her heartbeat.

Using all her strength, she turned toward the person sitting in the chair next to the bed she lay in. "Jack?" His name stuck in her dry mouth.

Jack jerked to attention, then leaned forward. The

dark scruff on his jaw seemed more pronounced and a river of lines creased his forehead. "I'm right here," he said, his eyes filled with worry. "You're awake."

Shifting, she grimaced as stabs of discomfort rippled along her side. She tried to recall the events that had brought her here, but the harder she tried, the more the memories blurred. "Mason took me to the loft. I hit him, then ran. I don't remember anything else."

He dropped his gaze to their joined hands. "Do you really want to know?"

She nodded. She needed to know the details, no matter how hard they were to hear. Not only to have closure but also to know if the words of love buzzing through her brain had actually been spoken or were just a dream.

Jack drew in a deep breath. "When I got to the loft, I heard a gunshot. By the time I was inside, Mason had just shot you. He'd picked you up. I thought I was too late." His voice caught, and he coughed to cover the crack.

"But you weren't. I'm a little beat-up but fine." She fought not to wince. He needed to see she was all right. That she wasn't another casualty he would blame himself for. She might have a physical wound, but he'd been wounded too. And she was the only one who could fix him. "You saved me."

He glanced up and the pain and concern shining from his watering eyes stole her breath. "You saved yourself. You bit his hand. If you hadn't acted, I don't know how I would have taken him down. You're a warrior, Olivia Hickman."

A faint memory fluttered back to her; the sweaty taste of Mason's hand combined with fear flooded her senses. His praise heated her cheeks. "You made me brave. I knew that if you were there, you'd make sure everything was okay. I just set things into motion."

"You give me too much credit," he said, looking up at the ceiling and pinching the bridge of his nose. He blinked, keeping his tears from falling.

"You don't give yourself enough." She yanked at his hand, making him look at her. "I heard you. You told me you love me. Those words stayed with me until I woke up. *You* stayed with me. From the time you showed up in the loft until I woke in this bed and everything in between. You kept me going."

"I've never been so damn scared."

"Me neither," she said with a short laugh. "And I want you to know, I love you. Even if you only said those words to me because you were scared and filled with adrenaline and didn't know if I would live or die. I loved you when we spent the night together and was just too nervous and insecure to tell you. I hope I don't scare you now, but life is too damn short to hide things in my heart. I know it's fast and crazy and—"

Jack pressed his lips to hers, pulling away and catching her chin in his loose grip. His face was so close, his breath warm on her cheeks. "I didn't tell you I love you because I was terrified of losing you. I said it because I mean it. And I was kicking myself for not telling you how I felt when I had the chance. I'm sorry I made you doubt where we stood. I'll never leave you questioning how much you mean to me."

Happiness flooded her chest, pressing against her insides until she nearly burst. "Can we get out of here? Not exactly the romantic moment I envisioned." Sure, fire burned a path up her side, but she'd rather deal with that somewhere a little more private.

"Sorry." He scrunched his nose and sat back down, recapturing her palm in his. "You had a small surgery to remove the bullet. You have at least one night here."

The mention of bullets sent another memory flitting to the surface. She bolted upright, and throbbing from her wound had her doubling over. "Christine! Edward!" she said through clenched teeth. "Are they okay?"

"They'll both be fine. You can't get riled up." Jack was back on his feet, his wary stare on the machine beeping beside her. "I went to the gallery before I realized Mason took you to the loft. I found them and called for medical help. They were rushed to the hospital. Edward has a concussion. Christine underwent emergency surgery, and she must have hit her head pretty bad when she fell. It was touch and go but she made it through."

Relief pressed against her sinus cavity, and tears blurred her vision. "They're here? Can I see them?" The last images she had of her friends were ones she'd rather forget. Although that would never happen, at least she could replace the horrible memory with new ones of them both on the mend.

"You'll have to ask your doctor about that," he said. "But when you're able, I'll take you to see them myself. I don't plan on letting you out of my sight."

She sank back onto the mattress and smiled. "I like the sound of that."

Jack trailed his knuckles along her cheekbone. "I mean it. I told myself I'd stay by your side until the danger was over. But even if Mason is behind bars, I still want you near. As often as is possible."

She wasn't sure what all that entailed, but the idea of spending more time with Jack lifted her lips and her soul. A sense of peace settled over her like a warm blanket. "I'd like that."

"Good. Because I don't want you to go back to that apartment and the loft holds too many bad memories. I want you to stay with me."

She sucked in a sharp breath, unsure of what to say. "You want me to live with you?"

Grinning, he gave a little shrug. "Let's just call it a detour while you figure out your next step. I don't want you to feel pressured to make any big decisions right now. You need to rest and heal. And I want to get to know you inside and out, while you do."

"What about your roommate? Won't he mind?"

"Nah. Nolan works all the time anyway. We're like two passing ships. But if you aren't ready, that's okay."

Her smile stretched her face so wide it hurt the corners of her mouth. "I never thought I'd be this happy again. You've shown me life goes on and finding love again is possible. You were there when I needed you most. I'll never be able to tell you how much you've given me."

He tucked a strand of hair behind her ear and pressed a long kiss to her forehead. He reared back an inch, keeping his gaze locked on hers. "You brought me back to life, Liv. We've both walked a somber path. Now let's be happy…together."

Jack stepped out of the home office with boxes stacked waist-high and slipped his phone back in the front pocket of his jeans. The room would have been great for setting up a desk and storing old files. But the light pouring through the multiple windows in the corner demanded it become Olivia's new studio.

A sacrifice he would gladly make, shoving his desk and work-related things in a living room that was double the size he'd left behind at his old place.

"Hey, babe," Olivia said. She sat in the middle of the kitchen floor, dipping into a box and pulling out more bubble-wrapped plates. "I hope we have enough room for everything. Who knew we had so much stuff?" She beamed up at him, her smile quickly falling. "What's wrong?"

He pulled her to her feet, wrapping an arm around the small of her back to hold her close. "Nothing's wrong. I just got off the phone with Max."

She drew in a deep breath. "Mason's trial ended today."

After Olivia had testified the day before, she'd decided not to stick around. Facing Mason had been too difficult. "Max filled me in on what happened. Do you want to know?"

She nodded.

He glanced around their new apartment, wishing their furniture had arrived so they could sit somewhere other than the tile floor in the kitchen. "He'll be in jail a long time. Charged in the deaths of Courtney Bailey, Priscilla Abbington, and Dave."

Tears sprang to her eyes. Tremors shook her body, and she buried her head in his shoulder.

He let her cry. The past four months since she'd healed from her surgery had been filled with plenty of questions and worry. He'd stood by Olivia as she learned more about Mason's intentions and how he'd orchestrated multiple murders in a sick attempt to get close to her. He'd confessed to killing Courtney and Priscilla as a way to remove intruders from what he viewed as his home—snapping after his grandmother passed and the home he'd known as a child was no longer there. He also admitted to following Dave and Olivia to Cold Spring, mowing him down with a rented vehicle when the opportunity presented itself.

Sniffing back her emotion, she smoothed her hands over his chest. "I can't believe it's officially over. He destroyed so many lives, and for what? How could he really believe I would love him?"

Jack shrugged. "I'll never understand why some people do what they do. Luckily, my job is just to stop them. But I do know, as much heartbreak as he dealt you, you survived."

She smiled. "More than survived. I found you, and you've brought me more joy than I thought possible."

Jack glanced down at the box by his feet and the shiny edge of a frame poking through its wrapping. "What's this?" he asked, bending down to scoop it up and unwrap a silver frame. A photo of Olivia and Dave holding hands, gazing into a sunset stared up at them.

She cringed. "Sorry. When the loft sold, I just packed everything I wanted and threw it in storage. I haven't gone through everything yet."

He rubbed his thumb over the smooth glass and a little sadness twisted his insides. "You have nothing to apologize for. You and Dave shared an amazing love, and that made you who you are today. You never have to shield me from any part of the life you two shared."

Her eyes widened, and she slid her arms to loop around his neck. "Thank you. How did I get so lucky to find you?"

A knock on the door turned his gaze toward the entryway. The door swung open, and Jason poked his head inside. "Hello? I've got some more stuff."

Jack raised his brows and aimed a pointed stare at Olivia. "I thought we locked that."

She scrunched up her nose. "I gave him a spare. Come on." She pulled him out of the kitchen to the front door.

Clara and Christine pushed past Jason, each offering her a hug and Jack a wave.

"Where can I put this?" Jason asked, arms loaded down with a large rectangular package wrapped in brown paper.

"In the living room." Jack captured Olivia's hand and pulled her along behind him.

"Did you hear anything about Mason yet?" Christine asked. She leaned on a cane; her limp not as pronounced as it'd been right after she'd been released from the hospital.

"Convicted for all three murders," Olivia said. "Including Dave's."

Jason propped the package against a wall, then straightened. He frowned, his hazel eyes a myriad of relief and lingering grief. "Good. Dave deserves justice. I just wish I would have listened to you, Olivia. I could have helped stop this before anyone else was hurt."

Clara stepped up beside him and rested a hand on his shoulder. "No more blame. Now is the time for healing. For all of us."

The smile on Olivia's face as she watched her brother and sister-in-law warmed Jack's heart. He was glad the two of them were working on their marriage, and he agreed with Clara. Blame wouldn't do anyone any good. "Good point, Clara. And thanks for bringing this over. I want it to be the very first thing that goes up in our new apartment."

Olivia shifted her weight to her tiptoes, trying to get a peek. "What is it?"

Jack tugged her forward. "Open it."

She jerked at the paper and revealed the painting she'd created so many months ago. The one that had spoken to him on such an emotional level, he couldn't tear his attention from it. He'd had it encased in a golden frame, and hoped she'd agree to make it a focal point on the deep blue walls.

A small smile played on her lips, and she turned to him with curiosity creasing her brow. "What did you do?"

"The first time I saw this painting, I saw you. I saw everything that was inside of you, and everything I wanted to know more of. I saw your sadness and your joy. Your kindness and your grief. I saw your heart and your soul." He framed her face with his hand, using the pad of his thumb to swipe away a lingering tear. "I meant what I said about your past making you who you are, and I love every single part of you. This picture symbolizes all those parts. It's a constant reminder that we are taking our hurts and heartbreak and mixing them with love and hope."

She leaned into him. The tears from earlier now slipping over the slopes of her face. "Oh, Jack. I love it. And

I love you. I couldn't think of a more perfect thing to put in our home."

He kissed her forehead and breathed in the smell of her. The smell of lavender and eucalyptus and home. She had given him so much in such a short time. She'd given him love and redemption and the promise of a bright future filled with all the happiness in the world.

* * * * *

Check out these other great murder mysteries from Harlequin Romantic Suspense:

Danger in Big Sky Country
By Kimberly Van Meter

Killer in the Heartland
By Carla Cassidy

Cavanaugh Justice: Up Close and Deadly
By Marie Ferrarella

*Available now wherever
Harlequin Romantic Suspense books
and ebooks are sold!*

Get 4 FREE REWARDS!

We'll send you 2 FREE Books plus 2 FREE Mystery Gifts.

FREE Value Over **$20**

Both the **Harlequin Intrigue®** and **Harlequin® Romantic Suspense** series feature compelling novels filled with heart-racing action-packed romance that will keep you on the edge of your seat.

YES! Please send me 2 FREE novels from the Harlequin Intrigue or Harlequin Romantic Suspense series and my 2 FREE gifts (gifts are worth about $10 retail). After receiving them, if I don't wish to receive any more books, I can return the shipping statement marked "cancel." If I don't cancel, I will receive 6 brand-new Harlequin Intrigue Larger-Print books every month and be billed just $6.49 each in the U.S. or $6.99 each in Canada, a savings of at least 13% off the cover price, or 4 brand-new Harlequin Romantic Suspense books every month and be billed just $5.49 each in the U.S. or $6.24 each in Canada, a savings of at least 12% off the cover price. It's quite a bargain! Shipping and handling is just 50¢ per book in the U.S. and $1.25 per book in Canada.* I understand that accepting the 2 free books and gifts places me under no obligation to buy anything. I can always return a shipment and cancel at any time by calling the number below. The free books and gifts are mine to keep no matter what I decide.

Choose one: ☐ **Harlequin Intrigue**   ☐ **Harlequin Romantic Suspense**
                   Larger-Print   (240/340 HDN GRJK)
                   (199/399 HDN GRJK)

Name (please print)

Address   Apt. #

City   State/Province   Zip/Postal Code

Email: Please check this box ☐ if you would like to receive newsletters and promotional emails from Harlequin Enterprises ULC and its affiliates. You can unsubscribe anytime.

Mail to the **Harlequin Reader Service:**
IN U.S.A.: P.O. Box 1341, Buffalo, NY 14240-8531
IN CANADA: P.O. Box 603, Fort Erie, Ontario L2A 5X3

Want to try 2 free books from another series! Call 1-800-873-8635 or visit www.ReaderService.com.

*Terms and prices subject to change without notice. Prices do not include sales taxes, which will be charged (if applicable) based on your state or country of residence. Canadian residents will be charged applicable taxes. Offer not valid in Quebec. This offer is limited to one order per household. Books received may not be as shown. Not valid for current subscribers to the Harlequin Intrigue or Harlequin Romantic Suspense series. All orders subject to approval. Credit or debit balances in a customer's account(s) may be offset by any other outstanding balance owed by or to the customer. Please allow 4 to 6 weeks for delivery. Offer available while quantities last.

Your Privacy—Your information is being collected by Harlequin Enterprises ULC, operating as Harlequin Reader Service. For a complete summary of the information we collect, how we use this information and to whom it is disclosed, please visit our privacy notice located at corporate.harlequin.com/privacy-notice. From time to time we may also exchange your personal information with reputable third parties. If you wish to opt out of this sharing of your personal information, please visit readerservice.com/consumerchoice or call 1-800-873-8635. **Notice to California Residents**—Under California law, you have specific rights to control and access your data. For more information on these rights and how to exercise them, visit corporate.harlequin.com/california-privacy.

HIHRS22R3

#2215 COLTON'S UNUSUAL SUSPECT
The Coltons of New York
by Marie Ferrarella
In the city that never sleeps, Detective Sean Colton is investigating one disappearance and stumbles across a body—a man whose daughter is certain her twin is the killer. But can the beautiful and earnest Orla Roberts be trusted?

#2216 GUARDING A FORBIDDEN LOVE
The Scarecrow Murders
by Carla Cassidy
When town baker Harper Brennan falls for Sam Bravano, the much-younger hunky carpenter who is working on her bakery building, the romance stirs up a dangerous obsession. Will their May to December romance withstand a man who wants Harper dead—as well as Harper's own insecurities?

#2217 HER TEXAS LAWMAN
Midnight Pass, Texas
by Addison Fox
FBI agent Noah Ross is on a mission to protect a woman who's being hunted by a dangerous criminal syndicate. If he can keep Shayne Erickson alive, she could be the key to the case that's haunted him since his wife's death...

#2218 THE PI'S DEADLY CHARADE
Honor Bound
by Anna J. Stewart
Kyla Bertrand, an up-and-coming attorney, risks everything to find her friend's murderer. An ex-con turned PI, Jason Sutton, is determined to prove himself a changed man by finding a missing teenager. Joining forces makes sense but doing so means they'll both have to deal with emotions and an attraction that will only lead to trouble.

HARLEQUIN
PLUS

Announcing a **BRAND-NEW** multimedia subscription service for romance fans like you!

Read, Watch and Play.

Experience the easiest way to get the romance content you crave.

Start your **FREE 7 DAY TRIAL** at
<u>www.harlequinplus.com/freetrial</u>.